Shappi Khorsandi is one of the ~~~~~~~~
having ~~~~~~~~~~~~~~~~~~~~~~~~~~~~
Edinburgh show, *Asylum Speaker*. ~~appi's career has taken her
to all corners of the globe, and she has appeared on countless
TV & Radio shows including *Live At The Apollo*, *8 Out Of
10 Cats*, *Have I Got News For You*, *QI*, *The Graham Norton
Show* and *Friday Night with Jonathan Ross*. She is the author
of the bestselling childhood memoir *A Beginner's Guide to
Acting English*, which tells the story of how her family were
forced to flee Iran and gain asylum in the UK.

NINA IS NOT OK is her first novel.

Praise for Nina is Not OK:

'Shappi Khorsandi is both funny and shocking, yet above all
writes with warmth, giving Nina an intelligent voice. This girl
could be you, or your daughter, or your friend, and I defy anyone
not to love the endearing, messed-up Nina as she finds her way
out of an alcohol-fuelled hell of her own making' *Daily Mail*

'Breathtakingly honest and laugh-out-loud funny . . . perfectly
captures the anxieties of youth' *Red Magazine*

'It's absolutely bloody magnificent' Marian Keyes

'Absolutely brilliant - funny, dark and terribly upsetting, and the voice is incredibly loud and true . . . a pure marvel' Jenny Colgan

'Astoundingly good. An important, touching, powerful and occasionally funny read' Adam Hills

'*Nina Is Not OK* is an entertaining, thought-provoking read . . . dark, honest, confessional . . . shocking, rude and dark . . . while being ultimately incredibly moving and hopeful. *Nina Is Not OK* will have you chuckling, gasping and welling up as you follow Nina's road to recovery and finding out what she needs to do to live the life she wants' *Psychologies*

'Unexpectedly moving, emotional and funny' Richard E Grant (on Shappi Khorsandi)

'I finished *Nina Is Not OK* in one sitting. Funny, sharp, and heartbreakingly honest, this is *Rachel's Holiday* for young adults' Louise O'Neill

'Moving, funny and shocking all at once, an almost perfect description of the empty highs and crashing lows of addiction' *The Telegraph*

'Shappi Khorsandi's debut novel, *Nina is Not OK*, is a moreish read . . . Shappi's writing is raw and connective' Gemma Cairney, *The Pool*

Also by Shappi Khorsandi:

A BEGINNER'S GUIDE TO ACTING ENGLISH

NINA IS NOT OK

SHAPPI KHORSANDI

EBURY
PRESS

3 5 7 9 10 8 6 4 2

Ebury Press, an imprint of Ebury Publishing
20 Vauxhall Bridge Road,
London SW1V 2SA

Penguin
Random House
UK

Ebury Press is part of the Penguin Random House group of companies
whose addresses can be found at global.penguinrandomhouse.com

First published in the UK in 2016 by Ebury Press
This edition published in 2017

www.penguin.co.uk

A CIP catalogue record for this book is available from the British Library

ISBN 9781785031373

Printed and bound in Great Britain by Clays Ltd, St Ives PLC

Penguin Random House is committed to a sustainable future
for our business, our readers and our planet. This book is made
from Forest Stewardship Council® certified paper.

For Andrew:

Keep travelling with me.

CHAPTER ONE

The burly bouncer was holding me by the scruff of the neck. I always thought that was a figure of speech, but he had my scruff in his hand and was marching me towards the exit.

An hour before, I'd flirted with this man and he'd let me, Zoe and Beth into the club with our dodgy IDs. Now I was being 'frog marched' by him. I held my head up high the way the very drunk do when they are trying not to seem very drunk.

I stumbled, of course. He put one hand under my arm to steady me. I was yanked up and dragged towards the exit like a haughty marionette. This was ungainly. No amount of front could hide from the other clubbers that I was being booted out.

We'd been drinking before we got there. It's loads cheaper if you get drunk at home. We'd had some wine – me and Beth – as we got ourselves ready. Beth had lent me her crazy, black minidress with crucifixes on it. It was gothy (Beth is a not-quite-committed Goth: a Demi-Goth) but had this scrunchy middle bit that somehow made my waist look tiny.

Zoe had also come over with a bottle of vodka and we'd had shots. Zoe had just come back from holiday and looked even more gorgeous than usual with her hair all tousled and sun-kissed. It sounds mad but with a tan she looks even taller.

It's Zoe who gets us into clubs, past the queues. Girls that look like Zoe never have to wait in line for anything. The bouncers come and get her, then me and Beth scuttle alongside her to the front. No door Nazi has ever said 'no' to me and Beth when Zoe has been with us.

She's smoking hot but has absolutely no sense of humour. I mean she doesn't get jokes. *Ever*. Beth cracks me up all the time and Zoe just smiles like we're both mad. She doesn't see what we're laughing at, and just goes, 'What are you two on?!' She's nice, though, never an arsehole to anyone.

Beth wondered if Zoe was a snob at first – she goes to our college but we only really got to know her last summer when we all worked at Pizza Paradise – but she's not a snob, she's sound; she's just not silly like we are. Zoe reads a lot and isn't a div like girls as pretty as her can be. Me and Beth have a theory that girls who are really pretty are often dull. They get attention without having to develop a personality. We've been friends, me and Beth, since we were ten.

We were all nicely tipsy by the time we got to the Boulevard. It was our last night out before term started on Monday and we wanted to make the most of it.

The reason I was thrown out was fairly clear. It was definitely something to do with me unzipping that bloke's fly by the bar and burying my head in his lap.

I'm not even a slag. I've only ever shagged Jamie White and I was *his* first too, so not slagginess at all from either side.

'Nina!' Beth had said. 'That guy over there won't stop looking at you.'

He was gorgeous. No doubt about that. He looked like a Benny Boy.

The boys from St Benedict's never usually looked at girls like me. They liked cool, tall, blonde girls like Zoe who don't say much and flick their hair. I'm short and have got crazy curly hair. It's long and never behaves unless I spend hours straightening it. I'm not ugly, I'm alright looking. My dad was half-Moroccan so I've got olive skin and big Arab eyes but my mum's thin English lips and my Auntie Jeanie's ski-slope nose. On a good day, I'm Pocahontas; on a bad day – most days – I'm a cavewoman.

This guy was tall, good-looking, with dark eyes and sexy, floppy indie-band hair. Guys who don't have the confidence to go for Zoe tend to go for me. I'm a fairly decent plan B. This guy definitely had confidence, but Zoe had nipped to the loo. I had to nab him before she came back.

I downed my Southern Comfort and Coke. He came over, or did I go over? Don't know. Someone went over to someone and then I don't remember what we said or did but the next moment we were in a dark corner, on a velvety sofa, and I was fumbling with his fly.

I had only given a handful of blow jobs before, mostly to Jamie White, my boyfriend. *Ex*-boyfriend. Jamie had left after his A level results and gone to live in Hong Kong for a year with his dad. He'd promised he'd write to me every day but I'd heard nothing for over two weeks. After I'd called and left a million messages and spent HUGE amounts of time crying to

Beth, he'd messaged, eventually, saying he'd met another girl out there called Marcia. This had been pretty devastating and so out of the blue. We'd planned a whole future together. I was having issues 'accepting' the break up, apparently.

I'd sent him endless emails. In one I'd call him a total bastard for five pages; in the next I'd send him seven pages of how much I loved him, how he was my hero and begging him to call me and get back with me. I'd texted him endless lists of what I missed about him.

I miss stuff about you that you don't even know I loved about you!

1. *The way you texted me in the mornings to tell me stop hitting 'snooze'.*
2. *Your Superman pants.*
3. *Your radish and tuna melts.*
4. *How sweet you always were with your mum when I am always ratty to mine.*
5. *The way you wrote down each book you lent people and demanded they give it back exactly two weeks later because 'if they haven't read it by then they can sod off'.*
6. *The way you always said 'when WE have kids, when WE go travelling, when WE become famous writers'.*

And on and on and on – to nothing, no replies. Silence. Then he'd posted pictures of them together on Facebook.

Beth had said, 'Well, that's a kick in the cunt.' But it hadn't been like that. It had been like a thousand kicks in the cunt and a giant fist around my heart, squeezing until it burst, again and again and again.

They'd been on a balcony on some fancy lit-up building. She's American. She's skinny with long, dead-straight blonde hair, and pretty. Not madly pretty, just normal pretty.

I'd stared at the picture. How could he love her more than he loved me? How is that possible? He'd always said that I was his exotic, dusky Arab beauty, even though I can't speak Arabic and have never been to Morocco.

Beth and Zoe had rushed round to my house because I'd been so upset. I'd showed them the picture, wanting them to slag this girl off, but Beth is a feminist and doesn't believe in pulling other women down just to cheer her friends up. She'd told me not to torture myself, to unfriend Jamie, to move on. Zoe is not a feminist and had said, 'Oh my God. He chose her over you? Well, he's blind as well as stupid!'

So this (probably) Benny Boy's hand was on my head, pushing it down into his lap, and I dutifully bobbed up and down. I don't know where Zoe and Beth were. Off dancing probably.

I remember hoping I was giving a good blow job. I read a thing in one of Zoe's magazines ages ago that to give a good one, you had to seem like you were really enjoying yourself and keep your teeth well out of the way.

Beth thinks glossy magazines telling you how to have relationships are trash but they are actually quite useful because how else do you *know* what makes a good blow job? You can't just ask, 'So how does sir like his cock sucked?' without him thinking you're mental.

So anyway, I think I was moaning a bit with pleasure (which is really embarrassing, but I was drunk, whatever) and wrapping my lips over my teeth. I must have looked like total granny porn.

Then I remember the commotion of the bouncer coming over.

Music and lights swirled around me, everything was blurry as I was manhandled out. This is what they did to blokes fighting; this did not happen to seventeen-year-old girls who had been predicted AAB in their A levels (As for English and history, the B is for philosophy which, if I'm honest, I find bloody boring and I wish I'd taken French instead but it's too late now).

Suddenly I was outside of the club with no coat and no phone.

I was cold, really cold, down to my bones cold. I needed to find Beth and Zoe. I tried to explain to the men on the door – the men who were disgusted with me – that I needed my friends, my coat, but I couldn't. My words were too slurred for them to think I was anything other than scum. Even though I was so drunk I could barely stand, I felt huge shame. I'd just given a bloke a blow job inside a club. Who does that?

'He's my fiancé!' I announced to the security guys, who had increased in number; the management did not want to risk me taking my whoriness back in there. 'We're getting married in a month,' I insisted. Yes. If they thought I had a steady relationship with the man I'd just fellated in public, they would judge me less harshly and let me go back in and find my friends. This was a stupid, stupid night.

My fake fiancé came out of the club to look for me. That was nice of him. He must really like me. Proof we were in love. The door staff would be ashamed of themselves now as he put his arm around me and giggled something to his friend. Why had he brought his mate? Perhaps they could lend me a phone. If I had a phone I could call Mum to pick me up. They were posh boys, both of them. They'll be from nice families, I thought, as he cuddled me close to keep me warm. Why was his mate following us? We walked – they walked me – a little way down the road, to the alley. My legs were so unsteady that the boys sort of carried me. Where was my other shoe?

Later – an hour later? Five minutes? – I was in a taxi. The guys were in charge, being sweet, making sure I knew my address and had enough money. I heard his mate call him Alex. They wandered off, back towards the club, back to the darkness, the music, the steamy bodies writhing oblivious to the outside world. I slumped in the back.

The cab driver was Muslim. He had one of those white skullcaps on. I clutched my knickers in my hand. They were nice ones. Part of a set from Topshop. Thank God I'd retrieved them. I wanted to put them on but I couldn't move. Why were my knickers in my hand? Did I fuck one of them? Both of them? Oh dear God no! Shit. No condoms. Not good. The gluey tang of spunk was in my hair. I wiped my mouth and pulled the gothy dress over my thighs. My eyelids were like lead. I mustn't sleep, I thought. It was dangerous to sleep. Was this even a licensed taxi? I passed out.

Suddenly Mum was on the street in her dressing gown. She was pulling me out of the cab. 'Come on, Nina, come ON!'

'She was asleep, you know? I couldn't wake her.' The cabbie must have gone to the door and fetched Mum. His Pakistani accent was soft and concerned. 'She is young. I thought I'd better get her parents, you know what I'm saying?' Later I would feel bad about thinking he might rape me.

My mother, Sandra Taylor, formerly Swanson, founder of Ealing Fields Running Society, leant me against our garden wall and began to fumble about in my handbag.

'My purse is inside,' said Mum when she couldn't find mine. She was flustered, wondering if she should just leave me propped up against the wall while she ran to get money.

'Please, miss, no problem.'

He waved away further offers of paying the fare, got back in his car and drove away.

I remember thinking 'he's too disgusted', before spraying the wall with Southern Comfort, red wine and spaghetti hoops. My shoeless foot was soaked. Everything went dark again.

Consciousness hits me like a hammer. I fly out of the black hole of the night before.

I am in my own bed, fully clothed. Good. The sun is bright. Urgh. It is a relief to be in my own room though who knows how I got here. Still, I am dressed so I can't have taken my clothes off and danced naked on a table, which is usually my worst fear when I come round after a blackout. I move a fraction to the left. Nausea rises. My dress is wet, stuck to my arse. I've pissed myself. The room spins, I make a horrible sound then splash my bed with puke.

The door opens slowly. Through the fog of poison rising from my sheets and sweating out of my body, I see my little sister, Katie, peep round the door. 'Go AWAY, Katie!' I manage to croak. It must stink in here. I am revolting. Katie is six and my angel. Katie cannot see me like this. She tiptoes out again.

A door slams downstairs. Mum has taken Katie to ballet class. Thank God Alan is in Germany. This would be a serious lecture with slide projectors and guest speakers.

I sink back down and lie, catatonic, in my bed of piss and puke.

By noon I have shuffled downstairs. Pieces of the night have come back to me and I am filled with shame so intense I wonder how I can remain alive. I could jump off a cliff? But I've been to Beachy Head. It wasn't all that sheer. It seemed like you'd bounce to death and it would hurt and I can't cope with that, not with a hangover. I want to pick up a saucepan and hit myself on the head with it so I can get last night out. Those boys and booze, the hard cock in the corner of the club . . . I want it all out of my head. There is an elephant sitting on my chest and I want to push it off.

Every movement is a monumental effort. Shame bombs go off one by one in my memory, making me shudder and clutch my face. I remember what I did, what happened. Not the bits outside, but the bits inside the Boulevard. Who saw?

Did Zoe and Beth see? Are they speaking to me? Or are they too disgusted? Where did they go? The whole world saw what I did, didn't it? If I turn on the TV or open a newspaper they will be reporting my behaviour: SEVENTEEN-YEAR-OLD NINA SWANSON HAS BEEN DECLARED THE MOST AWFUL, DISGUSTING GIRL OF ALL TIME AND NO ONE IN THE WORLD WANTS TO KNOW HER ANYMORE. Stupid hangover paranoia. No one else cares, right? No one else will ever know.

Suddenly I hear my phone. My quest to find it is a fine piece of slapstick comedy I am sad no one witnesses. I actually pick up a banana from the fruit bowl to see if the phone is under it. Katie isn't here to laugh but I put it to my ear anyway. I stumble and trip and eventually find my phone in Katie's little pink handbag where it must have been last night. I have missed the call. It was Mum. I have six missed calls and thirteen texts.

The texts are mostly from Zoe and Beth. '*Are you inside? Can't find you!*' And '*Babe, where ARE you? Reeeeeeelly worried now . . .*'

There is one message from Mum: '*I'll be home at lunchtime.*' Not '*I'll pop in at lunchtime*'. 'Pop' is a friendly word. 'Pop' would mean she's not really angry, just concerned. But no. Mum will BE home. I text back '*fine x*' then call Beth.

'You're not going to die,' she reassures me. 'You went out and got trashed. Everyone does it.'

'Beth! I went down on a guy IN PUBLIC! I got thrown out! *Everyone* doesn't do that!'

'No. They don't. You're right. But look, you've got a brilliant story to tell your grandkids. You'll be a rock 'n' roll grandma!'

I am not cheered by this.

Beth and Zoe had rung my mum to check I got home OK. I'm touched they care but Mum's lecture on 'sticking with your mates' was going to be an epic one.

'What the fuck happened? Those blokes said you got thrown out?'

'The Benny Boys?'

'They weren't Benny Boys! The one you were snogging, the fit one? He was an estate agent. He's twenty-one! He got off with Zoe after.'

'What?'

'Sorry, babe. He did though.'

'What a dick!'

'I know. Bloody rude. Not Zoe's fault though. Do you want me to come over? I finish at four today, I could pop round?'

Beth sometimes works at her dad's shop on the weekend. He has a kids' bookshop, Down the Rabbit Hole. I often take Katie there and Beth's dad is dead sweet to her. He lets her have a go on the till and he gave her a copy of *The Tiger Who Came To Tea* when she was three. He's young, Beth's dad. He's not even forty yet. My mum is forty-three. Ancient.

'No, don't worry; Mum's on her way,' I say although having Beth here might chill Mum out a bit. Beth's mum died of cancer when Beth was only two so Mum fusses over her a lot, knowing what it was like for me to lose a parent. Though at least I remember my dad. Mum thinks Beth is 'wise beyond her years'.

I strip and put my clothes straight in to the washing machine. I run upstairs, yank the sheets off my bed, shove them in too and turn it on. Mum would kill me for putting on such a small load but I need everything to be clean again. I keep getting awful flashes, scenes from last night. My head, his lap, the bouncer, everything comes back. I know the boys walked me to the alley behind the garages then later put me in a cab; what happened in between is a blank. I don't want to know. I don't want to think. They wouldn't have an STD, would they? I freak out for a while about chlamydia, herpes and HIV. Pregnancy is the least of my worries. But I don't even remember if I should be freaking out or not. I am not drinking again. I am never drinking again.

Naked, I go up the stairs to shower. As the soapy water slips off my head, down my grimy skin and tender, hungover flesh, I feel better. I stand and pray for total cleansing. I wash off the piss and puke. I try to wash off that boy.

'Do you remember how you got home last night?'

Mum's face is stone, but she doesn't shout or rant. When things are medium bad, she blows her top. When they are off-the-scale bad, like this, she is calm. She is trying to be understanding. We both have recent enough memories of Dad to know this is not unfamiliar to her.

'It's poison you're putting in your body. You have to be aware of how much you are having, and when you're tipsy enough to have a great time, stop!'

As though, when I am drunk, I can make this decision.

Mum is a health nut now. She hardly drinks and knows all about sugar and carbs and protein. She's not too boring with it; she's pretty cool, not that I'd tell her. She looks good for her age. Her hair is long and glossy and she dyes her greys. Her skin is smooth and fresh, not like some of her friends – the ones Alan calls 'the battle-axes'; Mum will raise an eyebrow to chastise him, but she doesn't really stick up for them. She loves him thinking she is hotter than her mates and he'll still make a lame excuse to take her upstairs on a Sunday afternoon.

'You OK down here while Alan and I have a quick nap?' It grosses me out so sometimes I say, 'Katie! Mum and Alan are going for a nap! Do you want to go too?' And Mum then glares at me and Alan turns purple.

'You're like your dad,' Mum is saying now, making me a cup of tea. 'You're a party animal.'

I like that: 'party animal'. So Eighties. Mum isn't a caner like Dad was. She is quieter, more traditional; she once told me that Dad's wild ways were what really attracted her to him.

No one ever wants to know about how sexy their parents find each other, but I can see it with Mum and Dad. Mum's family are conventional, middle class, very English. My dad and the whirlwind that came with him must have blown away what expectations she had of herself, of what her future might be like. Mum was intoxicated by Dad's charisma, his off-the-scale sense of fun, and despite everything, despite what his drinking put her through, I think she became as addicted to the excitement and drama he brought into her life as he was to booze.

With Alan, she has become boring. Though she doesn't see it like that. She has been to loads of support groups over the years and concluded that being 'loved' was a quieter affair than what she had with Dad. Mum and Alan go to dinner and she listens to Alan's opinion of every ingredient of their meal with such interest, like he's telling her state secrets.

I *know* she doesn't really give a toss about the Radio Four plays he's obsessed with. They sit there in the living room, listening to the radio like a middle-aged couple in the 1940s. I have music on in the shower or while I'm having breakfast or painting my nails or whatever, but who, under the age of ninety, sits in a room *just* listening to the radio? I know that's not the *real* Mum. It's what she slowly became after Dad died.

I can't blame her, not really. In restaurants, my dad never noticed the meal; he'd order a bottle of tequila and bring on the mayhem. Though his table was always rambunctious, waiters and other diners were disarmed by his charm and wit, which never left him in public, no matter how drunk he was. It also helped that Dad looked like a movie star.

'Your dad was always a riot waiting to happen,' my Auntie Jean said to me once. Auntie Jean is Dad's sister. She's a drinker like Dad but she does it quietly, on her own mostly. She's never married or had kids. When she was very young, she was travelling and met a peanut farmer in Burma and he's the closest thing she's had to a husband. She came back after a few years and the only thing she said about it was, 'There are only so many peanuts I could take.'

I have heard about Dad's legendary nights out from his friends who stayed in touch for a while after he died. They told me about the fistfuls of cash Dad would shove in the hands of managers of bars, and the fights he avoided with charm and fifty pound notes, when even his own buddies thought he probably deserved a kicking.

I would see him on those nights when he got home. He would be sprawled face down on the sofa fully clothed as I fetched my cereal and sat on the floor beside him and watched TV as he slept.

'But you need to know when to stop,' the Mum Lecture continues. 'The state you were in, Nina! Do you even remember how you got home? God, Nina! That taxi driver could have raped you!'

She looks straight into my eyes when she says 'raped'. Hers look terrified. She doesn't need blue eye shadow just because she has blue eyes. Why do older women think their eyelids have to match their eyes or, worse, their top?

I remember the cabbie. What must he have thought? Another pissed-up slag in the back of his car. Bit bloody judgemental. That's why I don't like religion. Other people thinking they have the moral high ground just because you get so drunk you pull out a stranger's penis in a bar and put it in your mouth.

Mum is stroking my hair. She's saying something about me being a role model to Katie. The bouncer flashes in my mind bringing with him a fresh attack of pain and guilt. 'You ought to be ashamed of yourself,' he'd said.

What would Mum say if she knew I'd washed cum out of my hair in the shower, from a man whose name I am no longer sure of?

'I got a daughter your age!' the bouncer had added.

'Yes, and I bet you fantasise about her mates.'

I possibly shouldn't have said that. That may have been the reason he'd gotten reinforcements.

Mum would freak if I told her I couldn't remember if I'd fucked a boy outside of a nightclub or if I'd fucked his friend too. I sip my tea. I sip my tea, then run to the toilet to puke, again.

By the time she has to go back to work, Mum is happy I have 'learned my lesson' and that the way I am feeling is 'punishment enough'. She kisses my damp head and gives me a relieved smile before she heads back out to teach English to her class of immigrants and refugees.

A text from Zoe: *'BABE. YOU OK? BETH SAID SHE TOLD YOU ABOUT ME AND THAT GUY. ARE YOU PISSED OFF WITH ME? ALEX SAID YOU WEREN'T INTERESTED. ARE WE COOOOOOOL???????'*

Well, at least I remember his name now. Alex. Slimeball! He can't have told her the whole story. Zoe didn't know about the blow job. I made Beth swear not to tell anyone.

I text back: *'All cool, babe. Alex who? ;)'* Sorted. Face saved.

You should be able to be honest with friends. You should be able to say, 'Oh, actually I'm a little hurt because you're prettier than me and you always get the good-looking guys. Boys don't look at me twice when you're around. That's annoying, Zoe, when they don't bother to consider my personality.' I should also be able to ask: 'What's it like, Zoe, to just stand there and have guys fall over themselves to get to you? They never check to see if you're funny or smart or nice, do they? Does that bother you or is it a relief not to have to make an effort?'

You can't say these sorts of things. You just have to always pretend you're fine.

What if they start going out and I have to meet him again? I would die. I would literally curl up and die and they would have to roll me into a coffin to bury me.

I want to scream, 'ASK HIM IF WE FUCKED BECAUSE I CAN'T REMEMBER!'

Zoe sends back kisses.

I call Beth. I tell her about not knowing if I fucked him and how I feel like the inside of a wheelie bin.

CHAPTER TWO

Monday morning. First day of term. English literature. *Sons and Lovers*. This book irritates me. I know it's brilliantly written and all that, but I want to scream, 'JUST SAY WHAT YOU BLOODY MEAN!' The character Miriam, in *Sons and Lovers*, is a drip and we spend the morning having to discuss why she is quite such a drip. She's basically an early version of an emo.

Zoe rolls her eyes up at me in class when Steve – this guy who always has to make a comment like he's the only one who understands what we are reading – says, 'I think Miriam feels things deeply and is much more emotionally complex than it at first seems.'

Miriam doesn't 'feel' things more deeply than anyone else; she's just a drama queen. I used to think quieter people were 'emotionally complex'. It's really disappointing when you realise they are not. I hung out with this girl L for ages last year. Her name was Louise but she introduced herself to people as 'L' and *always* explained, 'As in the letter, not the French for "she".'

This irritated Beth: 'Like a random person she's just met is gonna need to spell her name.'

L would come out with us and not say a word. Seriously, not a word. Beth would be like, 'Does she just hate us?' L shaved her head, so I thought she must be interesting. I thought she was quiet because she had really amazing thoughts on a higher plane of intelligence so couldn't engage on the normal chitchat level where the rest of us operated. But, eventually, I had to agree with Beth that she was actually dead boring. Now I never trust people who give *themselves* a wacky nickname. 'Call me by a letter!' It screams: 'I'm trying to make up for not having a personality!'

As it turned out, the extent of conversation you could have with L was: 'Do you shave your head every day?' and she'd say, 'Every other day', so I had to phase her out as a mate, which is not a nice thing to do but sometimes necessary.

People shouldn't shave their heads, have a cool nickname or mad tattoos unless they are genuinely interesting. They shouldn't be allowed to lure you in then waste your time.

Miriam from *Sons and Lovers* is tedious but at least she isn't bald. She's clearly pretty as hell. Pretty, misty-eyed and downbeat. I don't know how guys stand girls like that for a minute, but they seem to love it. Men love a damsel in distress, as long as she's hot, of course. No guy wants a fat girl with 'issues'. She is maddening though, Miriam. She's all intense and obsessed with Paul, and he's off shagging Clara.

I can't stand Clara either. She is not a heroine in this. She reminds me of Marcia. She's all secure and sorted and, compared to her, Miriam is a pain in the arse. Was that what I was? A pain in the arse for Jamie? And I just didn't realise? I was always there, always available and so he got excited by someone he saw as more confident, more sure of herself? Maybe he wouldn't have gone off me if I'd played it cooler, hadn't been so keen to go to Warwick with him. Perhaps if I'd said, *'Babe, I need my own space. You go to Warwick, and I'll apply to uni in Nigeria,'* we would still be together. Maybe if I hadn't sent him a compilation of heartbreak songs from his birth year with a note saying, *'This is EXACTLY how I'm feeling Jamie!!!!!!!!!!!!!!!!!!!'* he wouldn't have ignored so many of my calls and messages. And maybe, if I hadn't written and sent him bloody awful poetry, he wouldn't be sick at the thought of me.

> *I loved you to The Moon And Back,*
> *But you wouldn't stay with me.*
> *You tied my heart into a sack*
> *And threw it in the sea.*
>
> *Now my heart's adrift and cold,*
> *It shivers and it shudders.*
> *Your arms no longer there to hold,*
> *They are wrapped around another's.*

I actually typed that and pressed 'send'. I *actually* let him see it. I should have listened to Beth when she said 'burn it'. Writing poetry when you've just been dumped should be illegal. I should never have sent it. I should never have written it. He did not even reply.

Clara in *Sons and Lovers* wouldn't do that. It's Miriam who 'suffers'. Paul knows it and carries on cheating on her and being cruel. DH Lawrence is basically making it OK to treat someone who worships the ground you walk on like utter shit.

I didn't want to come into college today. I still feel Saturday night is this great big filthy beast that's following me around everywhere, growling, snarling and stinking.

I couldn't stay at home though. Alan is back from Germany today and I can't face explaining why I'm not at college. Mum has promised she won't tell Alan about 'Saturday night's shenanigans'. This means she *will* tell him, but he will promise not to let on to me he knows. He will find this impossible though. He'll be all quiet and brooding, feeling magnanimous; he's all about 'holding my tongue' and 'keeping my opinions to myself'.

'Nina!' Isabelle Christophorou, my English teacher, gently puts her hand on my arm as everyone leaves. I am wearing a vest top, and my skin is bare. Her fingers are warm and impossibly soft. She always smells like she's just stepped out of a bath with loads of nice products in it. I don't smell like that even when I *have* just stepped out of a bath with loads of nice products in it. She is sexy as hell. Small and slim with dark hair and big green eyes. I want to cuddle her to me. Her gorgeous wide smile is cute and girly. She is thirty-two but still gets mistaken for a student sometimes. I'd say I hope I look as good as her at her age, but I wish I looked as good as her now.

'Are you coming to our writing group at lunchtime?'

I couldn't stop thinking about her in the first year of college, like, in a full-on lesbian way. I don't think I am a lesbian, though, only when I think about Isabelle. I like watching lesbian porn, older women with younger girls, and I imagine Isabelle doing those things to me. I go off into sexual fantasies of me and Isabelle all the time. I'll be washing up and she comes up behind me, pulls me around to face her and kisses me intently then tears off my clothes and ravishes me on the kitchen floor. The only problem with this fantasy is that when I wash up, I always wear rubber gloves. This is problematic, porn-wise, because I don't find Marigolds sexy, so in the fantasy I always have to figure out a way to get them off without interrupting the flow. Even in my head I can't wash up with bare hands because I get dermatitis which gives me really rough skin and it would be on my mind the whole time I was being seduced. The details in my sex fantasy have to be absolutely accurate or it breaks my concentration and I can't come.

Last term Isabelle started a creative writing group at lunch-times for students like me who like to write. I went to the first one. She was wearing this white shirt with blue jeans and her skin looked so creamy and smooth next to the collar that I wanted to bury my face in her neck and kiss it and put my hands down her jeans.

I wrote this awful poem. I didn't realise we'd all have to read what we'd written out to each other. I nearly died. It began, 'Down the long lanes of the future, my tear-bedimmed eyes are peering.' I've blocked the rest of it out. I'm not even sure 'bedimmed' is a real word.

'Are you OK?'

Bollocks. I'm gawping, tongue-tied.

'Yeah,' I finally say. 'Just tired maybe. Heavy weekend.'

I try not to open my mouth too much because my breath still feels rancid with booze and sick. Hers, somehow, smells of flowers.

'I thought what you shared last term showed promise.'

Did it?

I'm standing here like a dickhead. I see Zoe out of the corner of my eye, hovering around, waiting for me. I blank her. I keep talking to Isabelle. I don't want to go to the class, not in this state, though I am blown away that Isabelle singled me out to say I have promise.

'Wow. Thanks! But I can't make today, I'm meeting my friend for lunch.' I desperately need to meet Beth and talk about the weekend and I *really* need to drink the miniature bottle of vodka I have in my bag.

Isabelle's beautiful face cracks a tiny, cheeky smile of mock disapproval that I'd put a silly lunch date before her writing workshop. I desperately want to kiss that smile.

'Aw, OK. Well, hope to see you there next week.' And she's off down the corridor, leaving a trail of her heavenly scent.

There are no big banners around the canteen announcing what I got up to on Saturday night. A relief.

Beth said all of this is a feminist issue and I'm not to feel any shame at all, and 'why the fuck should you?' She was right on her high horse last night when she came round, too. 'There were two of you in this: the sucker, and the suckee. Notice that *you* got chucked out of the club, not *him*. *Text book* misogyny.'

She went on and on about the 'slut-shaming' bouncer needing to be sacked. 'He *threw* you out! You were drunk and alone! Seriously, we should write and complain!'

Dear Sir or Madam,
    I'm writing to complain about my treatment by your staff on Saturday night.

> *At approximately 11.20p.m., I gave a young man I'd just met a blow job by the downstairs bar.*
>
> *One of your bouncers (I am afraid I cannot describe him, my vision was blurred) dragged me out and threw me onto the street without giving me a chance to call my mum, tell my friends, or finish the blow job.*
>
> *I feel this action was discriminatory as the bloke I was noshing off (I'm afraid I did not catch his name) was NOT asked to leave.*
>
> *Yours sincerely,*
> *Nina Swanson*

No. I did not feel like complaining. I felt like having another shower and scrubbing my skin with a Brillo pad.

It feels weird going into the canteen at college. Me and Jamie used to meet every lunchtime and get jacket potato, cheese and beans, and plot the next few years of our lives together. I still feel that lurch in my tummy as I walk in and see the white Formica table in the furthest corner with the orange plastic seats where we sat.

Me and Jamie went out from when I was a fourth year and he was in the fifth year. He got all A*s in his A levels, and got a place at Warwick Uni.

'Luckily you're almost as smart as me, girl, so work your gorgeous tits off and get to Warwick with me. It'll be NO fun without you, Nina, no fun at ALL.'

Jamie wanted to take a gap year anyway, so the plan was I would catch up and we'd go to Warwick together. The plan was *not* for Jamie to go to Hong Kong to stay with his dad and meet some American girl on the plane and fall in love with her. That was *not* what we discussed all those times in the canteen over our jacket potato, cheese and beans. We never mentioned boyfriend-stealing American girls when we curled up together in the corner of the pub whispering baby names to each other. I'd have remembered if we had.

Jamie and me were, well, we were 'me and Jamie'. 'Jamie and Nina' was one word for two years: *Jami-na*.

His dad is something big in finance and had pulled out all the stops for Jamie's visit, got him a job and a little rented apartment of his own. 'The old man wants to make me a money-head like him, but it's never gonna happen,' he'd said. 'But I'll go and work with him for a bit and save some dosh before uni.'

I didn't want Jamie to go all the way to Hong Kong. But he'd earn more with his dad than anywhere in London. Up until he left, we'd seen each other every single day, we did everything together. I spoke to his mum Hanna thinking she might be on my side. She had been divorced from Jamie's dad for years. Maybe she could persuade him not to go. Hanna is a lot older than my mum; she's an illustrator for science books. She's clever like Jamie and easy to talk to.

'I can't imagine a week without Jamie, let alone six months.'

'Don't they say "If you love something, let it go"?' Hanna had said.

'But I'll miss him.'

'So will I, Nina. But he will come back having had a wonderful experience. And there is Skype and email and, God forbid, actual letter writing.'

Hanna had said it was good for Jamie to spend that time with his dad.

'Teenage boys need to reconnect with their fathers, Nina. This will be a lovely bonding time for the both of them. Boys need their dads more than they let on.'

Not what I wanted to hear. It wasn't what I wanted to happen.

Going with Jamie wasn't an option. Neither his dad nor my mum would have allowed it. Also Jamie hadn't asked.

He had kept saying, 'It's an amazing opportunity', and when I'd said it felt like we were breaking up, he had been horrified and held me and said that he just had to 'have this adventure'.

'Chin up, Nina, absence makes the heart go wander!' his mum had said with a giggle. 'I mean grow fonder. It'll be good for you both. You'll come out stronger.'

I didn't hear from him at all for two weeks after we'd said goodbye at the airport. A whole two weeks of no Jamie. Nothing on his Facebook or Instagram.

I had called Hanna and he'd called *her* to say he'd arrived. 'Nina, please don't fret,' she'd told me. 'He's fine, I'm sure he'll call you when he's over the jet-lag and settled in a bit.'

Finally Jamie had messaged me. He'd met a girl on the plane. On the *plane*. He hadn't yet landed in Hong Kong and he'd replaced me. How? I imagined it:

'Excuse me, are you waiting for the bathroom?'

'Yes. You're pretty, I'll dump my girlfriend and go out with you instead.'

'OK. The loo is free. Shall we join the mile high club?'

27

'No, because I come too quickly unless I'm totally relaxed. Only my girlfriend Nina knows that . . . I mean my ex-girlfriend because I've just dumped her for you.'

Jami-na was officially dead.

Beth and Zoe had scooped me up and taken me to the pub after I'd texted them the news. I had sat there in shock.

Beth had said, 'It's shitty, Nina. This is so horrible. *I'm* in shock so God knows what you're feeling.'

Zoe had said, 'If you and Jamie didn't work, what hope is there for the rest of us?'

When I'd tried to talk, my voice squeaked and a sob choked me. I'd been too numb to commit to full-on tears.

Jamie had tossed me over the top of a tall building.

'He was besotted with you! I don't get it!' Zoe had said. 'I mean, how long after take-off did he . . .?'

'. . . meet someone so special that he realised he'd just been wasting his time with me? I have no idea, Zoe.'

Once he'd told me, his Facebook was awash with pictures of them. I've spent hours trawling through it to examine this 'Marcia'.

I found her page and it's full of pictures of herself, looking better than the one with just her and Jamie. She's got hot pants on in their holiday pictures. Her tanned thighs are supple and rounded and about half the size of mine.

She posts slogans like 'dance like no one is watching you' and loads of other bollocks about 'inner beauty', stuff Jamie would usually cringe at.

Her status updates are gushing and overly sincere and not funny AT ALL.

'*Watched the sunrise over this amazing city with my English gentleman #awe*'

#PUKE!

I check her page every morning. Her posts ruin my day.

'*My Jamie treated me to a "proper" hot tea today. I have learned that putting the water in BEFORE the teabag is a capital offence!!!!!!!*' then a million lame emojis.

She posted the picture of herself drinking the romantic tea. It was in Jamie's I LOVE BONO mug. I bought him that mug. I was all snooty about U2, but Jamie made me go and see them live and I loved them so much, I cried. On the Tube home he jumped up and shouted, 'Ladies and gentlemen! I'd like to announce that my girlfriend, Nina, LOVES BONO!' It was the funniest and most embarrassing moment. I found him the mug on the Internet. I was so touched when he said he was taking it to Hong Kong with him to 'think of you every morning when I have my tea'.

I'm surprised he hasn't unfriended me on Facebook after all the angry messages I sent him when I was drunk.

What does Jamie talk to her about? There is just no way she makes him laugh like I did, no way they would sit at a canteen table and piss themselves laughing at everyone and everything. I made Jamie laugh till snot came out of his nose. Bet she's never even seen Jamie's snot. Jamie doesn't go for girls like her. He went for girls like me, just me. How could he forget our plans? We'd finish uni then travel, get jobs then get married or something, I suppose. None of that can happen now because he's taking pictures of Marcia in hot pants drinking tea in his Bono mug.

I go into the loos and neck my vodka. The first one, neat like this, feels crisp and clean. I stick the empty bottle in the tampon bin.

I rinse my mouth, stick some gum in and go to find Beth.

Mine and Jamie's Formica table is now occupied by flamboyant drama students, draped over each other, having earnest conversations or inexplicably putting on regional accents and cackling loud enough so everyone can hear just how much fun they are having.

There are empty chairs everywhere, but drama students insist on sitting on each other's laps. Impossibly gorgeous Phoebe Simmons is draped over Martin Novak, who is camp, really loud and sort of dances everywhere. They are a tight gang, utterly self-consciously unselfconscious, who treat girls like me and Beth with polite indifference. I envy them and hate them.

Beth waves at me and I go over to where she has saved us a table.

'You OK, babe?'

'Better. Paranoid though. Has anyone said anything?'

'Nah,' Beth reassures me. 'No one else was there. Forget about it!'

Thank God it wasn't a guy from college. Thank God, thank God, thank God.

Beth says, 'You still don't remember if you fucked him or not?'

'No!' I tell her, 'I didn't!' Which is a lie because I don't actually know.

'I lost my shoe,' I tell her. I'm pissed off about my shoe. They were my perfect black go-with-everything-comfy-yet-sexy Mary Janes. I got them off eBay for fifteen quid.

'There you go. You came home with one shoe after a night out. You're not a ho, you're Cinderella!'

I smile but I feel like the rotten old pumpkin. I don't tell Beth how desperately I want to hollow out my insides and refill them with something fresh.

'When you're this hungover and can't remember chunks of your evening, it means you've had a good time, right?' I plead to Beth.

She grins. 'If your idea of a great time is waking up with spunk in your hair, puke on your clothes and your dignity left in an alleyway, then yup, you've had a marvellous time.'

I fold my arms on the table, put my head down on them and groan.

'I'm kidding, honey. Forget about it. In a couple of years' time you won't even remember Saturday night. Hey! You already don't remember! Result!'

'Shut up, Beth! You're not helping!'

'Well, stop torturing yourself then! It was one night. Do you reckon he's sat with a mate now going, "Oh my God! I let this drunk girl suck my dick in the club and I just don't feel pretty anymore. I'm such a whore!"'

'I get it . . .'

'He didn't feel ashamed; he strutted back in like King Cock and pulled Zoe.'

'So what's happening with him and Zoe?' I try to sound cool, chilled, not frantic. I'm not fooling Beth.

'Sorry, babe, but they were all over each other. She's seeing him tonight. She's worried you're pissed off with her.'

'I texted her yesterday.'

'I know, but she's worried you might think she stole him off you or something . . .'

'What? I got off with him, we didn't get engaged!' Classic face-saving, when the stupid truth is that I'm gutted about him and her. I shouldn't care, I know that. But still, he could have asked to see *me* again.

'Men always go for Zoe. It's boring,' I add.

'It's *only* because she's insanely hot and pretty damn smart. And nice. Men are shallow like that,' Beth says philosophically.

I scowl.

'Plus she doesn't jump into bed with them. She does the "make them wait" thing.'

'What, and I don't?'

Beth laughs. 'Course you do. How long did you make that Alex wait for a blow job after you met him?? Thirty seconds? You're dead Victorian.'

I blow a raspberry at her.

Zoe is sweet when she talks to guys. She can look like she's interested in anything they say. She would have been a bit shy with Alex, laughed at his jokes, tucked her hair behind her ear and nodded with a smile when he asked her if she wanted another drink.

'What did he say about me that night?'

Did he like me at all? I want to hear that he hadn't thought I'm just this *thing*. I want him to know I'm not just some slag. I want to drink the second vodka.

'Nothing. He said you were wasted, you had a snog, and him and his mate put you in a cab home. Was he a decent snog at least?'

I have no idea; I don't remember.

'I need the loo.'

I have a wee then drink the second miniature vodka bottle in the cubicle.

On my way out of the canteen with Beth, Phoebe Simmons calls out to me, 'NINA!'

I look over at her. From Martin Novak's lap she is animatedly pointing at my feet, elaborately shouthing 'Shoe, darling!' amidst girly giggles. I freeze. Does she know I lost a shoe last night? What else does she know? She keeps pointing, whispers something to Martin who looks over and laughs. Their whole table is looking at me now, some with a puzzled but friendly 'but how can this person be even remotely interesting to us?!' look.

'Your shoe,' Beth tells me, looking down. 'You've got bog roll on your shoe.' She steps on the long piece of cheap toilet paper and I lift my foot to disengage.

On Mondays I pick my little sister up from school. I try to get there a little early and watch them play through the window. I love seeing Katie with other kids when she doesn't know I'm there. She's in her own little world with her own little community, without me, Mum or Alan. She has made nice friends.

I was a bit worried when she first started school. Katie's fingers and toes on her left side aren't formed properly. She has digits missing and the ones she has are gnarled stumps. When she was born I'd kiss her little stumps more than anywhere else because I thought the more love I covered them in, the more she would love and accept them. Her friends don't notice. Or if they do they don't think to mention it. Her best friend Poppy holds Katie's left hand and doesn't bat an eyelash at how it feels different. Poppy and most of the other kids in her class were at nursery with her, friends since they were three. It breaks my heart knowing that one day other kids will start noticing. There will come a day when some kid will say something mean to her, or ask her something stupid, or in some way she will become self-conscious. When that happens, I will be there to make sure she knows she is the most perfect girl that was ever created and anyone who says anything different is to be pitied and ignored. But for now, Katie has no idea her hand and her foot might ever make anyone look twice.

Through the window, I see the kids packing away paper they have cut up, putting the pieces back on to trays to be stored neatly for the next day of 'sticking'. That's pretty much all she does all day: colouring in and sticking. What a brilliant life.

Lining up to come outside, Katie leans over in the queue to peer out of the door to see if I am there. When she spots me she grins and waves manically. Finally their teacher releases them and she flies into my arms. I am 'cool big sister' here, and not 'drunken slag'. Whatever else anyone ever thinks of me, my little sister thinks I'm brilliant.

Her friends spot me too. 'HELLO, NINA!' they bellow, jumping up at me like a pack of puppies. I jump as well and for a minute there is a gaggle of kids around me and we are all jumping and shouting and making a racket. I take Katie's hand and we walk home.

Katie never tells me about her day when I ask her. It's over, it's in the past, Katie wants to talk about RIGHT NOW.

'There's the moon! How come I can see the moon but it's daytime?'

'If I had a magic hat, I would be invisible and eat all the cake in the cake shop.'

'Look, Nina! That pussy cat looks like Oscar, except Oscar isn't orange. Oscar is grey and looks happier.'

On and on, my little sister prattles. I squeeze her hand tight.

At home I make her fish fingers and chips and sneak a shot of Alan's single malt whiskey without Katie seeing.

Once Mum is home I go to my room and lie on my bed. I have a text message from Trish who lives two streets away. She is a couple of years older than me and on a seemingly endless gap year before she goes to do some environmental studies course. She has a lip-ring, blue hair and wears dreamcatcher earrings, tasselled burgundy velvet skirts and listens to 90s indie music. She was meant to go travelling, but she got obsessed with this bloke in a band called Infant Skull Surgery and used all her money following them around on tour.

She went on and on about this singer, Shawn. She got it into her head he'd noticed her and fancied her and I had to hear every bloody detail of a 'look' he gave her or how he held her when she took a selfie with him after waiting ages at the stage door. She nearly wet herself with excitement once when he retweeted some gush she wrote after his gig. I told her he probably didn't do it himself, he probably had a Twitter butler who did all that for her, but she wouldn't have it; she was convinced they had a 'connection'. She managed to get backstage at the Forum and found his dressing room. She got chucked out by security and cautioned by the police. She never talks about him now. Trish is my emergency friend. For when there is no one else about.

'Old Vine? I'll be there at 8ish?'

I'm not going to get drunk, I just want to be out, have a couple of drinks, chill out and come home.

I have dinner with Mum and Alan at seven, then casually mention I'm off out.

Alan frowns. 'On a Monday night?'

'Yes. I'm going to Beth's. Studying.'

Alan nods his approval and thrusts another buttered new potato in his mouth.

Mum knows me better. She gives me a look. A look that says, 'After Saturday night, madam, you'd better not be skipping out to the pub.'

She can't say what she is thinking out loud. It would mean breaking her promise about not telling Alan. I'm putting her in an awkward position. I need a drink more than I need Mum to stop being sanctimonious.

'I've only got a tenner, Mum. It won't be a wild night.'

When I creep in later – not so much creep actually, more 'crash in like a baby elephant' – Alan is in bed. Mum is at the kitchen table. She is just sitting there, in her dressing gown, waiting for me to get home. I am shit-faced.

'Nina . . .' she calls, as I head straight for the stairs.

'Yup.' I try not to slur. I try to walk straight. I am fooling no one.

'Drink some water before you go to bed,' Mum says.

I do as instructed. Mum watches and with maximum concentration, I organise a glass, turn on the tap, pour the water and drink.

Someone has moved the kitchen wall. It's not in its usual place. I smack into it, reverse, find the doorway, and go to bed.

CHAPTER THREE

Katie breezes into my room first thing and starts nattering to me about her dream.

There is no preamble with Katie. She'll start with something like, 'When we found the fish, Abigail said we should put them in the pond,' and it takes me ages to work out what she is on about, who Abigail is, and whether she's describing a dream or something real.

Trish and Katie are two people who like to tell me their dreams. Trish bores me to death about weird stuff she has dreamt and what it means. She reads 'dream interpretation' books. She likes being weird, Trish does. I think she's deliberately weird.

Katie's dreams are never boring. She climbs into the bed with me, snuggles up then tells the story of her dream without stopping for breath. The detail is important to her so you have to pay attention. She will ask you questions and ask your opinion and if you haven't kept up, she'll go back to the beginning and tell it all again with the same gusto and without missing a beat. My hangover makes paying attention a challenge.

I try not to breathe on her. Six-year-olds must be protected from booze-breath.

Mum comes in.

I groan.

'It stinks in here.' Mum's voice is stone cold. She is trying hard not to lose it about last night.

'Then get out.'

Now Mum loses it about last night.

'Don't be so rude! How dare you! This is not a doss house, you know! Staggering in at God knows what time ON A SCHOOL NIGHT! AFTER THE OTHER NIGHT! WORRYING ME SICK!'

'College. Not school. Actually.'

It's gruesomely satisfying to hear the strain in her voice as she tries not to shout, though I feel Katie freeze in the bed next to me. Katie hates rows.

'Stop it, Mummy!' she whines and dives under the covers.

Mum yanks the duvet off the bed. Katie yelps. I'm still in last night's clothes.

'GET UP AND GET TO COLLEGE!'

She bustles Katie out of my humming room and soon I hear the front door slam.

Last night is a blur but I remember walking home. I think Trish was with me. That's good. I remember coming in AND drinking the water AND bumping into the wall. The pub, though, the pub is patchy.

I get out of bed and head to the bathroom. There is sick all over the toilet. Mum has deliberately left it there for me to see. A passive-aggressive action which will have meant she'd steered Katie to her and Alan's en suite bathroom. This will have delighted Katie because she is not usually allowed in there to meddle with Mum's potions.

I sink to my knees and puke again. Wet sick falls on dried sick. When everything is out, I dry retch for a while. This hangover blurs my vision. I am never drinking again.

I don't give the water time to run cold. I gulp down tepid, bathroom tank water, drinking deeply. I wash my face then grab the cleaning stuff and scrub the loo until every awful bit of orange and brown has gone.

My phone rings. It's Trish.

'You OK? You were wasted.'

'Was I all right in the pub? I can't remember it much. Did I make a tit of myself?'

'Not really. Well, a bit. You was going round getting all the old geezers to get you a drink. You sat with them and buzzed off to the next lot once they got you one. Oh, and you kept calling me "The Incredible Bulk".'

Oh my God, I did as well. Trish is quite fat. Oh my God. That's horrible.

'Oh God, Trish, I'm so sorry, I'm such a dick.'

'It's OK.'

My friends don't really get why I like Trish. This is why. She is dead sweet. She's weird and a bit embarrassing to be seen with, but she never gets annoyed with me. I'll be a total prick with her, and she doesn't mind.

Another text message. I almost drop my phone when I see a picture of an erect cock.

NINA IS NOT OK

'Dave from last nite here. Here's a taste of wot u'll get if you text back.'

I call Trish.

'I got a text from a bloke called Dave. Were we with a Dave last night?'

'Dave?' Trish says. 'Was that the old bloke you were snogging? You wanted to go home with him but he said another time because he lives with his mum.'

My memory slams into place. I went out for a cigarette with a guy, was that Dave? But Dave was old . . . forty, I think he said. I gave him my number, yes. I remember giving Dave my number. Why did I give him my real number?

The fact that Trish didn't mention Dave in our first conversation is so Trish. She'll tell you she preferred the old theme tune to *Doctor Who* while she watches a UFO land.

I block Dave's number.

How did I get so drunk? I only had a tenner. I get a flash of myself going round the pub, telling the old boozers it was my birthday. It worked: they did it . . . they bought me 'birthday drinks', these sad middle-aged men.

I finally get myself to college. On my way out of history, Zoe appears. She hugs me.

'I've been worried you've been avoiding me.'

'No, no I haven't honestly.' *LIKE THE PLAGUE.*

'I've so wanted to tell you about Alex, the guy I met?'

'Yes! You've seen him again?' I say with fake cheeriness.

'Twice! Look!'

She shows me a white DKNY watch.

'He bought this for me ON OUR SECOND DATE because I was late for our first!'

It's not jealousy. It's not. Just fucking infuriation. Why do guys go mental over tall, skinny women with blonde hair? Why do girls like Zoe get watches on second dates and I get pictures of dodgy men's cocks?

I don't know if she knows whether or not I fucked Alex. *I* don't know whether or not I fucked Alex. Would he have told her? She wouldn't be this cool with me if he had.

Zoe asks me to go to the cafe and have coffee with her. I sort of have to because it's hard to just say 'no' because she'll know something is up. I still feel like shit that Alex thinks she's girlfriend material and I'm just a drunk slag in the club. We start walking to Jumping Beans on the corner by the bus stop.

'NINA! NINA!' Someone shouts my name as we cross the car park to the bus stop.

It's Martin Novak and Phoebe Simmons. They are practically running up to me, which is baffling because they never usually talk to me. I feel kind of excited.

They are grinning and breathless when they get to me.

'Do you want to come over and play Scrabble? We're having a game at my house and we need a fourth team member.' Phoebe acknowledges Zoe. 'I'd totally ask you too, babe, but we only need four.' It's said so sweetly that Zoe has no choice but to smile understandingly at her rudeness.

The drama lot have never ever asked me to join in with them. I know some of them from my other classes, but they are never chummy with me.

But here they are all smiles and friendly, asking me to play Scrabble. I look at Zoe. I don't want to go for a coffee and hear her gush about that bloke.

I hesitate for long enough for Zoe to take the hint, and she says, 'Sounds fun! You go, Nina. We'll catch up another time.'

It's rotten of me. I'm basically blowing her out because something better has come along. Phoebe and Martin have taken an arm each and are pulling me away from Zoe. 'Come on, Phoebe's got her car,' says Martin. They are being rude as fuck. *I* am being rude as fuck. I throw Zoe an apologetic look and let myself be dragged away.

Phoebe's car is a Golf. It's red and smells of the drama corridor.

Phoebe is telling 'The Story Of The Car' without me asking. 'It was amazing! At my party, Mum distracted me, she told me to come in the kitchen to help with something random, and I was like "What's going on?" Then Dad got all the guests to go outside to the car and stand in front of it and sort of hide it, then I came out of the kitchen and was like, where is everyone? Then I went outside and everyone jumped back to reveal it, it was ah-mazing!'

The thing is about girls like Phoebe, they are actually all right. She is so completely into herself that she is never really horrible to anyone. Phoebe can be rude, but she can't be a bitch. She hasn't the time, she's too busy laughing at something 'random' or honking 'ah-mazing!'

'We have an ulterior motive for kidnapping you,' she tells me.

'Oh, don't tell her!' Martin says.

'What?' We are pulling into Phoebe's mum and dad's gravel drive. They live in one of the huge houses on Corringway.

Phoebe parks. She turns off the engine, unbuckles her seat belt, turns around and beams at me.

'I am playing Cupid, darling. Our friend, Robbie Goodman, has a HU-mungous crush on you, and I thought it would be AH-mazing to set you two up.'

'How do you know I don't have a boyfriend?'

Phoebe tilts her head and does 'sad face'.

'Darling, everyone knows you've been heartbroken about Jamie leaving. You two were so sweet together and it's poo that he buggered off and got with someone else.' She actually sticks out her bottom lip.

It was, indeed, 'poo'. It is also 'poo' that everyone knows about it.

This is, however, a good day. I know Robbie. Well, I know who he is; I've never spoken to him. He's quiet but good-looking. I'm excited. I quickly text Beth.

'I'm at Phoebe's house. She's setting me up with Robbie Goodman.'

Beth texts back: *'Fit. Though if you come back and call me 'darrrrling', you're sacked as best mate xxxx'*

Phoebe ushers us in. We say hello to her mum, who is really skinny and posh and wearing a silk maxi dress in the kitchen. Phoebe's mum looks and sounds pretty much exactly like Phoebe. She gives Martin an over-the-top hug, and he picks her up and twirls her round saying, 'Hello, Phoebe's mummy,' and Phoebe says, 'Mummy, this is Nina,' and her mum air-kisses me and says, 'Have we met, Nina? Have you been to one of our soirées?'

I have never been invited to a soirée in my life.

'I don't think I have.'

'Oh, Mum, stop interrogating her! Come on, Nina, let's go down to the playroom.'

'The playroom' turns out to be Phoebe's part of the house. She actually has her own flat there. It's down a small set of stairs and there's a bedroom, her own bathroom and a little living room.

'Oh my God, Phoebe, this is amazing!'

'Isn't it? I'm so lucky, I know I am.' She does full-on 'sincere face'. 'My friend Jessica had to share a *room* with her sister till she was twelve.'

Martin cackles. 'Oh my God, Phoebes, you're like SO a princess! My family are working class. Sharing rooms is normal, darling.'

Martin takes pride in being 'working class'. His dad was, but now he owns quarries; he became a millionaire before Martin was born.

Phoebe pours drinks from her retro cabinet – gin and tonics – and grabs ice from her mini fridge freezer. She's got posters of old movie stars all over the walls. In frames. I recognise Audrey Hepburn and Marilyn Monroe, and, of course, the blown-up professional photo of Phoebe herself.

'I know!' she shrieks when she sees me looking. 'It's a bit self-*indulge*, but I love it, don't you?'

Thankfully she isn't looking for an actual answer and puts on music on her state-of-the-art speakers. I don't know the band, but they sound old school. She pins her hair up and dances about with Martin. I sit on a pouf and drink my gin, feeling awkward as fuck.

After a few minutes of them singing along and dancing in that tiny room, Robbie appears. Phoebe is now all kisses and hugs. She holds his hand and makes him sit next to me. I smile and say 'hi'. So does he. Phoebe gets him a drink.

'Are we going to play Scrabble then?' I ask.

Phoebe giggles. 'Oh my God, Nina, don't be so boring. Robbie, tell her not to be so boring . . . Let's play strip poker!' And she pulls the arm of her top down to reveal a shoulder, then collapses giggling like it's the funniest thing anyone in the world has ever done. She hasn't even had a drink. She does this stuff totally sober.

I crunch my ice. Hoping she will offer me another gin and tonic. She doesn't.

Robbie hasn't said a word. He's making no effort to talk to me or look at me or anything. It's excruciating, actually. We both know what's going on, that we are being set up. This means absolutely no normal interaction can go on between us. In fact, in these situations, when two people fancy each other, the person who seems least interested, wins.

While Phoebe and Martin inexplicably have a pillow fight, Robbie gets me another drink. He's brought beer. He sits next to me. Finally we start chatting.

'You're not in their drama group, are you?' he asks. I've never actually heard Robbie speak. He's northern. Yorkshire, I think.

'No, I'm in Phoebe's philosophy class. You are, though, aren't you?' God, I sound so formal, like I'm bloody interviewing him.

'Am I fuck. I'm not a bloody luvvie. I do psychology, politics and economics.'

'Oh, wow,' is all I can come up with.

'Phoebe's mum and my mum are best mates. From primary school in Halifax, so when we moved down to London last year, I started hanging out with her. I didn't know anyone else.' He grins when he says that.

Eventually, after a few beers, me and Robbie are properly chatting. Just nonsense, nothing deep. He's nice. Sweet, funny, cool without being an arsehole. Phoebe said he likes me but he doesn't make a move, though I guess it's hard with Martin and Phoebe around. Their animated conversation is peppered with shrieks and spontaneous dancing. It doesn't leave me and Robbie much privacy.

'Can I walk you home?' he asks suddenly, smiling. That's it! His move!

We say goodbye to Phoebe and Martin, which takes way longer than it should, and slip out with a little wave to her mum, who is draped over her kitchen counter with a glass of red wine in one hand and her mobile in the other. She blows us kisses as we leave.

'She and my mum are so different,' Robbie says.

I can't take the piss out of Phoebe and her mum with him. That will have to wait until I see Beth. They are Robbie's old family friends, and although he clearly knows they are dicks, it would be disloyal to laugh at them and I don't want him to think I'm a cow.

So instead I say, 'Do you fancy the pub?'

And he says, 'I would but I've got a bit of reading to do tonight so best not.'

If he liked me, he'd come to the pub and get drunk with me. If he fancied me, he wouldn't stop at a couple of beers with me, he'd get plastered and we'd jump on each other.

He doesn't ask for my number. Nothing. Just says, 'See you around.'

Alan and Mum have 'news' for me when I get home. I don't go straight in to see them. I go up to my room, get the bottle of vodka from under my bed and drink three capfuls. As I'm swirling mouthwash over the sink, Mum is already calling up.

'Nina, can you come down as soon as you're able. We need to talk to you about something.' It doesn't sound like I'm in trouble. Mum has her upbeat 'please don't make a fuss' voice on.

I hope Mum isn't pregnant again. She's forty-three, for God's sake. Surely it's no longer medically possible?

Katie has been settled in front of CBeebies and Mum is putting the kettle on.

'Tea?' I say, sitting down. 'Whoa! This must be serious.'

'Well, it is serious,' Alan says, 'but we're rather hoping you'll think it is also good news.'

'Are you breaking up?!'

'Nina!' Mum scolds.

Mean, I know. Katie would be upset if they separated. She loves her dad. Little kids have no idea.

Alan is letting Mum do the talking. Clearly they have 'discussed' how to have this discussion, and all the possible outcomes of it. Being organised, 'belt and braces', dull as shit Alan, he will have weighed up the pros and cons of whatever they are going to tell me. He will have gone over the 'best course of action' and he and Mum will have discussed 'the best strategy for how to tell Nina'.

Mum stirs my tea and puts it on the table for me.

'Darling, you know Alan's company have opened a branch in Germany.'

'Really? I didn't hear this on the news.'

Mum ignores my sarcasm and ploughs on the way she does when she wants to ignore the fact that I'm being an arse. 'They've offered Alan a partnership, which means a year in Germany getting things off the ground.'

Then there is a gushing explanation of 'great opportunity', 'significant pay rise' and other over-enthusiastic blah blah blah. You'd think by the way Mum talks about Alan's job that he is about to go on tour with Beyoncé instead of going up a notch in his dreary IT job.

A year with no Alan *is* pretty good news in my book, but a bit selfish given Katie adores him.

My own dad died when I was nine. I came home from school one day and found I'd never see him again. The living-room curtains were closed. This wasn't too unusual because Dad was an alcoholic and sometimes a hangover would last longer than a weekend.

But this time, I'd sensed something dreadful. I went in and Mum was crying. I wasn't allowed in the living room; there were medics in with Dad.

You couldn't always tell he was an alcoholic. He worked, made decent money and he was popular. Dad was loud and lively when he was drunk. He filled the house up with mates from the pub, mates from work, mates from down the road, mates from wherever he had been and boozed.

I loved my dad. I loved being loved by him. He was funny and warm and everyone thought he was like that all the time. There were times, though, when Dad was mad with a hangover, when he would shout at me and Mum over nothing, and we'd tread on eggshells around him.

When he was growling and mean, Mum would gather me up and take me out and tell me not to bother my dad.

Sometimes it would take a few days for him to be nice again. In those few days he'd go mad at me over something little like my dropping a fork or forgetting to say 'thank you'.

When this mood passed, he'd say he was sorry and give me grins and cuddles and Mum and me would be so relieved that Dad was himself again.

I could tell by the way he turned his key in the door what mood he was in and whether or not to make myself scarce.

When we went out, this big handsome man, who everyone adored, who was popular in the way the drama lot could never dream of being, would pull me to him in front of everyone and say, 'Isn't my princess beautiful?' I was special in that room because my dad said so.

It was pancreatitis. He was only thirty-seven.

I was nine so not exactly a baby, but I didn't believe he had actually died. I mean obviously I knew he must have because there was a funeral and everyone cried. But how could you never see someone like Dad again? How could it be possible that he had left for ever? The grave, the flowers, the hugs and the tears all implied he had gone, but I couldn't make that *my* reality. There must be a different explanation. I mean how could he just *go*? How does someone who is a part of you disappear? Where did all of Dad's love, his noise, his laugh, his energy all go? I could still smell his 'dad' smell of aftershave and cigarettes all over our house. I think that's why my screaming fits started. Not long after the funeral, I woke up, in the night, screaming, and didn't stop for ages. I'd taste blood in my throat. This kept happening.

Mum took me to this special grief counsellor for children and eventually I stopped the screaming.

Auntie Jean was at Dad's funeral, of course. Auntie Jean is a year older than him. Mum is polite to her but she doesn't like her. She finds her tricky because Auntie Jean does not do polite or tactful, and she doesn't do politically correct. It was Jean who was the first person to say anything around me about Dad being an alcoholic. She said at the funeral, 'He poisoned himself to death and broke all our hearts. Don't you ever get into the drink, Nina.'

Now Dad is dead, Mum keeps a terse distance from her sister-in-law.

Am I over Dad dying? I don't know. I look at Katie with Alan and I think how can you get over your dad dying? Katie adores Alan. He may be as dull as dust, but he's a lovely dad to her. He never shouts and is always ready to play, as long as it's educational or quiet. He wouldn't pretend to be an aeroplane and whiz around the room like my dad did, but still, if he suddenly disappeared from her life . . . I don't even want to think about it.

So I say now to Alan, 'Katie isn't going to like you buggering off to Germany. When you go for even two-day trips she misses you. It's selfish to go away and leave her and Mum.' I enjoy the rare opportunity of being sanctimonious towards Alan.

'No,' Mum says. 'We're going to live in Germany for a year. All of us.'

What?

'A whole year? And you want to go with him? And take Katie?'

'Of course,' Mum says.

'What about me?'

What the fuck is Mum talking about? I'm now aware that I drank quite a lot too quickly. More than I would have from a miniature bottle. It's kicked in. My voice is loud, my mind a bit fuzzy and my cool is out of my reach.

'Well, darling, you could come with us.'

'I'm in the middle of my fucking A levels.'

Alan finally contributes instead of letting my mum deal with everything. 'That language is uncalled for. Your little sister is next door.'

'She doesn't have bionic ears. You're buggering off to Germany with my mum and my little sister, that's more "uncalled for" than some minor fucking swearing!'

Alan's face hardens awkwardly. He absolutely refuses to ever lose his temper with me, or show he is narked by my behaviour. 'If you really want to come, you can defer your A levels and spend a year improving your German.'

'If I *really* want to come. Wow, Alan, what an invite. That makes me feel so warm inside. I feel so wanted.'

'You got an A for your German GCSE,' Mum chirps, encouragingly. 'Surely you'd want to live in Germany for a bit?'

'I got an A for physics too, Mum . . . doesn't mean I want to go and live on the fucking moon!'

This is a step too far for Alan. He will now take 'appropriate action'.

'I must insist you mind your language, Nina.'

'And *I* must insist you don't turn my life upside down so it suits *your* poxy job.'

Alan is very red now. I brace myself. Will this be the moment when Alan finally calls me a vile brat?

'Nina, my "poxy" job pays the mortgage and when the time comes will pay your university tuition fees.' His voice is shaking, ever so slightly. A triumph.

'I don't want your bloody tuition money. I'll get a job and support myself, I'll be a prostitute, I'll do anything just to get out of this shithole!' I am snarling, ranting, my rage is bigger than the room. Alan and his 'let's keep things civilised' manner doesn't stand a chance.

Katie comes in. Mum tries to usher her out but she has heard the commotion.

'Why are you shouting?'

My baby sister is the only person in the room in that moment that I don't hate. I do not want to spend a year apart from her. My heart may explode. I manage, with monumental effort, to tether my fury and stay silent.

Alan cuddles her to him. 'Nothing at all, poppet. Nina is not quite herself.'

I almost scream 'fuck you' but Katie's presence stops me and instead I hiss, 'I am *very* myself and I am NOT coming with you.'

I storm out and leave Alan to discuss the failings of the discussions with Mum and how best to go forward. Alan is a bellend.

I have a can of Coke in my room. I open it and mix it with vodka in my toothbrush mug. I don't have an en suite bathroom, but I have a sink. Mum really tried to sell this to me when we moved into Alan's. She went on and on about it as though a sink in a bedroom made it the height of luxury and not a prison cell.

I'm properly pissed now and message Jamie. *'Hey! Just popping by to say hi! How goes it? My mum and Alan are moving to Germany so I'll have the whole house to myself! Parties? Think so! It's going to be amazing! Other than that, same old same old here. Drama students have colonised our spot in the canteen. You have to come back and help me reclaim our land! Speak soon! Nina xxxx'*

I know I sound like a total dick, I know I will regret it, I know he will see through my chipperness and will not reply, but I still press 'send'.

I text Beth. *'My mum and Alan are wankers. Wanna go out?'*

Beth writes back straight away. *'Coursework, babe.'*

Beth is being a fucking swot. I have no money left. I think about texting Trish, she buys me drinks, but it's too lame relying on her for a night out again. She'd depress the hell out of me and men never come over to our table when I'm with her.

But I want to drink and I want to be out. My phone is in my hand. I find the number I blocked earlier and 'unblock' Dave.

'So, where are we meeting?' I text.

I cringe slightly at how quickly he texts back: *'Lol, I knew ud wanna see me again. Vine?'*

I hear Mum putting Katie to bed. Katie has been upset with all the shouting. Poor Katie, but it's Mum and Alan's fault. I put on an old pair of knickers and leave my legs unshaven, stubbly. This means I'm less likely to shag someone. 'Modern Chastity belt,' Beth calls it.

I creep downstairs. Alan is watching some documentary in the front room. Mum is still with Katie. I leave, ever so quietly.

I don't recognise Dave. I was too smashed to remember his face. But then a bloke in a freshly washed and ironed shirt and still-damp-from-the-shower hair waves at me from the bar. Oh God, he's made an effort. He is clean-shaven and apart from a missing tooth at the side of his mouth that you can only see when he grins and an illegible tattoo on his neck, he's all right looking; I'm not totally repelled.

'You seem pissed already, young lady,' he says as I stumble, clinging on to the bar stool.

He gets me a beer. I drink it quickly and we are on to another. I can't remember what we talk about, I just know we aren't in there long. I make us leave. We walk through Steeples Park and I say I need to sit down so we do, on a bench. I tell him I'm cold so he cuddles up to me, my hand now somehow in his. I look up at him and we start to kiss. He's a good kisser; I'm really drunk but it feels nice. He's a man, I'm kissing a proper grown up, it feels different, sexy. He's confident. He puts his hand up my skirt and between my legs, gently touching over my knickers. I think how lucky he must feel to be touching a teenager like this. Our bench is out of sight from the path, surrounded by some big shrubs and bushes. He pulls down my top a bit and starts kissing between my breasts. I catch a glimpse of a wrinkle roll on his neck. I quickly close my eyes again. I wish I'd worn nicer knickers. I want a drink. I pull vodka from my bag. I offer him some. 'God, girl, you're hard-core!' he says as we take turns to swig. I get up, take his hand and pull him behind the bushes. I'm not sure what to do now. I don't know where I'm going with this. I can't just leave him hanging. I get on my knees, put my hands on his thighs and wait, a bit awkwardly, as he unbuckles and unzips his fly. Finally, he gets it out. I close my eyes as he puts his hand on my head and pushes his groin forward. The park starts to spin. It's cold. I sink deeper into drunkenness and for a moment I sleep or pass out. Just a second. I can't keep his cock in my mouth. 'Sorry,' I murmur.

'Are you OK?'

Yeah, yeah, I assure him. I want to get on with this. I pull him on top of me and we kiss on the grass. I wriggle underneath him, pulling down my tights and knickers. When he realises what I am doing, he helps me and he is touching me and I turn around so I'm on my belly and he is on top. He gently pulls me up on all fours. I'm so cold. I shiver. Thank God it's dark and he can't see my knickers. I hear the rustle of a condom packet. He sorts himself out, and then he's inside me. My hands are on wet leaves; they hold me steady against

his polite thrusts. I close my eyes; nausea rises. Oh God. Oh
no. There's nothing I can do. I puke on the dark ground. He
carries on as I retch and splash my hands. He goes harder for
just a few seconds, then shudders. My face is ice. Strands of my
hair are wet with puke and stuck to my face which I can feel
has gone deathly pale. He withdraws and hands me tissues to
wipe my mouth. He has loads of tissues on him, in a proper
pack, not just bog roll. He puts himself away and helps me up.
He sounds worried, slightly panicked. 'You OK, love?'

I nod, not daring to speak because my breath is foul.

We walk back out of the park. He asks again, 'You sure
you're OK? I didn't realise how plastered you were!'

I am shivering. I am sobering up. I need to be home, I
need water. We are back outside the Vine. I only live ten minutes away.

'I'll be OK walking home by myself,' I tell him.

'I'll walk you back.'

Oh God, no. I need to get away. I tell him I am fine and
I just go.

He doesn't follow.

CHAPTER FOUR

I jump out of bed and frantically search my Facebook messages. Oh God no. I didn't dream it. I actually wrote the lamest message ever to Jamie. The most 'Hey I'm fine, but obviously not' message. Not only is there no reply, but I see I wrote another message last night when I was drunk. 'HIYA again!' I can hear my own fake chirpy voice. 'Just wanted to see if you got my last message?' Of course he got your last message, you idiot. The 'read' icon on the app is up.

There are three texts from Dave.

He's the first person I've fucked since Jamie. Well, the first person I remember fucking since Jamie.

'U ok babe?'

'U get home OK?'

'U wanna meet 2nite?'

It's Saturday. I crawl back into my bed. Alan and Mum have taken Katie to Alan's parents for the day. I was invited but no one woke me up this morning. I know Katie would have wanted to come into my room but Mum would have stopped her. The way I lost it last night is a big deal in Alan's world: I used the 'F-word' in front of him and my mum. God knows what he would think if he knew about me in the park with Dave. The shock would kill him. To be fair, though, I think the shock might be killing *me*.

I call Beth and tell her I got drunk and fucked a forty-year-old bloke in the bushes in the park, then I have to calm her down because she immediately thinks it's date rape and is all like, 'Don't shower! I'll go with you to the police' and 'No means no!'

'Beth, I knew what I was doing. He was nice. He didn't make me do it. I just did it.'

She calms down.

'Forty? Wow. Could he get it up? They can't at that age sometimes.'

'Your dad's going to be forty soon; he can get it up still, I bet.'

'ARGH!! Why put that image in my head? Delete! DELETE!'

We're laughing. I shouldn't have done it. I know I shouldn't have done it. My knees and palms are grazed and I feel disgusting, like proper disgusting.

I don't tell Beth this because she'll go off on one again about 'He won't be feeling shame, why should you?' blah blah blah.

Why did I do it? I was turned on because I was pissed. I wouldn't have done it if I wasn't drunk because actually Dave is someone I wouldn't normally even talk to. I don't want to tell Beth I was sick. But when she comes round later, it's the first thing I tell her.

'Beth, I puked while we fucked.'

I'm an idiot. When you don't tell people stuff, it hasn't really happened.

'Jesus, Nina. What did he do?'

'Carried on . . . it was from behind.'

'Cl-assy.'

'He said he lives with his mum.'

'Sex-y.'

'Maybe he's lying and is actually married.'

'Let's hope so.'

'Oh my God, Beth! What have I done?'

'Was he an actual tramp who *lives* in the park?'

'Shut up! It's not funny!'

'I'm just asking!'

You can't undo a fuck. That is the problem.

I show her the texts from him. There are two more now.

'Cud u text back? Just say ur safe. Worried.'

'Hello?'

Beth shudders and drops my phone back on my bed. 'Yuk. Hate it when old people use shortened texts. My dad never does it. It looks so lame. You have to text back.'

'What shall I say?'

'That you're not dead.'

'Then he'll keep texting me.'

'Well, text him and say you ARE dead.'

I text back.

'Hello, I'm fine. Got home OK.'

I get a text back immediately.

'Few! I was worried.'

Beth squeals. 'Babe, you can't ever see this guy again. I won't let you fuck anyone who can't spell "phew".'

Another text.

'Can I cu 2nite gorgeous?'

'He spelt "gorgeous" right.'

'Then you must marry him.'

'Shut up.'

'Why does he want to see you again? You PUKED while he was fucking you. I'd take that really personally.'

'Maybe I should get him a "sorry" card.'

'Maybe. Did you piss yourself too? Bet he'd be into that.'

We crack up.

I text back. *Sorry. No. I've got homework.*

He writes back, not as quickly as the last time. *Homework? How old are you?*

'Oh my God! He doesn't know your age?'

I shook my head. 'He never asked. I told him I was a nanny.'

'Text back "15", freak him out, the pervert!'

I giggle.

I text back *'17'.*

He doesn't text back for a while. Then he says: *I didn't realise u r so young. Thought 20s. Your 2 young. Sorry luv. Bye. X*

Beth squeals with laughter and pounds the bed with her fist. 'You've just been dumped. You've just been dumped by a tramp in the park.'

I say thank God he used a condom, Beth says thank God he didn't murder me. Then she adds, 'I'd rather die than get pregnant by a guy who fucks me while I'm puking.'

I hit her with Henry the teddy which Katie has left in my room.

He texts again. *I am shocked by this. I got a daughter a bit younger than you. Please take better care of yrself. Treat yrself with more self-respect.*

'What a patronising arsehole!' He should be impossibly flattered that I went anywhere near him, he really should.

'He's got a point though,' Beth says.

This stings because I *know* he's got a point. I *know* what happened last night was not cool. I know it's serious without Beth getting all serious.

'No, he hasn't. What point has he got?'

'Well, babe, he's too old. You gotta think why you did it, why you got so drunk that you shagged someone old enough to be your dad, in a park when you had just met.' Her tone is no longer jokey.

'He wasn't that old!'

'He's *forty!*'

'Guys get with younger girls all the time. Any of the blokes in college, if they shagged a forty-year-old woman everyone would be like wey-hey!'

'Forty-year-old rock star, yeah; forty-year-old that doesn't live with his mum, maybe. But this guy was a random crusty in the Vine!'

'He was nice to me, he bought me loads of drinks.'

'So you had to thank him with your vagina?'

'Oh my God!' I get out of bed. I feel disgusting and grab a towel and my toothbrush. I need to wash. Now.

'You're supposed to be a feminist, Beth!'

'I am, doesn't mean I have to think everything you do is OK. It's not OK because *you* don't feel OK about it.'

'Who says I don't?'

'Er, because I know you, and I know you feel like shit about this. You didn't own what happened, you weren't in control.'

The problem with Beth *always* speaking her mind is that sometimes she doesn't get that she should just shut the fuck up.

'I don't feel like shit, I had fun, and if you're a "feminist"' – I'm so angry I actually use finger quotations for 'feminist' – 'then you shouldn't be so fucking judgemental.'

Accusing Beth of being judgemental is the meanest thing I can think of saying to her. Beth lives her life 'not judging'. It's annoying. We went to a house party once and Zoe brought her cousin Sian. Sian was dressed in practically nothing, showing off her boobs and arse, and she flirted with all the guys and didn't make an effort to talk to any girls. Someone said she was a slag. I think it was me. Beth was outraged and said it was judgemental and 'slut-shaming'. I don't think it was; I just thought Zoe's cousin *was* a slut.

So I am proper angry. I never fight with Beth, but I shout at her now. 'Do you know what? *YOU* are *FULL* of *SHIT*!'

I've never shouted at Beth before. We've been moody with each other but not like this. I'm not sure what to do so I stomp out of my own room and go into the shower. I hear her leave. She doesn't slam the door. She shuts it quietly.

Showering feels good. I come out and call Sammy Houghton. I was at primary school with Sammy and now she's at the same college as me and Beth. Her mum is a TV producer and Sammy knows loads of celebrities. We are sort of friends even though Sammy is obnoxious. She's not the type you'd choose as a life-long friend but she always knows a cool party to go to if you're in with her. She's rich too. Like she'll wear £200 jeans in art class and not care if she gets paint on them.

Beth and Sammy do not like each other. Sammy wore a Kurt Cobain T-shirt once and Beth asked her what her favourite Nirvana song was. Sammy couldn't name a single one. Not even 'Smells Like Teen Spirit'. Beth is a massive Nirvana fan and gets really annoyed when people do lame things like wear a band T-shirt when they don't know their music.

So Sammy hates Beth and the feeling is mutual. She's intrigued when I tell her me and Beth have fallen out. We are quite famous for being inseparable. When I went out with Jamie, some people called us 'The Wheelbarrow', which Beth hated.

I kick down the sickening sense of disloyalty as I tell Sammy the massively distorted version of our argument. We laugh at how right-on Beth is and how up her own backside she is, and how she dares to judge me when she's too boring to have the kind of fun that I have.

'Babe,' Sammy says, 'she's probably jealous because you're out getting some and she's not.'

I left out the bit that Dave is forty, has a tooth missing and that I puked while we did it.

I arrange to go out with Sammy and her lot that evening to a house party, some girl called Tamara from her old school.

In the kitchen I see Katie has left me a handful of Jelly Babies on the table with a little note: 'Roses are red, violets are blue, you're still asleep, and that's boring of you!'

For some reason they make me cry. The Jelly Babies and the note break my heart. I sob as I get some Drambuie from Alan's drinks cabinet. I get pangs of shame and pain when I remember how Jamie ignored my messages.

Alan will notice the Drambuie has been drunk, but who cares? It's sweeter than whiskey and goes down easy. Before I can stop myself, I've drunk more than half of what was there. I take the whole bottle. I will buy another before he notices. I put on make-up and wear heels to look older, not that I usually have much of a problem buying booze.

I'm sweating as I walk to the shops; my armpits are soaking and I can feel damp patches growing. I haven't enough money to buy a whole bottle of Drambuie, so I've swiped six pound coins from Katie's piggy bank. I will replace that too. I think I smell of BO but I *have* to replace the booze.

CHAPTER FIVE

'I don't know who you are, can you please get OUT of my parents' HOUSE!'

I open my eyes. There is a girl staring down at me, her hand is on my shoulder, having shaken me awake. She has long blonde hair, freckles and wide blue eyes that look in this moment icy and angry. She is really pretty. I'm on a hard floor with a dark pink carpet, under a sleeping bag. I try to sit up. My head spins. The girl who woke me goes and busies herself with clearing up her parents' home. I squint at her. It's Tamara's older sister, Geneva, and, from the sounds of it, Tamara is in huge trouble.

There is someone sleeping next to me, sharing the sleeping bag. A black girl with really long false eyelashes. She's more than just next to me. We are cuddled up close. She senses me stirring and she does too. She holds me closer and puts her lips on mine and she kisses me gently without opening her eyes and I know we must have started all this last night, but I can't remember anything. I stop kissing her because I'm sure my breath is vile and I need to get out of here. She turns her back to me and sinks back into sleep.

Geneva is trudging through the bodies on the floor and waking them up. I hear a loud 'All right! Chill out,' and Tamara whining as her sister scolds: 'Mum and Dad TRUSTED you!'

There is no Sammy or anyone else around that I know. I'm literally in a stranger's house, surrounded by strangers. It's a huge house. Miraculously, my bag and my coat are in the corner of the first room that I look in. I don't stop to pee or look in a mirror, nothing. I just find the front door and go. I don't know what time it is but it's early. The streets are deserted and the air is so fresh, the sun can't have been up for long. I don't know where I am. I don't know how I got here, when I got here, or what I did here. I remember meeting Sammy and two of her mates in the park; we had bought drinks to have there before we went to the party. But that's it. My phone battery is dead. I've got my travel card, though, in my purse. I keep walking until I reach a main road and find a bus stop. I'm deep in the belly of Wimbledon. It takes me over an hour to get home to Ealing, but I finally find a connection of buses and tubes.

I did not text Mum to say I'll be out all night. I always text Mum if I'm going to be out all night. Alcohol is still rampaging through my bloodstream. Still pissed, I avoid eye contact with the mums and dads taking their excited kids, laden with scooters and footballs, to the park.

I feel like an alien as the city wakes up, stretches, and gets moving. My hair is a haystack, I have last night's make-up sliding off my face and my mouth tastes like a drip tray with fag ash in it. At least I woke up alone, well, apart from eyelash girl who I try to tell myself doesn't count because my knickers are still on. My first experience with a girl and I can't remember it.

When I walk in the house, Mum goes all kinds of mental. She hears my key in the lock and rushes into the hall, a mad look in her eye – fear, I think it is. She is pale and looks a hundred years old.

The police have been called, Beth's dad has been called. He and Beth are right here in my mum's living room. When she sees me, for a second Mum's face is the most relieved I have ever seen, like she thought I was dead, then found out I'm alive.

After a beat, though, she screams at me. Katie runs and clings to my leg, begging Mum. 'Stop it, Mummy! Stop shouting at Nina!'

Alan tries to calm Mum down. Mum swears. Mum never swears. Mum screams: 'I've been worried sick! WHERE HAVE YOU BEEN? WHERE THE FUCK HAVE YOU BEEN?'

'Just some party,' I tell her. 'Don't know where.' At least that is honest.

She throws a mug at the wall, quite carefully.

She starts to cry. 'I don't know what to do. I just don't know what I'm supposed to do.'

It's mayhem.

Max, Beth's dad, sort of takes charge because Mum is a mess and Alan prides himself on not interfering. He thinks being a spineless twat means he's being a good person. He clears up the miraculously unbroken mug.

'She's all right,' Max says. 'That's the main thing, Sandra, yeah?' He looks at me. 'I don't think you realise what you've put your mum through, Nina.'

Max sits down on the arm of the sofa, puts his hand on Mum's back and gives it a rub. 'Sandra, Nina is safe, OK?'

Alan bristles awkwardly. 'I'd better inform the police. We don't want to waste any more of their time.' Then off he goes.

I untangle myself from Katie. 'Get off now, I need to go upstairs.'

'Mummy was crying loads and saying, "I want my baby back,"' Katie explains. 'I thought she meant me but she meant you. You're too big to be a baby!'

Mum has her head in her hands.

'Sorry, Mum.' I do feel sorry. 'My battery died.'

Mum cries. 'I thought YOU had died!'

'You go on upstairs, Nina. I'll make your mum a cup of tea.' Max is so chilled.

'Can I have a cup of tea as well, Dad?' Beth grins at me. I grin back. I'm so glad she's here. She comes over and hugs me and I want to cry.

'Sorry I was a total dick yesterday.'

She kisses the top of my head. 'Dad? Can Nina have a tea too even though she's a total dick?'

Max rolls his eyes, smiles and goes to the kitchen.

He 'gets' things, Max does. He gets how Mum and Alan are overreacting and it's actually normal for a seventeen-year-old girl to have a few drinks on a Saturday night and end up on the other side of Wimbledon, in a strange house kissing a girl with massive long lashes and have no idea how she got there.

I tell Beth I went out with Sammy.

'Sammy? Blimey, you must have been *really* pissed off with me.'

'Don't remember anything, the whole night's a blackout.'

'Then are you *sure* you were out with Sammy? Might have been Satan with a wig on. Oh no, wait, that *is* Sammy.'

'She didn't stick around, she just left me passed out at a random person's party.'

'What a wanker.'

I tell her about the girl in the sleeping bag. Beth knows about me and girls. She says I'm a 'lipstick lesbian'. Beth thinks it's cool. She is VERY straight. No matter how pissed she is, she'd never get off with a girl.

'I am never, ever drinking again.'

'Just stop being *such* a caner.'

'What do you mean?'

Beth looks at me and I know whatever she's going to say next isn't going to be all jokey.

'Don't stomp off and be a nightmare again. You get to this point where you're no fun anymore. You're a right laugh when you're a bit pissed, but then you don't stop drinking and you're not *you* anymore. You're gone and the next time I speak to you you've been in some drama.'

'What do you mean I'm "gone"?'

'I dunno . . .' Beth says. 'You get this look in your eye that says Nina's gone.'

Beth and her dad leave soon after we've had tea. Mum stops being so mad and gives me a long hug. Alan takes Katie to the shops for milk when we already have a full four-pint bottle in the fridge. He has no imagination.

I have a shower and charge my phone. There are a million messages from Mum, of course, getting more and more frantic. There are no messages from Sammy. I call her up.

'Babe, I can't talk, I'm out shopping with my MUM.' Code for: 'Can't talk about anything much right now.'

She doesn't ask how I am, or how I got home.

'Hon, what happened last night? I've got total blackout.'

'Oh my God, you were so wasted. We got to the party and you were so off your face I was embarrassed because, like, I invited you and my friend Tamara was like "what the fuck" and then you and this girl Rachel were all over each other. Like properly *eating* each other's faces. It was so gross. We got a taxi home, I told you when we were going but you didn't want to come. Your mum's put loads of messages up on Facebook trying to find you, by the way. I'd DIE if my mum did that! This morning was manic – I had to get my nails sorted before I came shopping so didn't have chance to write back to her. You better give her a call, I think she's worried. By the way I totally didn't know you're gay!'

'I'm not actually gay, Sammy. Don't go around telling people I'm gay!'

'Oh my God, Nina,' she says, laughing, 'it's not a problem. Just don't, like, come on to *me* ever, because I'm so not into that.'

'You're heterosexual, does that mean you want to get off with Archie Barfoot?' Archie Barfoot is this huge fat guy in college who always sits on his own at lunch, always wears the same dirty, baggy T-shirt, and he smells.

I'm annoyed with myself for calling Sammy. I feel a cow for using poor Archie Barfoot to call out Sammy's ignorance.

I'm not ashamed, I'm just not gay. I'm bi or whatever, but who cares? If you fancy girls sometimes, then idiots like Sammy think you fancy ALL girls. And I don't. I fancy ten guys to every one girl, me and Beth worked that out once, so I'm only ten per cent gay.

Mum wants to 'spend time' with me. We have a nice day actually. I feel rough but she takes me out for sushi and a milkshake, and I feel better. We go shopping and she buys me a new top. I love my mum when it's like this. She can be cool. Very cool. I miss it being just us. I can't imagine my world without Katie, but Mum is different now. She's got to look after Katie and Alan; they're her priorities. 'You're not a little kid anymore,' Mum always tells me, as though that means I'm no longer her responsibility.

I'm glad Mum has someone, of course. I'm glad she's not lonely, but. . . Alan? She's way too cool for Alan. She used to be quite wild, I think, when she was with my dad. She's got loads of pictures of them at parties and festivals. He looked so fit; that's a creepy thing to say about my own dad, I know, but he was, and she was beautiful and young. Both of them are always holding cans of beer or glasses of wine in the pictures, looking in love and happy. Now, though, now she is sensible and does yoga, and says things like, 'Now I don't think that's a good idea,' and watches her salt intake.

She used to talk about my dad a lot when I was younger, and when she didn't have Alan. She met Dad at uni. Well, when *she* was at uni. He had a band and they played in the pub where she worked. The band was called Dirty Snow. They didn't get anywhere. Dad eventually got a job doing websites, but they still played pubs.

Before she had me, Mum went with him to his gigs and loved everyone piling back to their little flat afterwards for a party, but when I came along, Dad didn't stop partying and she wanted their lives to be more normal. Mum says that loads of other girls were jealous of her because everyone fancied my dad. I think she liked that; I think she liked being the special one who got him. Not sure how special she felt when he wet the bed or shat himself after he passed out drunk on their bed.

She doesn't talk much about him, these days. I suppose it was ages ago and I suppose she doesn't want to drag him around in her new life. I get that. I don't get much when it comes to Mum and Alan, but I get that he was the one to catch her when she finally let go of Dad.

I've got a stack of things my dad wrote and drew for me. He was a really good artist. On my first birthday card he drew a cartoon of himself, Mum and me where Mum is looking madly dishevelled. I, as a baby, am wailing in her arms; all you see is a gigantic screaming mouth. Dad has his thumb out, hitching. He has huge bags under his eyes and is holding a card out with his destination written on it: 'Land Of Nod'.

'You're really like your dad, you know. Not just your hair,' Mum says.

My hair is jet black like Dad's was. Mum and Katie are both blonde.

'Your dad was always stumbling home at all hours. We both were. He was always the one to start the party when there wasn't one happening. But, darling, he didn't know when to stop.'

I know all this. Dad fell on me once. I was about four and sleeping on the floor next to the sofa at a party and Dad thundered on top of me and Mum shouted at him. It's one of my earliest memories. I can't imagine Mum or Alan EVER letting Katie curl up on the floor and sleep where adults are partying. I can't imagine Mum and Alan having the sort of party that doesn't involve place settings and a Waitrose cheeseboard.

'He didn't know when to stop so there was heartache all round.'

I know this too.

'Do you think your drinking is a problem? Do you get drunk when you don't mean to?'

I always mean to.

Dad always had a glass or bottle of some kind of booze in his hand. He was a happy drunk with his friends. Dad worked in Soho with loads of single people in their twenties and thirties. He was always drinking after work and going to events and parties. Mum got upset on the nights he didn't come home at all. She would scream and scream at him when he finally came back, then lie on her bed and cry, and he would spend days begging for forgiveness and promising he'd never stay out again. Alan never makes her cry.

We don't talk, me and Mum, about the times he wasn't nice. We don't talk about the times he would scream and shout over nothing and bully me and Mum until he'd slammed every door a thousand times and thrown a few things at the wall. Me and Mum never talk about those things, because those things weren't dad. Dad was wonderful, Dad was funny, the absolute best dad in the world.

'When was the last time you had an entire day without drinking?'

There hasn't been a day for ages without me drinking. I haven't got pissed every day but I always have a few shots of vodka and pinch booze from Alan's cabinet when I haven't got any of my own.

'Loads of days. I don't drink every day. No way.'

Mum sighs. 'Alan does notice alcohol going missing, you know.'

Oh Christ. Knowing Alan he'll have marked it and done a bar chart of when, what and how much has gone missing.

Then Mum wants to talk about Germany.

'I'm not coming,' I tell her. Again.

'I get that. But Alan and I *must* go.'

'Can't he go on his own and come back at weekends?'

'Do you have any idea how much that will cost in both money and time?'

'Everything is about money with you.' Mum can't win this.

'We want to be a family so Katie and I must go with him.'

'And I'm not family suddenly?'

'Oh, Nina, don't be stupid. Don't be deliberately stupid.'

I'm not being stupid, I'm being an arse. I'm being a brat. It's hard to stop once I start.

'I've got my A levels and I'll just be stuck out there. What about my friends?'

Mum tries her irritating best. There is an English school, I am bright, I'll adapt, Beth can visit, it will be an adventure . . . and then she says this: 'It might be a good way to start afresh, Nina. Stop all this drinking. Be a completely new person.'

I suck my chocolate milkshake down to the bottom. My mother thinks I need to be a 'completely new person'.

'I'm going to be eighteen in a month.'

'I'm aware of that; I was there when you were born.'

'I can do what I like without your permission then.'

'Yes, but not without our money.'

'I'll stay in London and stay with Beth and her dad.' I'm pretty sure this will be OK with Beth and Max.

It didn't take that long to convince Mum this was a solution. She made a good show of thinking it would be best for me to go with them, but I think she was quite relieved when she spoke to Max and he backed me up on my idea.

Alan, I think, behind his 'whatever you and Nina think is best, Sandra' exterior, was doing cartwheels on the inside at the thought of having Mum and Katie to himself and not having to deal with my crap for a year.

Mum's main concern was my partying. I promised her I would stop drinking so much. I was so convincing. 'Come on, Mum! I think I've learnt my lesson after the gruesome hangovers I've had lately.'

Also Mum knows I really want to get into Warwick Uni still. 'I've got to get AAB, Mum, I won't have time to drink!' That's the grades I'll need to do English literature. I don't see why I should give up on that just because Jamie messed up our original plans. I am going to go there and have an amazing time and prove I don't care about him and Marcia one bit.

Beth and me were excited about living together. 'Maybe we can get Dad to move into the shed and it can be like our own pad!'

Then all the plans were put into place in Alan's efficient-as-fuck style. He's rented the house out to a Scottish family for the year. I had to take down all my posters and completely clear out my room and what I didn't take to Beth's went into storage. My room at Beth's is tiny so I could only really take my clothes and books and a few photos.

'It's just for a year,' Mum kept reassuring me. 'It'll fly by.'

I am to work in Max's bookshop when I can, to help earn my keep, as long as it doesn't eat into study time. Max and Mum came to other arrangements with money for my food and stuff and for generally taking me off her hands.

Mum told me and Beth to make sure we 'give each other space'.

'Living with friends can be a challenge, however close you are. You learn new things about each other, so try to be tolerant.'

'You don't know how close we are, Mum. Please don't give me advice about my friendships.' I can't help being an arsehole to Mum at every opportunity.

Katie and me pack up my room together. I give her my old jewellery box, full of junk I don't wear anymore. She sat for a whole afternoon admiring her loot.

Mum's work don't want to lose her and have told her they'll keep her job open for her. The refugees of London will have Mum fighting their corner once more but for now, she is off to Düsseldorf.

Max takes them to the airport in his people carrier. With me, of course. I cry the whole way. I sit in the back holding Katie, who has fallen asleep.

It only really hits Katie that I'm not going with them when it's time to go through security. Then she starts to sob and clings to my waist and I try so hard *not* to cry now because I want to be strong for her. I've bought her a book to read on the plane, one I'm sure she will love called *Cats, Bats, Frogs and Logs*.

'You read this, Katie, and when you're finished call me and tell me what you think of it. OK?' She nods and cuddles Henry, her bear. Then she and Mum and Alan go through the gate.

CHAPTER SIX

I've been going every week to Isabelle's creative writing class. The others dropped off one by one and now there's just a little group of four: me, Zoe, Steve Lambeth, this Goth guy who is really sweet and has acne, and Lucy Charles, who is a total brain and definitely going to Oxford or Cambridge.

Zoe is still seeing Alex. I haven't met him. Well, of course I've *met* him; I mean I haven't seen him with Zoe, and I don't want to. He doesn't want to meet her friends either by the sounds of it. Zoe goes to cocktail bars and dinner parties with him.

'He can get on the guest list for practically any club in London,' she gushes as though picking up the phone and blagging stuff with your public-school confidence is in any way cool.

She's changed a bit. She wears smarter clothes, stuff he's bought her. I've never seen Zoe so into a guy; she's usually so, 'yeah whatever', but with Alex she constantly checks her phone and worries about what he'll think of stuff. She has stopped saying 'homework', she now says 'coursework', and she says 'tutor' instead of 'teacher'.

Beth doesn't trust Alex. 'How can you go back into a club, after what he did with you, and just pick someone else up? If it's that easy for him, *I* wouldn't trust him.'

But Zoe doesn't know how far that night went. She just thinks we had a bit of a snog then I went home.

'Should I tell her?' I ask Beth.

'God no. If you were going to tell her, you should have done it at the start. Bit late now. She's in too deep. It'll upset her.'

I miss Mum and Katie like mad.

'You're the first person I know who has left home,' Beth says.

I didn't leave home. Home left me.

Sometimes I'll see a little girl about Katie's age and I swear I'm going to just go up to her and cuddle her and freak her parents out.

Me and Beth have a little mini dinner party as my 'house warming'. Max cooks for us and goes out somewhere to leave us to it. He's brilliant. He does loads of sweet things like that for Beth and they're never pissed off with each other.

I thought all families fight and scream and that the ones that seem OK just don't do it in front of you, but Beth and her dad are polite and chilled with each other all the time. She never screams 'GET OUT OF MY ROOM' at him like I do to Mum. She's got no reason to; he doesn't just barge into her room to nose around on the pretence of 'collecting laundry' like my mum does.

We get some people we like round. Just girls. This was my idea so Zoe wouldn't ask to bring that Alex guy. We have to invite Trish, of course, and Lucy, from my writing class, and Dana, from Beth's philosophy class. She's loud and funny and does brilliant impressions. We eat, drink wine and play Trivial Pursuit and I totally win even though I'm a bit drunk.

We all rip the piss out of the drama lot. Even Trish is laughing and she isn't even at our college.

Dana does drama with Phoebe and dramatically re-enacts the time Phoebe ran out of a lecture crying because *Miss Julie*, some play they were reading, 'feels like the story of MY life'. Dana throws herself about on the sofa in mock woe and cries, 'No one understands JUST how hard it is to be quite this beautiful and quite this rich. Beth, be a darling and cry for me, I'm too tired.'

Trish announces she can read palms so we all take turns to hear her sincerely delivered, totally made-up bullshit about our life lines. She tells Dana: 'You're gonna be an actress.'

Dana says, 'But you know that because I'm doing drama and, er, everyone knows I'm gonna be an *actor*.'

'Yeah,' says Trish, 'but what you want isn't necessarily on your hand. You could *want* to be an actor, but your palm might say "plumber", though in this case your palm says "actor", not plumber, so you're lucky.'

Trish doesn't mean to be funny, which is what makes her hilarious.

I go to bed pissed and happy but not so pissed that I don't remember going to bed. A rare thing for me.

We are in our final college year. We take our exams next summer.

'That's gonna be my last blow out for a while,' Beth says. She is determined to do well in her A levels. She wants to be a barrister and work in human rights, of course, and she will,

I know she will. I'm not focused like her and want nights like this all the time.

Isabelle tells me I'm making 'real progress' in the writing class. She likes my poems. She tells me I should go and watch some performance poetry as it will 'inspire me' to go in that direction. I have watched some on the Internet; some of it is awful but some has been so amazing it's made me cry. I think I'd die before I could read a poem out loud like that though; it's hard enough in our little class.

Steve Lambeth even asked me if I could go for a coffee with him and talk about my 'writing technique', so we went for a drink. I don't know if I even have a writing technique. Katie likes writing. She writes cute little poems and stories. She says, 'You just have to let all the dumb stuff out.' This is her writing technique, I tell Steve. He doesn't get how cute and clever a kid saying something like that is.

We went to The Mash Tun, a sort of grungy pub with indie band posters everywhere. My dad was a big fan of bands like The Stone Roses and The Wonder Stuff. I like seeing their posters when I go in. My dad liked pretty cool bands. We walked in and Isabelle was in there with a mate, a lesbian. At least I assumed she's a lesbian – she had a LESBIANS DO IT BETTER T-shirt on.

My belly flipped when I saw her unexpectedly like that. I got a proper rush. My cheeks went hot and my palms all sweaty as I tried to pay the barman. She smiled and beckoned us over and so we went. It was amazing, really; she's a teacher and she was having a drink with us and we talked about writers we liked and what we had read. I haven't read nearly as much as Steve, but Isabelle said she'd lend me some books she thinks I'd like.

We finished our pints and Isabelle bought us another drink, Cokes though – she knows I'm seventeen. I felt a tingle, a proper tingle between her and me, like she directed all her questions at me, well, mostly, and every time I looked at her, she was looking at me. I actually thought I was going to faint.

I was gutted when her mate – I didn't catch her name – said they had to leave. I thought we were all settled in for the evening. Once they'd gone, we could get beers though.

Steve and I ended up getting drunk, with him telling me how lost he would be without his writing and how much he hates his stepdad.

I could have slagged Alan off to him, but weirdly, I didn't want to. I sort of felt loyal to Alan just then. He wasn't the arse Steve's stepdad seemed to be. So I just listened. For ages and ages, and he was getting a bit soppy – 'you're so easy to talk to' kind of soppy.

He insisted on walking me home so I snogged him on the way. I was pretending he was Isabelle. Well, trying to but it didn't work because he's six foot two and really skinny with a little goatee. I closed my eyes but it was still hard to pretend he was a sexy girl. He was a clumsy kisser too, tongue all over the shop, and kept grinding against me with his hand on my arse. Thank God I wasn't too drunk. I pulled away and went inside Max's place without inviting him in.

Max has a rule that boyfriends are allowed to sleep over at weekends with 'prior consent'. That's exactly the sort of thing Alan would say, but not in a jokey way like Max.

They can sleep over if they're proper boyfriends that we have all met, and not EVERY weekend. Not that I wanted a one-night stand with Steve. The rules applied to all of us, he said, but I reckon he laid down the law for my benefit, because Beth has never had a one-night stand and Max, Beth has told me, never brings a woman back to the house unless she's going to be a regular fixture. There have only been two since her mum died. One is now Beth's god-mum, Sandy, who I've met loads. She's an artist and lives in Devon and is really cool. The other is a woman called Sonia. Max is now *her* little boy's godfather. They all get along and have stayed friends and it works because Max is the nicest man in the world. Beth reckons the reason his relationships haven't lasted is because he's still in love with her mum; he's never gotten over her.

In my tiny, cosy room I Skype Katie and Mum almost every night. If Katie is in one of her chatty moods, I just leave Skype on for ages and mooch about my room and chitchat to her.

Max isn't strict about going out at all. Not that Beth wants to go out much with so much coursework to do. I stay up sometimes and join Max for an end-of-the-day glass of wine. He only ever has the one.

Beth takes the piss. 'Ergh! You don't have a crush on my dad, do you?'

I throw a pillow at her. She can be such a dick.

Mum asks me about my drinking every time we Skype. Not directly. Never directly. It's never, 'Hey Nina! I'm still worried sick about you becoming an alcoholic like your dad. On a scale of one to ten, how much do you need a Jägerbomb right now?' It's more subtle, more like, 'Are you taking care of yourself? Are you going out a lot?'

Mum seems happy there. They all do. Alan sometimes pops his head in when we are Skyping and says hi. Bless him. He makes an effort. Katie says she hasn't learned ALL the German words yet, but when she has she will speak them to me.

Mum might not always say it out loud but she's got 'Freaking Out' written all over her face whenever I mention I'm going out. So I don't tell her I was pissed in Communications class.

I had gone to the pub up the road at lunchtime. It was a really warm day and the whole place was pretty much taken over by our college. Beer goes to my head quickly in the heat.

On the way back to school I took a swig from my hipflask – I've got a proper old man's one now. It works out cheaper than carrying miniature bottles of vodka around. So I had too much and, back in class, I was a bit of a mess. Just giggled a lot, nothing major, but then I got emails asking me to see the college counsellor, Gwen.

I had counselling before, when I was a kid, when Dad died. I panicked that Mum was going to die too, even though she wasn't ill, even though it was explained to me over and over again why Dad died and why Mum didn't have those same problems. I still lay in bed, awake all night, wondering what would happen to me if my mum went.

I still think that. Obviously Katie would stay with Alan, but who have I got? Who have I really got? Beth and Max, I know, but if people aren't family there's a limit to how long you can stay with them, how much they can help you, and what you can help yourself to from their fridge without asking.

Dad's family are all in Morocco and I never hear from them. Except for my Auntie Jean; she lives on Portobello Road. I visit her. Not often. The area is so cool, but she and her flat depress me. She hasn't cleaned it or thrown anything away for years. Even making a simple cup of tea is gross because her cups are grimy and the tea bags are from another century.

Turns out that even though they hadn't talked for years, Mum called Auntie Jean and told her about Germany and asked Jean to keep an eye on me. So she calls me and says, 'I hear she's abandoned you. Come over and we'll have a cup of tea and a chat.'

So I go. I'm always trying to get her to clean her place up a bit, make it look nice, but it's like wading through treacle. You clear one lot of stuff and it just makes room for other junk to spill into the space. She's kept boxes and boxes of Dad's stuff. His books, his clothes, pictures, records. I like having a rummage through them. Dad's clothes smelled of him for ages but now they all smell of Auntie Jean's flat. There's new stuff in there too, junk Jean's bought off the Internet that she'll never use. Weird stuff like baking equipment and quilt-making sets. She gets loads of useless junk like that online and it just sits there. You have to walk sideways, pressed up against her wall to get round it all and go to the loo, which is a whole other nightmare. Hygiene isn't Auntie Jean's priority.

'You don't mind mice, do you?' she asks as she sweeps some droppings off the table and we drink cloudy tea.

Auntie Jean will eventually be that mad old lady who shuffles around muttering to herself. She's not *quite* there yet, but close. She knows every stallholder down Portobello and they're all nice to her. She boozes. Of course. I go round sometimes and we drink together. I try to tell her she drinks too much but she just says, 'You mind your own stuff, missus. It's too late for me, but you've got your life ahead of you.'

I want to bring Katie here one day, show her my dad's pictures and records, tell her about him. I'd love her to meet Auntie Jean. She is a bit smelly and bonkers, but she is the only link I have to my dad.

Dad was born in Casablanca but he didn't like making a 'thing' about being half-Moroccan. I don't think it was something he wanted to keep being reminded of. He wasn't exactly emotional about that side of his family. His mum, Salma, was the Moroccan one. She died when he was three. His dad, my grandad, Joe, was an English businessman but he died before I was born. He met my gran when she was a dancer or something in Casablanca and Grandad Joe was there for work.

It's not quite the romantic family history you'd hope for. He met Salma in some club. She already had Auntie Jean who was nine and had never known her real dad. My gran, Salma, got pregnant, they married and when Dad was still a baby,

Grandad Joe moved them all to London. Salma can't have liked London much because she jumped in front of a train at Morden station a year later.

No one knows why my gran chose Morden; they lived in North London, in Kentish Town, the opposite end of the Northern Line.

Auntie Jean told me all of this. 'So I was left with no mum and with a bloke who wasn't my dad trying to raise me. Your grandad got stuck with me.'

Dad never talked about any of this. He only ever said, 'My mum died when I was three and I dunno what I would have done without your Auntie Jeanie.'

'I was like a little mum to him. He was so small when Mum died and your grandad was always away . . . left us with whatever twenty-year-old he'd picked up.'

I still think my grandad must have been a *bit* cool to raise Dad and take on Jeanie too. I mean it's not what he planned: his wife killing herself and leaving him to it. I think about what it was like for my gran, those last few seconds before she jumped. Her suicide has been a dark rain cloud over my life for as long as I have known about it. Not too oppressive, but it's there. I haven't got a grandmother, not because she got cancer or had a heart attack, not because she was killed in a car accident, but because she found her life so unbearable she jumped in front of a giant hunk of metal moving at high speed.

'Nowadays people talk and talk about depression this and depression that; everyone's got bloody depression,' Jean tells me. 'But back then, my mother wouldn't have known there was a word for what she was feeling. Must've been ter-rifying, eh?'

Jean didn't directly blame my grandad, but she obviously thought he could have done more to help her. 'He was an educated man. My poor mother was not. She was just happy a nice English man had come to her rescue. Ha! What a "rescue"!'

I look like my gran. Well, I've got her Arab eyes and crazy curly hair. I've got just one picture of her. She's preg-nant and in a wedding dress. She has a big Hollywood star smile and I stare at her face, trying to find a clue of what was going on in her mind. But I just see dark, pretty eyes. She looked calm.

Auntie Jean's photos are in a big dusty box which she pulls out from under her bed when I go to see her, and then brushes off the hairs of a cat long dead.

I find a picture of me, aged three with Dad. We are looking at each other and I am giggling. He has a big smile on his face, a cigarette in one hand and a drink in the other as he balances me on his knee.

Our flat was where Dad's mates all gathered. An endless rabble of 'drinkers and thinkers'. Mum never knew where he met half of the people who trooped in and out of our home. Some were from work, staff and contacts. Some were just peo-ple Dad had met in a pub, at a gig, anywhere they'd had a laugh and he'd invited them back.

Dad did his best to look sheepish the next day when Mum complained about having to clear up after strangers, getting into a huff at the state they left the flat in. 'Who puts their fags out in a kid's sippy-cup?' She would clear up while Dad sat hungover, in his dressing gown, watching TV with me tucked under his arm eating the chocolates he'd bought on his early morning stagger to buy cigarettes.

Dad would gently calm Mum down. Not all of Dad's hangovers made him mean. Eventually Mum would allow him to make her laugh and then they'd disappear into the bedroom for ages which meant I could watch TV and eat chocolates for as long as I wanted.

The college counsellor is called Gwen and she is comfortingly posh with kind-old-lady blue eyes.

Her room is a sweet little carpeted one at the far end of the college with dusty books on a big bookshelf and big goldfish swimming around in an old tank with slightly green water.

'Nina, how much would you say you drink?'

'No more than anyone else.'

'And how much does "everyone else" drink?'

'Probably a bit less than me,' I admit.

She moves on from talking about drink pretty quickly and we talk about Mum and Alan and Katie moving to Germany. Before I know it, we are talking about my dad.

If your dad dies when you're only nine, then everything you fuck up after that ends up being because 'her dad died when she was nine'.

'She's hit another kid!'

'Well, her father's died.'

'She didn't do as well as she might in the exam!'

'What did you expect? Her father is dead.'

'She got smashed and showed her knickers in Communications class!'

'Well of course she did, her father's dead.'

Poor Dad. He gets the blame for all my fuck-ups.

I manage to convince Gwen that I'm not about to move to a park bench and drink meths and start shouting at the air.

Gwen's suggestion is: 'Try alternating your drinks. One drink, then a glass of water, alcohol, the next one, water.'

I promise her I will try this great idea. I am all smiles and 'no problem', then I leave without having to make another appointment.

I get a message from Jamie. Finally. I have 'liked' a million of his comments and photos (not the ones with Marcia in them).

'Hey, Nino, good to hear from you. Sorry I've taken so long to reply.'

A flash of hope enters my mind. Perhaps the next sentence will be, *'I have broken up with Marcia.'*

But it isn't.

'Have been really busy.'

I hate that. I hate it when people say they haven't been in touch because they're 'busy'. It's like they're saying you're *not* busy. President Obama is busy but I bet he would return a message from the girl he said was his soulmate until he buggered off to Hong Kong.

'Glad everything is cool.

Love Jamie x'

That's it. That is the whole message. Nothing else. I stare at it for ages, my heart weighing a ton and feeling like it's going to drop into my stomach.

I put my shoes on, grab my bag and go to The Mash Tun. I don't tell Beth I'm going out, I just go.

Ordering a pint, I glance around for Isabelle which takes about a second because it's not busy. She isn't here. I really want to see Isabelle. I drink. I sink pretty much the whole pint in one go right there at the bar. I remember what Gwen said about alternating drinks with water. I catch the barman's eye.

'Can I have a glass of tap water, please?' He nods, grabs the glass, and I add quickly, 'And another pint too, please.'

The barman must think I'm a dickhead, drinking in a pub on my own.

'Are you waiting for someone?' he asks. It's just a friendly question, not a 'hahaha, you've got no friends' thing.

I tell him the truth. 'No. I just fancied a drink.'

He's nice, the barman. A bit older than me. He has an entire arm tattooed, a shaved head and he's fat. We chat. I tell him my boyfriend is in Hong Kong and has met another girl.

'Well, he's not your boyfriend anymore then, is he?' He's Irish. I like his accent. It's soft and sing-song.

'I guess not.'

'Not "I guess not". He definitely isn't.' He smiles at me. 'I'm Derrick.'

I smile back. 'I'm Nina.'

'Nina,' Derrick says, 'my shift finishes in fifteen minutes, do you want to wait and have a jar with me?'

I do. I wait at the bar. I drink the second pint, and the water. Once he is done, he buys me a drink out of his tips and we sit. He's nice, an art student at St Martin's College, like in the Pulp song. He has little beads of sweat that keep forming on his brow and he wipes them off.

We have another pint. He's funny, sweet, gentle. He's twenty-one and wants to be an animator. I tell him how much Katie loves *Wallace and Gromit*. I tell him I write and he says I should write a story for Katie and that he could animate it and it would be like the next *Gruffalo* and we'd be millionaires. I love him knowing about the same kids' stuff that I do.

'I've got loads of nieces and nephews,' he tells me. 'Whenever I'm home I overdose on kids' TV and books. I like it more than adult stuff.'

He asks me if I want to go back to his for a pizza.

'My answer to pizza is always "yes".'

He shares his flat with three other art students. We go back to his; the others aren't home. I stumble when we get in. Drunk. It's early, only about six o'clock. I put my arms around him and giggle. 'Are you gonna kiss me?'

I feel his belly against mine. It puts me off a bit which is horrible because me and Beth are always annoyed with guys who never go out with fat girls.

He is surprised, in a good way. He is smiling, though not putting his arms around me.

'Do you want me to?'

I smash my lips on his, he puts his hands on my back and we are kissing. He is a lovely kisser.

Then he stops, gently pulls back and says, 'I'll whack the pizza in the oven, shall I? Do you want tea?' I follow him into the kitchen. He puts the kettle on.

'I want another drink,' I say. 'What have you got?' A rummage in his fridge unearths a half-empty bottle of wine.

'That's my flatmate's, but sure have it. I'll replace it with a full one.'

'We will, to be sure to be sure.' I giggle.

'Oi, missus, that's racist.'

We go into the living room. ''Tis not racist!' I say in the worst, piss-take Irish accent. 'I don't have a racist bone in my body!' I'm being a dick. I'm often a dick when I'm pissed. I think I'm being funny; other people think I'm an arse. Luckily Derrick smiles and rolls his eyes as he sits down and picks up his guitar.

When I tell Beth about this she's going to cringe. 'Argh! He *serenaded* you?' But it's all right. Not too cheesy. Some song I've never heard about riding with Lady Luck. 'Tom Waits,' he tells me when he's finished. 'You like him?'

I've never heard of him but I nod.

The pizza is done. I follow him to the kitchen. The wine's inside me now, and I sort of jump on him and kiss him again. He kisses me back for just second, then pulls away. 'Nina, c'mon, you're pissed.'

'Come on, let's go to your room,' I say. Somewhere in the back of my mind I know I'll feel bad afterwards. I know I'll feel guilt and shame and I'll swear I won't do this stuff again, but right now there is no return.

His room is messier even than mine; there are a load of things on the bed.

He finds condoms and we eventually get each other's clothes off. I am noisy, and at one point he tells me, 'Shhhh. I think my housemate's home.' I like his bigness in bed. When he is on top of me, it's like he absorbs me, consumes me, like I've disappeared. It feels good to be held tight afterwards. He holds me really close and strokes my hair and kisses my face and tells me, with his accent even more gentle after sex, that I am beautiful and that he'd noticed me when I'd gone in with Steve and had thought Steve was my boyfriend. We fall asleep.

I'm still in his arms like that when my phone rings and wakes me up. He stays fast asleep. My skin beneath his is clammy. He is sweating as he sleeps. I sort of have to lift his heavy arm off me and wriggle out. I dress quickly and leave his room.

I have a missed call from Beth, then a text: *'Where did you go!? Dad and I are getting a takeaway.'*

I go into the bathroom. It's a messy boys' bathroom. The toilet looks like it has never been cleaned. There is a sliver of soap and a threadbare old towel. I wash as best I can. I open Jamie's message again. I write back.

Jamie: I feel like shit that your message is so short. I wrote you loads! Aren't we friends anymore? Because if we aren't then tell me and I'll stop embarrassing myself by staying in touch.'

I press SEND. It feels good.

Beth has been saying for ages I should just be honest with him. Beth and Jamie have kept in touch a bit since we broke up. They'd been good mates. She has never called him a dick for going off with someone else. Instead she says, 'Babe, maybe it all got too intense for him. We're not even at uni yet. He probably wants you to have some freedom when you go, instead of being tied to a relationship. You don't want to not make the most of uni because you've practically got married before you've even got there.'

I get all that. I get all that from people who aren't in love . . . people who don't have what me and Jamie had.

There is chatter and laughter coming from the living room. As I go down, this guy comes out of the kitchen carrying beer.

'Hello! Who are you?' He is gorgeous, really hot. Like a model. Or a rock star, tall with a lean body, floppy, dark hair and a sexy-as-hell face, all high cheekbones and amazing blue eyes.

'Nina, I'm . . .' I've sobered up so am suddenly self-conscious that I look like I've just fucked his mate. 'I'm a friend of Derrick's.'

'Derrick? Is he in? DERRICK YOU BASTARD GET DOWN HERE! YOU NICKED MY FUCKING WINE!'

He hands me a beer and tilts his head towards the living room. 'Join us.'

There are about ten people in there. All art students, all about twenty and really cool. I drink everyone's booze and have a few drags of a joint. I'm not good with drugs. My head's foggy, really foggy. I try hard to hold it together, not wanting to be the dickhead teenager who can't handle her gear.

Derrick comes in and there are cheers from the others. He sits next to me and tries to put his arm around me, but I don't want that. I don't want the people in the room knowing that we've done anything. I don't want them to think I'm his new girlfriend. I'm wasted but consciously make efforts to turn away from him and talk to other people.

Elliot is the gorgeous guy from the hall. I try and talk to Elliot. Elliot is loud and funny but I can't get his attention to myself. The other girls there are nice and I'm trying not to seem so young. I drink more.

I'm not exactly sure how, but I end up in a bedroom with their other housemate, Gus. I've not talked to him much at all. We just started kissing. He's tall and really skinny, bony even, with reddish-blonde hair and wide, mad blue eyes.

He's kissing me in his bedroom and putting his hands under my top and scratching down hard on my back. We fall on the bed and he murmurs something about a condom once he's between my legs, and we have to stop for a sec, but it's good. The sex, I mean, it's really good. I'm more stoned than drunk. I fall asleep for a bit, I think.

I open my eyes. He isn't in me anymore; his face is pressed against mine and he's saying, 'Hello? Hello? Are you awake, girl? I need you awake, it's more fun if you stay awake.'

Although he's pasty and skinny, he's strong and sort of rough and gentle at the same time. He pins my arms down so I can't move at all, then kisses my neck and murmurs stuff that's a bit cringy, like, 'Who is this princess in my bed?' Stuff that puts me off and I have to kiss him to shut him up.

He goes down on me for ages but I can't relax; I haven't exactly planned this and have already gone with Derrick so I'm not sure what state I'm in down there. I push his shoulder gently and shuffle up the bed so he stops. He gets up, finds my hand and pulls me up. He turns me round, over his desk and starts fucking me from behind. By now all I want to do is sleep. The desk is covered in charcoal sketches. The black rubs off on my boobs and our hands and after, when he pins me down on the bed again, on my arms and face.

He finishes before me. I don't mind, but he carries on with his fingers. It's nice. Then he stops and says, 'You've fucked someone else tonight?'

What? I don't want him to know about Derrick. Has Derrick told everyone? What an arse! 'NO! Of course I haven't,' I lie.

'Are you sure?' he says.

I'm properly awake now, and I'm laughing a little unnaturally. 'I think I would know.'

'I've just fished this out of you,' he says and holds up a mucky condom.

I get dressed quickly and walk to Beth's. I want to get there as fast as I can. The morning air is too clean, it's 7a.m. I got out before Derrick or Elliot saw me. They live about a twenty-minute walk from Beth's place. I am freezing and my phone battery is flat.

He tried to be nice, Gus, but I could see he didn't want me near him again. Why would he? That was seriously scummy. That was not something you can come back from. I made him swear not to tell anyone. 'I don't even know how that happened. If you tell anyone I would die so please don't.'

'You're pretty rock 'n' roll,' he said. 'Also, if I were you, I'd get the morning-after pill. Unless you want a cute little half-Irish baby. That might be quite nice. You could call it "Oops".'

No one can blame my dead dad for the used condom inside me. My knickers felt revolting when I put them on then pulled my jeans over them.

I get in and I see takeaway boxes stacked up with a note from Beth saying 'EAT ME'.

I plug my phone in and shove an onion bhaji in my mouth.

I stand at the kitchen table grabbing food out of the boxes like a pig. I'm starving. The second I hear my phone beep back to life I grab it and check my messages. Jamie has written back.

Nina!

I'm sorry I was abrupt! Marcia is totally cool but she thinks it's weird for me to stay in touch with you. She thinks we should have a clean slate so I've promised her I won't, but you kept messaging me and I didn't want to keep ignoring you. I'll always be your friend in the universal sense of the word . . . how could I not be, mad woman:) But mate, I can't chitchat like we did. Don't think Marcia is a cow, she isn't, she's amazing, really fucking AMAZING, I didn't know what being in love was until I met her so I don't want to fuck it up.

Please understand, please don't go all mental.

Look after yourself.

Jamie x

I think I'm going to be sick, then there is just a dullness where all happiness, all joy in my body, has sunk into a black hole. Beth is asleep. My mum is in bloody Düsseldorf. Why haven't I got more friends? I want to die. And I stink.

I run upstairs and shower. I wash Gus and Derrick off my skin and the smoke and the weed out of my hair. Still in a towel, I run back downstairs and look at my phone to check the message again. Perhaps it's a joke; perhaps I read it wrong. No. He is cutting me off because he loves *her* so much. *Didn't know what being in love was until he met her.* I want my heart to stop, my brain to turn off and my lungs to collapse. They're all in agony. What can I do? A doctor can't help; the police can't help. Why is stabbing someone illegal but setting fire to their feelings is not? How can I be in this much pain and still be alive?

I'm crying, really crying. I bend over the kitchen counter and a sound comes out that I have not heard myself make before. It's a very deep howl.

I don't hear Max come in. He pulls me upright and holds me to him but not for long because I'm in a towel so it's a bit weird.

'Hey, hey! What's wrong? What's happened?'

I try to tell him about Jamie's email but my sobs and snot and hiccupping make it hard.

Max sits me down. He gives me a glass of water. I cry for a bit longer then I start to calm down. He makes me tea. He tells me it's shitty. He tells me I don't deserve this and I have to be kind to myself. He tells me this is no reflection on me, it's just that Jamie is on a different journey.

Why doesn't this end? We broke up so why does this pain resurface again and again, each time more painful than the last?

'Where's Beth?' I whine.

She's out, he tells me. She went out last night and stayed over at Zoe's. They wanted to be up mega early to revise. She'd called me to drag me along. I never called her back.

'You want to get dressed? I'll drive you over.'

'It's Saturday. I'm working at the shop.'

'I'm your boss. I say take the day off.'

I shake my head.

'I want to go to the shop.' I do Story Time on Saturdays. I sit in the corner and read a book to the kids. Their parents bring them especially and I dress up in a mad clown outfit and do all the voices. The kids love it. I get them to roar like lions and snap like crocodiles: whatever or whoever is in the story, we act it out. We jump up and down and go through the actions. Pretty much all the parents stay and buy books afterwards. I don't want to be on my own or go to Zoe's to revise. I get dressed; I wear a jumper Jamie gave me, with a badger on it. I re-read his message, I sob again.

'Weeping woman in the kitchen!' Max says. 'I'm just a bloke! This is the mother of all awkward!'

I laugh because he is making such an effort to cheer me up. Max makes me drink some herbal tea thing and pretends to read the back of the box: 'Calm and soothing, scientifically proven to mend broken hearts.'

I drink it. It's disgusting and Max says, 'You can't really mend a broken heart with tea, despite what the packaging says. But c'mon, you can spend the day having tea and biscuits and glaring at customers. Just take things easy.'

The shop, and Story Time, *do* cheer me. The mums and dads come in and their kids mess up all the books. It makes me miss Katie like hell but it's nice to have other kids to talk to, to make giggle. Sometimes they are the only people I can stand. It's not just because they're cute (because some of them, to be brutally honest, really aren't), it's because they care that you're interested in them. As long as you want to hang out with them and like talking to them, they like you. They don't mind what you look like or what you got up to when you were off your face. You just have to be nice to them and they're up for hanging out with you.

'I can count to ten in Spanish . . . *uno, dos, tres* . . .'

I smile at the little girl. She's about six with her two front teeth missing so she lisps.

'That's so good! Have you been to Spain?'

She ignores my question. I love it when kids do that. She doesn't want to talk about her holiday, she wants to count. 'I can count in French too . . . *Un, deux, trois, quatro, cinco* . . .'

How can you forget someone who still feels a part of you? How is it possible that he's able to cut me off? All those chats, late into the night, still talking as the sun came up. All those cuddles, holding each other for hours, moving only to kiss an earlobe, shoulder, forehead, locked perfectly into each other, not caring that we're getting clammy, two giant pieces of marshmallow moulding softly into each other, drifting around heaven together. WHAT IS HE THINKING? GOING OUT WITH SOMEONE THAT IS NOT ME?

'You're so smart, so good at languages,' I say to the little girl who can't really count to ten in French or Spanish. She smiles then runs off back to the pile of books she has heaped on the floor. Max's shop is like that. You're allowed to make a mess of books and look through them as though it's a library. Max doesn't make much money, I don't think, but everyone loves Down the Rabbit Hole. He has a tiny area we call 'the coffee shop'. It's got three little tables and one of those kids' shop counter things where you can buy plastic tea, coffee and cake with fake money. I love Max for thinking of a little thing like that.

Max says my pain is palpable. I look up 'palpable'. Yeah, I guess it is.

When I ask Max if he thinks I should call Jamie and talk to him, he says, 'You're never going to get the answers you want from him. It would be like sticking your hand in the fire again. He can't help you get through this. You're dealing with sadness and loss. Mourn him, feel sad for as long as you need to feel sad. There's nothing wrong with having the blues. The most beautiful poems, songs and films were written by people trying to express what you're feeling now. You can't change it. Perhaps you will be friends with him and talk to him in the future, but while you're in so much pain, it won't help.'

Max knows about sadness. He lost Beth's mum like I lost my dad. That's proper loss and sadness. But they're dead. Jamie is not.

I pathetically whine my 'phone Jamie' argument . . . if he just heard my voice . . . if I could just get him to click with me the way we used to.

'Maybe I should fly out to see him? I could get an overdraft to pay my ticket.'

Max stops me with a big 'Whoa!' He talks about being intrusive and how I should respect Jamie's wishes to leave him alone.

'But he hasn't specifically said "leave me alone", he's said *he* can't contact *me*.'

'C'mon, Nina,' Max says. 'He's in a tricky position. He doesn't want to have to spell it out. Don't put him in the position of having to, and he will, darling, believe me he will, and that will make you feel ten times worse. He's in love. When people are in love, they're under a spell. You can't break it, and if you go near him, you will get hurt. You'll get hurt again and again and again and once more for luck.'

Beth and Zoe come into the shop and Max lets me go to the coffee place next door with them.

Zoe is still seeing that bloke but I don't care today. It seems like a long time ago. I'm over it. Or at least I'm too fucked up about Jamie to think about it.

Beth pretty much repeats what Max has just said and again doesn't let me slag Marcia off.

'Don't hate on her, babe, cos the only person feeling that hate is you. It's not her fault. She can sense you want him back so she doesn't want him to talk to you. That's fair enough. She's not deliberately hurting you.'

I show them pictures of Jamie and Marcia on Facebook.

'Why are you torturing yourself? Don't look!' says Zoe, peering at a picture of Marcia in a flattering pose. 'She's got good legs.'

'Gimme that phone.' Beth snatches it from me.

'Desperate situations call for direct action.' She starts tapping on it.

'What are you doing?' I try to swipe my phone off her, but she pulls it away in time and runs to the loos.

'There,' she says when she comes back in. She has deleted Jamie from my phone on Facebook, Instagram, everything.

Zoe is impressed. 'Wow, Beth. Love the tough love.'

I take my phone in a panic. 'Jamie and I had pages and pages of funny messages and stuff!' I have copied and pasted the main ones on to a file; if I hadn't I think I'd have stabbed Beth with a fork.

'Shake him off. Friend him later, when you're married to a rock god and sipping cocktails in your pool. I just hate seeing you all busted up.'

My phone feels lighter. It *is* a relief.

'We made so many plans.' I'm crying again.

'Make new ones,' Beth says. Her face is stern, no mollycoddling.

Even though Beth is probably right, she has never had a relationship, not a proper one. She is chilled and upfront about sex. She can sleep with a guy and not get all emotional about it. The closest she has had to a proper boyfriend was a French guy called Sebastian. He was on an exchange program in England and they had a summer of love, then he moved back to France and they are just mates now. No drama. She actually went to France to some music festival with him. She said they just hung out like normal friends because he'd just started seeing someone new in France. She was cool with that. I would have been outraged. Dragging someone all the way to France, then telling them you're not going to fuck them, is really rude.

I tell Zoe and Beth about last night. I tell them I got with two art students in the same house on the same night.

'What? Like a threesome?'

Sammy had a threesome on holiday last year and told us it was more funny than hot. She said porn made it look easy. 'But when you actually do it, you realise how six feet in one bed get everywhere they shouldn't be.'

No, I tell them, not like a threesome. Weird that having sex with each guy separately made it seem more slutty.

Beth immediately asks if I used condoms.

I want to forget it happened, but I tell them about Gus, the skinny guy, and the condom in my fanny. Zoe drops her panini. Beth covers her eyes and wails 'NO!' We laugh. It's funny, right? I'm not boring. No one can accuse me of having boring nights out.

'Honestly, you think you know what the word "mortified" means but you don't. Not until that happens.'

Beth runs to Boots then and there and gets me a morning-after pill. 'Jesus, they're expensive! And I had to endure twenty questions from the pharmacist. No wonder Britain is the Teen Pregnancy capital!'

She hands the bag to me. 'Here. Have this. Don't be a statistic. I'm not ready to be Auntie Beth.'

'Be careful, Nina,' Zoe adds, 'you don't know where guys have been.'

She clearly has no idea where *her* guy had been. It's safe to say she still doesn't know why I got kicked out of the club. He hasn't told her. Thank God.

'I did *try* to be safe. It's not my fault it slipped off.'

I'm not worried about STDs because Derrick can't have slept with that many people. I know that sounds horrible, but he probably hasn't.

Zoe knows Derrick because her sister used to work at the Mash and hung out with him.

'He's a really sweet guy, Nina. You should see him again.'

This kind of thing annoys me about Zoe. She's gorgeous and always gets really gorgeous guys. Then she says stuff like, 'He's a real sweetheart, you should see him again,' about a guy like Derrick, knowing she herself would never go out with him.

She has a Prada shirt on that Alex has bought her.

Beth changes the subject, to talk about my party.

Max, the coolest dad ever, is letting me have my eighteenth at their house. He gets it, he gets me and Beth. Not like Alan who I think was born middle-aged. If he ever *did* let me have a party in the house, it would be 'six guests maximum' and orange squash to drink.

'Is it OK to bring Alex to the party? I really want you guys to meet him properly.'

Oh, God.

It's not OK for Zoe to bring Alex. It's weird. I have only just started being comfortable hanging out with *her* again; I'm definitely not OK about the guy from the most shameful night of my life coming to my landmark party. I don't want to see him; the thought makes me feel sick with anxiety.

'Sure,' I tell her.

The party is ruined already.

'Great! It took me ages to persuade him,' Zoe says without thinking what a massive insult this is. 'He finds people our age immature.'

Beth stands up for our generation. 'We're not immature, we are at exactly the level of maturity we are meant to be; it's *him* that's too old to hang out with us.'

After I help Max shut up the shop at six, I dive into the Mash; it's really near Max's shop.

Derrick is working. I don't know why I jumped in there really. I smile at him and he's quite cold with me and says, 'Hi, what can I get you?' Like I'm just a punter and he has to be polite.

'A pint of lager,' I say.

'Can I see some ID?'

What a dickhead! I'm old enough to fuck but not old enough to be served a beer.

'Coke then.'

He serves someone else and comes over. 'I'm surprised you WANT to drink again after last night.'

Gus has told him. He must have told him.

'What has Gus said?' I demand, like I have a moral leg to stand on.

'Nothing. He didn't have to, you were all over him . . . I saw you.'

'I was wasted last night, I'm sorry if I . . .'

Derrick waves his hand and interrupts me: 'Ah, sure, was a bit weird like.'

'I'm really sorry.'

'No need to apologise, you're not my fecking girlfriend . . .' He hands me my Coke and leaves me to it.

It's Saturday night and I have no plans. Everyone is studying.

'Nina, are you OK?' I turn and it's Isabelle and I nearly fall off the bar stool. She looks amazing in really tight jeans and this lacy black top that falls off each shoulder, better clothes than she wears at school.

'Hi!' I squeak. Why do I squeak when I see her unexpectedly?

'What are you doing here on your own?'

I gesture across the bar to Derrick, who is completely ignoring me. 'I'm sort of friends with the barman.' Then I whisper, 'I got off with him last night and I came in to sort of say hi but it's mega awkward.'

She grins. 'Ack, you crazy kids.'

Isabelle is waiting for her friend, and when she arrives it's a different girl than last time. This one is dead pretty like Isabelle. 'Nina, this is my girlfriend, Sian.'

She says 'girlfriend' as in girlfriend, not a girl who is a friend but as in a lesbian she goes out with. Isabelle just introduced me to her lesbian girlfriend. They kiss, on the lips, and I nearly collapse.

Because I'm a twat, and because I fancy Isabelle so much, I am so surprised that I actually blush and probably look a bit homophobic. 'Oh! Hi! God! I didn't know.'

'Didn't you?' Sian says. 'Isabelle, you mean you don't announce to your classes that you're a lesbian on the first day of term?'

'Ignore Sian,' Isabelle says, 'she thinks she's hilarious.'

Sian grins. I die.

'It's just a shock to find out your teacher has a sex life,' I hear myself say.

Phew, they laugh. That's good.

'Can I get you guys a drink?' This is awkward as hell and not just because I don't have enough money to buy a round.

Isabelle smiles. 'No, thanks. You're under-aged and I'll get the sack.'

'God, yes, sure. I'm not here, I'm going. BYE, Derrick!' I call out, waving too maniacally. Derrick continues ignoring me. I'm actually sweating. I want a drink so badly.

I walk home past the supermarket and I have enough money for a can of ready-made gin and tonic. I open it, gulp it down and suddenly there are tears streaming down my face because gin and tonic is Mum's favourite drink and I miss her and I miss Katie and I even miss boring old Alan. I want to be home again, in my old room with Katie sitting on my bed and chatting to me as we thread bead necklaces together – it's one of the few things she can't do on her own, with her hand. I want Mum buzzing around, doing her mum stuff like asking us if we want mash or chips with our fish fingers and trying to get me to join her running club.

I call Mum. It goes straight to answering machine. For a split second I think about calling Katie, then remember she's six and doesn't have a phone.

I call Alan's phone.

He sounds surprised. Surprised I have his number at all.

He's awkward for a moment, then worried. 'Nina? Are you all right?'

I tell him I am but I can't tell him much more because the sound of his voice makes me miss my family so that my throat seizes up and a load more tears turn up.

'Are you crying? Has something happened?'

My voice is thick as I try to control it and I tell him nothing has happened, the house hasn't burned down or anything and that 'I just want to speak to Mum and Katie. I miss my mum!' I know me and Alan will be embarrassed about this later and neither of us will ever mention it again.

'Oh dear, well, she'll be sorry to have missed your call but I can assure you that your mother misses you tremendously, and Katie chatters about you to everyone we have met. We're all missing you.' That makes me full-on bawl.

Alan does OK. Actually, he does really well. I've always made a point of not talking to him about much, ever, and he 'respects that' and the fact that he 'respects that' has always irritated the hell out of me. He's being so nice. Has he always been like this and I've been determined not to see it? I don't feel like going home. The booze has kicked in.

CHAPTER SEVEN

Max is standing over me, watching, worried as an older man and a young woman both crouch beside me in green paramedics' uniforms. It takes me a few seconds to realise I'm on the kitchen floor.

'Can you tell us your name?'

'Rumpelstiltskin,' I murmur, and giggle. I can't move. My head is full of cement.

'Can you tell us if you've had anything other than alcohol? Have you taken any drugs? Any substances?'

I haven't had drugs, but something must have happened because I am on the floor without knowing how I got here.

'No drugs,' I manage to tell them.

I can't move my limbs but I'm able to hear and grunt answers.

'Was this bottle full?' The paramedic, the bloke, is holding up an empty bottle of vodka in front of me. Their tone isn't 'I can't believe you've drunk all this!' but more 'We just need information so we know what we are dealing with and how we can help you.' Amazing people.

'Yeah.' I drank it. I remember buying it. I bought it on the emergency credit card that Mum gave me with pay-with-your life-if-you-disobey-me instructions not to use it unless it is an actual emergency.

I'm not sure if being absolutely desperate for a drink *was* an emergency. It felt like it at the time.

'Anything else?'

I tell them about the gin and tonic.

'These?' they ask, showing me some of the cans.

There are three or four empty ones in my bag. I must have bought them too. I should probably feel embarrassed, apologetic, but I haven't the strength.

All I remember is being homesick for my family, upset I couldn't speak to Mum and going into the supermarket to buy the booze. Sitting in the park with it, I thought I'd have a little drink before I went home. I didn't imagine I'd drink all the vodka; I was going to save that for my party.

I sort of pass out again.

They do a few checks on me to be sure I'm not going to die on the spot and they tell Max to leave me to sleep it off. Fine by me except I'm on the kitchen floor, in everyone's way, so the paramedics pick me up and move me to the sofa, then leave. I'm conscious but can't move.

Beth's around. I see her somewhere. She's pissed off. 'This isn't normal, Dad,' I hear her growl.

I try to tell her I agree with her but when I open my mouth a stream of pure liquid puke comes out and splashes onto the floor.

I close my eyes and sleep.

*

When I'm better – and this takes a full twenty-four hours of further puking and sleeping – Max asks me if I can understand why he needs to tell my mum about this.

'She left you with me so I have a duty of care to tell her when you're not OK.'

'But I AM OK!'

Beth is at college. I can imagine her response. 'Yeah, I've always got an ambulance on hand when I'm "OK" too.'

When Beth does come home, she pops her head round the door for a quick 'hello', then locks herself away in her room revising. She reckons she's got to do extra studying so she can 'justify time out to party', which is the most boring thing I have ever heard.

I'd begged Max not to tell Mum. Max said he *had* to tell her.

Mum had gone mad on the phone. She called me as soon as Max told her. 'As though Alan and I haven't got enough to cope with in a new country. You wanted to stay, we *trusted* you to behave. You're seventeen, not seven. Katie is more sensible than you are.' Mum went on and on. She doesn't need this. Her priority is her life with Alan. I think Mum feels she's done her bit with me. She didn't rush back to London to look after me; she left that to Max.

'Mum, I hadn't eaten, I didn't realise how strong the drink was.'

'Mum, I'm so sorry I've worried you like this, it breaks my heart to see you this upset because of me.'

I did it, it worked, I convinced her I was just being a typical teenager and had learned my lesson.

Max wasn't so easy to persuade. I found out stuff I didn't know about that night. I'd passed out on the pavement outside Max's house. Some woman knocked on the door to ask Max for help, then helped him carry me in. I'd been drinking in the street.

'You have a drink problem, Nina, you know that, don't you?'

This is clear. Max is the first person besides Mum to say this out loud. I'm not an idiot; I know this isn't exactly normal. I go into a tunnel with drink and that's it: 'See you on the other side!'

When I'm at a bar, I tell my mouth to say 'Diet Coke, please' but it disobeys me and I hear 'Pint of lager, please'. I'll get the drinks down me before my mind has an opinion on what I am doing. I drink and shut my mind up. I drink until I go into blackness. The alternating drinks with water doesn't work. Not for me.

I'm a different person when I'm drinking. Sounds mad, because it clearly *is* me, but it's not *me*. I want to stop. I want to be able to just drink normally and have fun.

I never was this bad when I was with Jamie.

Max gives me a leaflet. 'Please read this, Nina. Have a proper read of it and see what you think.'

It has a list of questions to tick, like: 'Do you get drunk when you don't mean to?'; 'Do you drink to make yourself feel more confident in a social situation?'; and 'Do you drink when you wake up in the morning?'

The first two are normal; everyone does it. The third, all right, bit weird. I don't do it *every* morning. I don't always have booze in my bag so I sometimes have to wait until lunchtime when I have been to the shops. It's not that unusual; loads of people my age drink. Admittedly not often on a park bench on their own to the point of blacking out.

Max hands me more leaflets and I promise to read them. He calls the college counsellor for me and an appointment is made. I promise myself I will not drink again. I have a problem, but I'm not an old tramp sitting in the park. Not yet.

I'm behind on college work. My teachers have had a summit and have called me in for a 'word'. My predicted grades are good. I've always had good grades without – even if this sounds big-headed – working that hard. But all the teachers have noticed I'm slipping. Not quite hitting marks like I used to. My essays are sloppy and I am behind on work when in the past I was the Deadline Queen. No one is hard on me and I'm given extensions and lots of understanding. The good thing about going to the college counsellor is that everyone thinks you might top yourself at any moment so they're extra nice to you and give you a bit more time to get work done. There is no way I *would* top myself, for the following reasons:

1. *It's too dramatic.*
2. *I don't want to traumatise whoever finds the body.*
3. *People like Phoebe Simmons would fall about crying and pretending she knew me much better than she did in order to make it all about her.*
4. *I haven't thought of a guaranteed pain- and gore-free way to do it.*
5. *I would miss Katie.*
6. *Alan would give me a budget funeral.*

I get defensive of the gran I never met, the one who jumped at Morden station. People say, 'It's selfish to kill yourself by jumping in front of a train; it causes delays and traumatises the driver.'

If your mind was clear enough to consider these things, you probably wouldn't go through with suicide. I doubt any suicidal person ever thought, 'I can't go on with life, but I don't want to make people late for work.'

Social etiquette, I imagine, goes out of the window.

Sometimes, when I'm on the underground, and I hear the rumble of the train in the tunnel, I press my back right up against the wall, as far away from the edge of the platform as possible, just in case, at the very last second as the train hurtles past the platform, I go mad and jump.

Beth is being weird with me. She was angry about the whole ambulance thing.

'It's a really stressful time with all our coursework count-ing towards our exam grades, Nina,' she informs me.

It's a stressful time when your family bounce off to another country in the middle of your A levels. I don't say this, though, because I'm in her house and I actually do feel bad. It was intense, that whole drama.

Then I find out the other reason Beth is being weird with me.

Jamie calls. Jamie *actually* calls me, from Hong Kong.

'Hey, mate, you OK?'

I'm shocked when I hear his voice, properly shocked. I had a billion things I've been desperate to ask him, tell him, but they all leave me in an instant.

'Jamie!' I say, 'Jamie, oh my God!' I'm laughing. I'm shocked and happy and laughing.

He is too; I love his chuckle. His voice is the same, everything is the same. We chat, he asks me if I'm OK, I tell him yeah, yeah, I am.

I tell him stupid things that I know will make him smile. I hold my phone so tight to my ear as though it is HIM I'm grabbing. I feel a warm rush because it's Jamie and it's me and we are talking and having a laugh.

He says he's sorry he's been a dick about us. He says Beth called him and said I was having a tough time.

'Are you still going out with Marcia?' I just blurt it out.

He is, of course he is. They're planning to go travelling around South East Asia together, starting off in the Philippines. Jamie lived there for a year when he was eight and always said he wanted me and him to go there together. I don't mention this. Even though I want to scream it. They might come home for Christmas, he says. I never want her to be in London. I never want her in England. I don't tell Jamie that. I say 'wow' and 'cool' and 'that's amazing'.

I am honest with Jamie, though. I actually am, now that I can hear his voice and not just see words on a stupid screen.

'Jamie, I don't want to cry, and I am happy for you, but I'm not going to pretend I'm not hurt. You dropped me, you just dropped me.'

I don't want to scare him away, I don't want him to disappear again, but I need to tell him how he made me feel. Gwen, the counsellor, kept asking me, 'Do you tell people what you're feeling?' Turns out I never actually do.

'I was hurt Jamie, I AM hurt.'

Jamie doesn't run away from the phone. Jamie tells me that he's sorry but he hadn't planned it. He tells me we were too young. Jamie tells me that Marcia is two years older than him and she has made him grow up a lot.

I tell Jamie I'm not fucking interested in how fucking old she is or how much more fucking marvellous Marcia is than me.

Jamie says he didn't call up to have a fight and if I am rude about Marcia, he will hang up.

I say I'm sorry. I'm not his girlfriend anymore. He doesn't have to deal with me again if I lose my cool. I cannot lose my cool.

He throws a bucket of relief over me when he says, 'I was really worried about you when Beth called.' So what we had WAS real. If he's worried about me it means I didn't imagine the whole 'love' thing. I can still worry him. That means I'm not just a nuisance; I hated thinking that I was a nuisance to him.

'Are you pissed off I called him?' Beth asks me later.

'No. I'm glad you did. He said he was worried about me.'

'Yeah, he feels guilty.'

No, it wasn't just guilt. He meant it . . . he loves me. He's not with me, I know, but he loves me and I'm not being a psycho thinking he'll come back to me, but I do know that he loves me.

'I thought you needed "closure".' Beth says 'closure' in an American accent.

'Oh God, don't. You make me think of Marcia.'

'Sorry, babe.'

'What do you think she's really like?' I ask her.

'What do you care?'

'Do you think he'll stay with her for ever and ever?'

Beth gives me a 'look'. 'Stop obsessing.'

'She stole my boyfriend!'

'Listen, Nina, I'm going to have to go all Oprah on you now, but you can't steal people. You can't. They go of their own accord. Look, babe, this is going to hurt, but if he felt about you the way a boyfriend is meant to feel about you, he'd have admired her arse from afar, gone to the loo, had a wank thinking about it, then LEFT IT.'

'Oprah would never, ever say that!'

'It's the truth!'

'You're a crap Oprah.'

'I am an oracle. I am wise and practically holy.'

Beth and I had to do some serious work on Max to let me still have a party. Max thinks it might be too much for me. I promise him I have learned my lesson with booze . . . that I have read the leaflets he gave me and realised I don't want to be that girl – that I'm not that girl.

'She's seeing the counsellor regularly,' Beth pleads. Beth really fancies this guy she's invited who works in the bakery near the bookshop on Saturdays. He's on his gap year and saving to go travelling. He's called Matt and he's totally Beth's type: not good-looking, but quirky. Beth really wants this party to happen.

Max sits me down and tells me he wants me to have fun, but my number one priority should be looking after myself.

'I WILL look after myself, Max.'

Max speaks to Mum and they decide to go ahead with the party, but Max is to stay the whole time and not just come back at midnight.

Beth groans at this but I'm cool with it. It's not my house; he's not my dad. It's better than not having a party.

I do cut down on drinking. I actually do some work. I'm bright; I'm not big-headed, but I know I am. I know I'll do well in my A Levels if I work hard. I've always been in the top streams in everything at school and got A* in all my GCSEs.

'Darling, you can't get complacent,' Mum tells me on Skype. 'People as intelligent as you are always in danger of being complacent.'

'I'm OK, Mum. It's fine. I'm revising, I'm exercising my amazing brain.'

Mum has got a job in Düsseldorf at Katie's international school and has joined the local cycling club.

I don't really like this news – she's settling there, completely. But then Mum is always going on about being 'more than just a wife and mother'. Now she is a wife, mother AND a teaching assistant AND a keen cyclist.

There is lots to be done before the party. What if no one comes? What if EVERYONE does?

Zoe is in a bit of a state at college. She's usually so chilled. It's a bit weird when she clutches my arm and whispers, 'Alex won't pick up his phone!'

Alex, it turns out, is away with his work at a conference. It's in a hotel in the countryside. She has called him all last night and all day but he's not answering. Not even a text. I've never seen her like this.

'Well, if he's had an accident you would have heard.' I know she's not worried about accidents; I know all she can think of is him in a bar with a pretty girl and him in a bed naked with that same girl. She's trying to be calm. She's not doing very well.

'I know he hasn't had an accident! But where is he? What's he doing? Shall I call his work and find out what hotel he's in?'

'NO! Don't do that!' Zoe going out with Alex means I can't properly forget about that night and have to deal with the hideous inevitability of seeing him again. Even so, I don't want her to make a total arse out of herself. 'Don't call the bloody hotel! Just be cool. When he sees he's got a couple of missed calls from you, he'll call when he can.'

She shows me her phone. He's had twenty-eight missed calls from her. And twelve texts.

'Blimey, Zoe, you've turned into me!'

'I know! I sound so desperate!' She's too involved in her own little drama to realise she's just slung an insult my way.

He texts her eventually, towards the end of class. Zoe's whole face changes. The relief almost makes her cry. He said he had *'no signal at the hotel, babe'*.

Zoe is all breezy back when she replies: *'Yeah sure babe'*. Then she goes back to being normal Zoe. But I can tell she regrets my seeing her lose her cool like that. Zoe is determined that Alex is her dream man.

I don't believe for a second that he's had no signal.

I see the drama lot in the canteen. Phoebe is all like: 'Hyped about your party! What's everyone wearing? Is it feather boa, or like sexy-cool?' I've invited her and her lot so that I can invite Robbie too.

The good thing about Phoebe and her friends is that they're loud and colourful and, even though I hate to admit it, the right people to have at your party because they will always break any ice.

'Wear what you like,' Beth says, 'it's just a chilled party. Just be yourself.'

'Oh, God! No way! I spend my whole life trying very hard NOT to be myself! I'll come as my alter ego, Marilyn Monroe.'

I have no idea if she is serious or not.

CHAPTER EIGHT

I put on false eyelashes; my eyes look even bigger and darker than usual.

I am eighteen. In a few hours' time, I will look back into this mirror and I'll be a proper, full-on, all-rights, adult. No one can tell me what to do. I can legally buy booze. I can vote, get married without parental consent. And I'm not mega skinny, but I'm not fat either. I am behind in coursework, but I've still got a bright future ahead of me because my mum thinks I'm super smart.

I am not going to get drunk tonight. I'm drinking water and having ONE drink every hour, on the hour. That is my plan.

Me and Beth have tidied up and put everything valuable or breakable away in Max's room with a KEEP OUT sign.

We put out the food and fill a garden bucket up with ice for the beer and cider. I'm wearing an outfit bought especially for tonight with birthday money from my mum. It's a short, black, retro dress with the back open down to near my bum, with cute little ties. It swishes when I move in it. It's the sexiest thing I've ever worn and Beth gives a wolf whistle when I come down to the kitchen. 'Lez!' I say, grinning.

'You look very nice,' Max says, 'very Sixties.'

I've straightened my hair and slashed red lipstick on and plenty of smoky eye make-up. I look good. I know I do. I hardly ever feel like I can actually say that, but I can tonight. Me and Beth take photos of each other. I make her put them up on Facebook then and there so Jamie can see. (We are now 'friends' again, after Beth deleted him from my virtual life.) Steve has made us a playlist of cool music, mostly indie rock, and we put it on and dim the lights and we wait.

We told people to come at eight. And at exactly eight o'clock, Trish comes with a bottle of cider and plonks herself on the sofa and tucks into a big bowl of crisps.

For the longest time, no one else comes. It's just the three of us. Max comes home from somewhere or other and says, 'Relax, it's still only early,' and starts cooking a big batch of pizzas.

I want to cry. It's half past nine. I'm thinking, 'What if no one comes?' Everyone is revising. 'What a stupid time to have a party,' I say, and Beth says, 'Relax, only saddos come early to parties,' then she dies a little because she remembers Trish is here and Trish arrived at eight. But Trish doesn't mind. She says, 'I once got to a party half an hour late. They said they couldn't let me in, too many people already or something. I don't take chances now.'

I'm properly nervous and panicking, then at ten to ten *everyone* arrives. Me and Beth are laughing with relief. We open bottle after bottle of wine, we pour drink after drink, we throw bottles of beer people have brought into the ice bucket. The house is rammed with everyone from college we invited, and some we didn't. But it's cool. Everyone is happy, people are dancing, the playlist is perfect.

The drama lot sashay in with their usual flamboyance of high screeches and fake accents. I'm glad to see them. They're all dressed as movie stars. Phoebe wasn't joking. She's come as full-on Marilyn Monroe. Martin Novak comes as Angelina Jolie. Others come as different stars I can't actually name, but they're in ball gowns and fake diamond jewellery.

Behind them, dressed normally, looking a bit embarrassed, is Robbie. I had invited him but hadn't heard back and so find myself struck with both excitement and shyness at seeing him unexpectedly. I smile and he gives me an awkward little wave, then comes over.

'All right, Nina. You look incredible. This party is good. It's really good.'

'We've brought our own theme, honey. Hope you don't mind!' says Phoebe, planting two kisses on the air near my cheeks.

There is vodka, there is tequila. I take a beer from Robbie and we are talking for a bit until I'm called away by a load of people because someone has been in the loo for ages and won't answer the door. It's Trish. Of course. She's in there drinking cans and reading a magazine because, 'It's the only place I could get peace and quiet.' Trish is in hyper-odd mode. When I finally persuade her to come out, I leave her at the top of the stairs talking to no one in particular about the bands she's really into.

I come back down, I reach into the cupboard downstairs where me and Beth have got our secret stash of beer. One for me, one for Robbie. I squeal to myself in excitement that he is here. I quickly check my face in the hall mirror. My hair is behaving and my mascara hasn't run yet. I find him in the kitchen, locked into a chat with Sophie Swartz, one of Beth's mates. Sophie is giggling into her hand at something Robbie is saying. It's noisy, I'm drunk, he is leaning in towards her, his mouth close to her ear as he talks, with a huge grin on his face, then they both laugh and she grabs his arm like he is so funny that she may just fall over. I want to hiss and spit. I want to grab Sophie's arm and drag her out of the house and slam the door in her face.

Totally unreasonable of me, I know. I don't know why I thought he might be standing like a lemon where I'd left him. *I* had been chatting to Robbie, they didn't even know each other, and now she is laughing and joking with him and I feel like I can't join in because I'd be interrupting something. I open a beer, pretty much down it, then I have the other one too. Neither cut through the horrible feeling I have of wanting Sophie to spontaneously combust.

I start dancing like an idiot near them with the drama lot and neck vodka from a bottle. It's a supermarket own brand.

I make myself a vodka and Coke with more vodka in it than Coke. I drink it like it's Ribena. Sophie and Robbie are chatting in a group of other people now. They're still standing next to each other, though, like they're a couple entertaining their friends. Sophie is nice. Sophie would never be mean to anyone. I hate Sophie.

The party is noisy, friendly and full. Yet suddenly all I can see is Alex out of the corner of my eye. I freeze. There is a cold *whoosh* inside me even though I knew he was coming.

I absolutely didn't want to be standing on my own like an idiot when I saw Alex, but here I am, standing in the doorway of the kitchen, alone at my own party.

I have thought so often about how to play this. Scenes from that night bounce around in my head. Me, wasted, head in his lap, trying to keep his cock in my mouth, the bouncer yanking me up, then later, outside, when everything went blurry and I don't remember anything until I was in the taxi, with the Muslim driver, holding my knickers in my hand.

Alex grins at me. ''Ello,'ello, I remember you.' He pulls me to him and kisses me on each cheek.

I thought I might not recognise him, but I do. He's really good-looking. Out-of-my-league good-looking. So I'm the average-looking slapper, good for a quick blow job but he's here with his *girlfriend* Zoe, who looks completely stunning in a Gypsy Purple top and tiny hot pants and wedges. She looks at me all patronising, and her eyes are saying, 'AW! So glad there's no hard feelings despite the fact you thought my hot-as-fuck boyfriend might actually be interested in you.'

Alex is super nice to me, super friendly, like, 'Don't feel embarrassed about what a whore you were that night. We both know it was never going to be any more than that between someone like me and someone like you.'

I think I'm smiling but I'm not sure. He smells of after-shave, a subtle, trendy aftershave. I can't talk.

'Ah! You're not shy now, are you?' He's posh but not snobby. He's cocky, self-assured and glances over people as he talks to them.

'My God, Nina,' Zoe says, 'you look amazing! That dress is so cool.'

Alex hands me a bottle of proper champagne. 'Happy birthday, this is from us.' Then he and Zoe go to get drinks.

I find Beth. She's snogging Steve from my English class in a corner. She's forgotten all about Matt from the bakery who has consoled himself by taking charge of cooking the pizza. She is all over lanky, earnest Steve. The terrible kisser. I told her that. What is Beth doing? I feel tears coming. I need her, now.

'Hey, you OK?' someone asks, don't know who. I can't breathe. I have a huge sob, a huge raging sob inside me, and it's fighting to get out but it can't so I'm gasping for breath, wheezing with my eyes full of tears. I go upstairs.

There are people in my room. I grab a glass of wine. I don't care whose it is, I drink it. There is an 'Oi!' as I leave.

Beth's room is full of the drama lot. They are singing sea shanties. When they see me they switch to 'Happy Birthday to You!'

Beth appears, suddenly. 'Oh my God! Steve is so lovely. He's the guy you snogged once, right? Is it cool? Do you mind?'

'Course I don't mind.' I'm irritated that she asked. 'Alex and Zoe are here,' I blurt. I grab her hand. 'I *need* to talk to you.'

Beth is looking around for Steve. He's in the loo. Beth shouts to someone: 'Tell Steve I'll be back in five.'

We sit on the stairs – not the best place to freak out but the house is too rammed.

'I'm supposed to be all normal, but I'm talking to this guy and I don't know if we fucked or not. And he's swanning around my party with Zoe like it's nothing.'

Beth is calm. 'Ask him. Just ask him. Just say you've got a blank and need him to colour things in.'

Beth is right. But how can I in front of Zoe? Beth goes back to snogging Steve, not without giving me a hug first and saying, 'It's your birthday, this is an excellent bloody party, don't let that "Daddy's-got-a-yacht" twat ruin it!'

I stay away from Zoe and Alex. They are in the garden having a deep and meaningful with Trish of all people. I bet she's telling them about something weird that she's fascinated by, like crop circles or something. They are holding hands, listening, Alex in his expensive jacket and slicked hair; he'll be listening, nodding, asking questions, knowing that he will take the piss out of her later and Zoe will dutifully laugh. I suddenly feel very protective of Trish. She *is* weird, but she's nice; it never occurs to her to be horrible. She unifies Alex and Zoe in their smugness, their coolness, their good-lookingness. This is a trip to the zoo for them; they are humouring the dumb animals and will then be enchantingly dismissive.

Poor Trish. She thinks she's made friends when, really, people hang out with her either to take the piss or because she is the only one who is always on her own and is grateful for company. I realise that I am guilty of the latter.

I make myself a huge vodka drink in a pink glass. Vodka, cranberry and orange juice.

It's a *very* good party. People are actually dancing, which almost never happens at house parties.

I try to dance, but I'm too unsteady on my feet. 'I'm dad dancing! DAD DANCING!' I laugh and fall over. Arms come down to pull me up. People are congratulating me on my disarray. I am the drunkest person at the party so, to my own mind, I'm somewhat of a superstar.

I stagger around. I pick up cups that aren't mine and drain them. I can't find Robbie. I find Sophie. 'Wherish Robbie?' I slur.

'He's just in the loo.' Sophie smiles. 'He's walking me home.'

Robbie reappears.

'Are you walking her home? Why are you walking her home?'

I want him to stay; he is here for me.

Robbie looks slightly taken aback by my question. Sophie looks at her feet. I am not being nice.

'Cos I'm northern and so I'm a gentleman,' Robbie replies, 'and I've got to be up mega early. I'm doing a half marathon tomorrow.'

Sophie is holding her coat, quietly delighted at being walked home by gorgeous Robbie. She had no business hogging him all night.

I'm not sure how I get to the Mash. I must have walked but so much booze has made it seem like I just suddenly appeared there.

Derrick is closing up. On his own, thank God. He lets me in. He won't give me a drink. I puke in the loos. I look in the mirror. My hair still looks good but my mascara has run, panda eyes, and my face is sweaty and my eyes red from the puking. I rinse my mouth and sort out my face. I'm staggering about doing all this, the pub toilet spinning.

When Derrick finishes up he finds me falling asleep on the toilet floor. 'I've got a cab waiting, Nina. Let's get you home.'

I have no idea how long I had been gone. It seems like five minutes and three years at the same time. The house is quiet. The party guests have gone. Max had sent everyone home after people noticed I was missing. Beth and Steve and Zoe and Alex have been out looking for me. When I get in, Zoe and Alex make to leave.

Alex gives me an awkward pat and says, 'You look after yourself, yeah?'

Zoe is cold, which is not like her. 'She always does this. She HAS to be centre of attention. It's so immature.'

I can't speak. Beth is pissed off with me. I've ruined the party.

'Oh, don't be like that! Where's Steve?'

'Dad made Steve go too,' she tells me. Then she goes straight to bed.

'Not cool, Nina,' Max says to me. 'Drink water, go to bed and I want you up in the morning to help clear up this mess.'

Then suddenly I'm sobbing. 'Everybody hates me!' I stand in the kitchen crying like Katie does, unselfconscious about the hiccups and snot. 'Please don't be angry with me. Everyone is angry with me.'

I cry and Max comes over and hugs me.

'No one is angry, Nina. We're worried about you. Everything feels like a calamity now so just go to bed and you'll feel better in the morning.'

Max sits me on a chair and gets me water.

I drink it and he goes up to bed, not before telling me again to do the same.

It's a mad thing that I decide to do. 'Decide' isn't really the word. I don't think. I just do it. I go upstairs a moment or two after him and take my dress off and fling it on my bed. I'm just in my bra, pants and heels. I look at myself in the mirror. I look OK. I put on lipstick, hold in my stomach, then go into Max's room, without knocking. He has already taken his trousers and shirt off; he's in his boxers. I shut the door.

'What are you doing, Nina?' Max is shocked.

'I'm doing everything, Max.' I can't believe the words just come out of my mouth, but I'm pissed to the point of insanity and I suddenly want Max like I can't even believe. I put my arms around him and I kiss him on the mouth. For the briefest second, he puts his hands on my hips, then he pulls away, but I press myself against him, I put my hand on his crotch and kiss him again.

His 'Nina! Don't!' is in a tone of voice I haven't heard from him before. It is scared, almost.

It makes me bolder, more powerful. 'Why not?' I ask, then jump on his bed and put my hands down my knickers. It used to really turn Jamie on, watching me play with myself; it was his favourite thing.

Max grabs my arm and tries to pull me up. 'Nina! Stop it!' I giggle and let him hoist me up, then hurl myself at him again. I shove my hand into his boxers. I grab his cock, clumsily.

'Nina! Fucking stop it!' He's aggressive now. So am I. I keep trying to reach his face to kiss him and I keep my hand on his crotch. He pushes me away, hard, and I fall on the bed, giggling again. I try to pull my knickers down but fall asleep instead.

I wake with a jump when the morning light comes in through Max's bedroom window. I'm cold, really cold and it takes me a few seconds to remember where I am and why I am here. My pants are still halfway down my thighs. I look around, for a second thinking Max might still be in the room. But hours have gone by and he isn't. I would give my life for this to be a bad dream. I wait. It's not.

This is the worst thing I've ever done. Without a doubt. Maybe worse than what I did in the club. I knew what I was doing this time, though. I must have done because I remember everything I said to Max. I remember falling onto the bed. A scream roars silently through me. I get up. I wait for the walls to stop spinning, then I go to my own room.

I hold my phone in my hand for ages, wanting to ring someone, but not knowing who, not knowing what to say. I get a text.

It's from Derrick. *Just checking to see if you're OK, Nina. And you left your purse at the pub. I'll take it home with me, not working tomorrow. Pop round and get it.'*

I get dressed, quickly, and I rush out to go to Derrick's house before I can bump into Max. I don't know what time it is, but the sun is properly out.

Derrick, in his dressing gown, opens the door. He's sweet to me. He gives me my purse back, then makes me a cup of tea.

'You've had quite a night by the looks of it,' he says.

'It's my birthday . . . I'm still having it. You got any booze?'

'Nina, it's seven o'clock in the morning.'

'So?'

Derrick hands me a beer from the fridge. He leaves while I sink it and comes back dressed.

'Nina, I have to go to the pub for a delivery. Come with me? Get some air? Have a chat.'

'Can I have a cuddle?'

Derrick gets up, I get up, and we cuddle. He's so lovely and his arms are strong and thick. I look up at him and we kiss. It's nice. I pull him closer to me and kiss him harder. But then he suddenly stops. 'Nina, no, this isn't good. I think you need help.'

Derrick grabs his coat and his keys and goes to the door. 'A walk?' he suggests again. 'Are you coming?'

I shake my head. 'Is your flatmate home?'

'Jeez, Nina, you know how to flatter a guy, like. Gus is away, just Elliot upstairs.'

I stand there, and say nothing, waiting.

He leaves.

Elliot is the really good-looking flatmate. The one I met on the first night I was here. I find his room, take off my clothes and slip into the bed beside him. It takes him a moment to stir and realise I am there. I kiss his shoulders. He turns around sleepily, rolls on top of me. He opens very tired eyes, looks at me confused and croaks, 'Derrick's mate?'

'Yeah.'

Then we kiss and he grabs a condom from his bedside table and without him even knowing my name, we fuck.

At nine Elliot says, 'Er . . . I got my mum visiting today. You gotta bounce, babe.' Just like that.

'Oh my God! I'm not a prostitute! You can't just turf me out!'

'Excuse me? You crept into my bed uninvited and sexually assaulted me, which I thoroughly enjoyed, but now you have to go because I've made plans.' Which is fair enough.

I'm so tired now I shuffle like an old man back to Max and Beth's house. I've nicked a bottle of beer from Derrick's place and I drink it on the way. I creep into the house without seeing anyone, thankfully, and apart from two quick dashes to the loo to pee and drink water, I stay in bed all day and all night.

The next morning, Max knocks on my door. 'Nina, it's time you came out.'

I wish I could pass out, faint, something like that so I'd have to go into hospital. I want something to happen to make all this not my fault. I want to not just be hungover, but to be properly ill.

'Nina, I would like you to get out of bed, get dressed and come downstairs.' When I hear him go, I get up and get in the shower.

Beth has texted me. *Sorry I had a go at you last night. You were being mental though. I'm out with Steve today . . . bit of a surprise turn! My dad is NOT happy!*

Then another text:

'I mean he's not happy with you. He's cool with me and Steve. Just to clarify :)'

She doesn't know. Oh my God, good.

Again I am sat like a dickhead with my phone in my hand, wanting to contact someone but not knowing who. I text Derrick. *'Thanks for this morning. Hope you enjoyed the walk.'* Stupid thing to say.

Derrick calls me. 'Are you OK, Nina?'

I don't know the answer to that question so I say, 'Yeah, course, I'm fine.'

'Are you at home safe?'

'Yeah, I had to leave early because Elliot's parents were coming.'

'Elliot? Oh God, Nina.'

I shouldn't have said anything.

Derrick is silent for a second. 'Erm, Nina, Elliot's girlfriend is coming to stay this morning, not his parents.'

A sickening thud in the pit of my stomach. I'm such an idiot. I'm such a bloody idiot. My voice cracks as I say, 'Oh, right.'

'I'm sorry, Nina, he's a lovely fella . . . doesn't usually do this kind of thing. It's going to be a bit awkward having Lara to stay, knowing what's gone on. She's a great girl.'

I'm jealous of Lara. I'm jealous of Marcia and I'm jealous of Zoe. I'm jealous of all these 'great' girls who are 'girlfriends', who don't drink so much and don't fuck someone just so they can have a cuddle. I'm jealous of these girls because the men who tell me to leave their house don't want *them* to leave. They are free to wear his dressing gown, help themselves to his toast and coffee, have a laugh with his mates and he will see them to the station instead of leaving them to scuttle out of the house like a burglar without so much as offering to make them a cup of tea.

I shower. I dry off, I get dressed and I want to jump out of the window. I want to do anything I can to avoid what is coming.

I go downstairs, finally.

Max is in the kitchen. With my mum.

CHAPTER NINE

I want to cry with relief at seeing her, but she is stony-faced and pale. She does not smile at me. She still has her coat on, like she's just arrived or is just leaving. Her little overnight bag is at the door.

'Mum!' is all I say, then I start to cry.

I go to her. I cling to her. She is stiff at first, then relents and absorbs me, puts her arms around me. I sob and sob into the collar of my mum's coat and I smell our old house on her, I smell Katie, I smell all the nights she snuggled me to sleep.

'Mum, I'm sorry, I'm really sorry.' Mum has heard these apologies before, not just from me. Was it me that Mum had run away from? Did Mum see this coming and so moved away so she didn't have to go through it all again? The thought crosses my mind as she detangles herself from me, blows her nose, and starts on about us 'needing to talk'.

Max makes tea, rinses dishes with his eyes down. He is polite, too polite. Not all jokey and funny. He doesn't want to be in this room. He and Mum give each other a 'look', then Max says: 'I hope you understand, Nina. After what happened it would be irresponsible of me to continue having you stay.'

I nod. Max leaves the kitchen and leaves me to Mum.

Mum being here is a big deal. I mean she didn't make my eighteenth birthday but she obviously felt this was too huge to ignore. I can imagine Alan shaking his head as he buys her ticket online, driving her to the airport, insisting he park so he can see her onto the plane. Katie would be crying because Mum was going and she wasn't going with her, and Alan would have bought her an ice-cream to soothe her and taken her to a park for the rest of the day to keep her mind off Mum not being there.

It's her duty, as a mum, to make sure Max did nothing wrong. She needs to know I'm not protecting him before she decides how to feel about me.

'Max says you were drunk . . . that you came into his room.' Mum is calm, businesslike. She wants facts. She knows Max is telling the truth, but she has to launch a Professional Parental Investigation. 'And he didn't respond? And he told you to leave? And *did* you leave? Nina, did he lay a hand on you . . .?'

I answer all her questions truthfully and Mum sits at the table and puts her head in her hands. I stand there. Her life would be so perfect without me. Mum has it all without me. She has the doting husband, the pretty house, adventures abroad, and, of course, the sweetest smartest little girl in the world. But here she is, having to exit all that and deal with the reality of me.

Once she is satisfied that her eldest child has not been taken advantage of, she is not an investigator anymore, she's a furious parent. 'What were you thinking? WERE you thinking? You put Max in such a compromising situation, you abused his trust, you've humiliated me, humiliated yourself. We *trusted* you.' Then Mum starts to cry. Quiet, angry tears.

I'm still just standing there. I'm stone inside. I look at Mum and I don't care. I don't care about any of it, actually. Max can kick me out and Mum can go back to Germany and I won't care, I'll sleep on a park bench if I'm this much trouble to everyone.

Mum is 'collecting herself', which means putting all her crying and shouting in a bottle, corking it and putting it to the back of her mind.

She washes her hands, rubs them over her face, then uses a tea towel to dry. She looks old. She looks tired and old.

'You can't go on like this, Nina.'

I know this. But I can't tell her I know this.

'Like what, Mum? I'm sorry. I've said I'm sorry.'

'You're a drunk, Nina, or you're in danger of becoming a drunk. You need help and I can't help you.'

'Mum, I won't drink again, happy? You can check up on me, I'll call you every night.'

Mum's gone weird; she's not really listening. She says calmly, without looking at me, 'You're going the same way as your dad. It can be hereditary, you know. Did you know that?'

Yes, I did fucking know that, Mum; I'm living this.

'You're so like him and you're so convincing when you need to be, but you need help. I can't help you,' she says again.

I remember Dad, happy, always laughing, picking me up and whirling me around, making me laugh until I couldn't breathe. Then I remember the time when he burst into the bathroom while I was brushing my teeth. I was taking too long – 'What the fuck are you doing in there?!' – and he snatched my little purple glittery toothbrush and he slammed it so hard on the edge of the sink that it snapped in two, and I cried and he grabbed my arm and yanked me out of the bathroom. I was about four.

'You DO know you have a drink problem?'

I tried to get off with my best mate's dad. I can't really argue with anyone who says I have a drink problem.

'Mum, I can stop . . .'

Mum has got her 'been there, done that' face on. 'You have to take responsibility.'

'Ha! That's perfect, from a mum who has fucked off to Germany leaving her daughter all alone in THE MIDDLE OF HER A LEVELS.'

Then it starts, a huge fight. Her screaming that we'd *talked* about this, me screaming that, no, *she'd* talked about this.

Then her shouting – 'You have a drink problem!' – then me shouting – 'The only problem I have is *you!*' – and on and on and on. Then she screams, 'You need rehab!' and I go mad. 'I don't need fucking rehab. You're fucking insane! There's nothing wrong with me!'

Mum does something really mental suddenly. She grabs my hair, and screams in my face, 'You are not going to end up like your dad. You're going to rehab or you are NOT my daughter anymore.'

I struggle. 'FUCK OFF!' I try furiously to untangle my hair from her clutches. I kick out at her, wild with rage. I kick and hit. I am fighting my own mother.

She lets go; she's snarling, breathing hard, shocked at her own loss of control. She manages to spit out, 'I mean it, Nina.

You go to this place, you let them help you or you will not see me again and I will not let Katie have anything to do with you.'

I saw Mum crazy like this a few times when Dad was alive, not since though. This is our old life.

I break. I howl. I sit on the stairs and sob. I've had enough of fighting. I want my mummy to stop being cross with me. Even though I'm eighteen, I just want my mum the way Katie has her.

She softens, of course. She's relieved I'm crying. Mum sits next to me and puts her arm around me and I turn into her shoulder, and we're snuggled up and I sob and she cradles me and strokes my hair and whispers, 'My beautiful, precious girl.'

When we have wiped our tears and are organising tea again in the kitchen, Mum says, 'I don't think you can stop by yourself. Let's get you help.'

Mum has been researching. She's got printouts of a rehab place. She shows me. This is surreal. Rehab is what pop stars do. I look at the pictures and it's all leafy and pretty. She shows me the website. It's a place for alcoholics and it's just outside London in Surrey.

'Imagine . . .' she says, 'imagine what life would have been like if your dad had gone to rehab.'

I forget, sometimes, that Mum misses Dad too.

I'm exhausted.

'I meant what I said, Nina. I can't be here for you unless you do this, unless you take this big, brave step to help yourself.'

She makes lists and makes some calls. She's gone into full-on organisation mode. Mum needs a ritual, she needs to organise something to stop herself falling apart. She calls my college, Alan, the rehab centre. She makes 'all necessary arrangements'.

This will mean deferring my A levels. There will be forms to fill in when I get back. Everything is to be put on hold.

People will know I'm a total fuck-up but – I hear Beth in my head – 'They probs know that already, babe.'

Beth comes home while Mum is here and Mum is all happy to see her and cuddles her for ages and for some reason this pisses me off and I go upstairs and start packing for this place even though I have no idea what to pack.

Beth chats with my mum for a good long while then comes upstairs. I don't know what she knows but I can see by her cold manner, she knows something.

'Your mum says you're going to rehab. I think that's for the best.' She doesn't say it in a caring way. She says it in a 'You're a total arsehole and I want you out of here!' way.

I want her to put me out of my misery. I nearly blurt out 'YOU KNOW I TRIED TO FUCK YOUR DAD, DON'T YOU?'

But I don't.

'Yeah. I drink too much, apparently.'

'It's not "apparently". You do. You do drink too much. You smash it down till you're a fucking disaster.'

I am a low-life; it seems important for everyone to let me know this. Uselessly I defend myself.

'Everyone drinks, Beth. Everyone gets off their face from time to time.'

'Babe, there's getting off your face and there's getting off your face and, er, trying to get off with my dad.' She mimes retching.

I don't think I could feel any smaller or more ashamed. This is Beth, usually my buffer against me and total humiliation, the one who will tirelessly search each avenue to declare me blameless in my every mishap. Now she's looking at me like I actually *am* as awful as I feel inside.

'Did Max tell you?'

'No, "Max" didn't tell me. Your mum did. My poor dad is in a state of shock.'

Max has barely said a word to me at all since it happened.

'What did Mum tell you?' Mum doesn't even know the details.

'She said you were "inappropriate" with Dad, and that you went into his room naked.'

'I wasn't naked! I had pants on!'

'Oh my God, Nina! I don't want to hear it! My dad won't tell me *anything*, which means it was pretty serious.'

It was an eighteen-year-old girl hitting on her best mate's dad in *the* cheapest porn way possible. Yeah, it was pretty serious.

'Beth, I was so fucking drunk . . .'

'How would you feel if I said, "Oh, hey Nina, I was off my face and got off with Alan! Soz!"'

'Alan is NOT my dad!'

'All right then! What if I got off my face and fingered YOUR FUCKING MUM!'

She throws a cushion at me. Violently. Beth has lost control. I don't know how to handle it. It's like me and Beth are now on the other side of the wall around our normal life. I don't want to be here. I want to be safe where we were but I don't know how to get back.

She is snarling.

'Did you stop to think about the situation you put my dad in? He took you in, looked after you, treated you like a daughter, so all of this is pretty disgusting, plus, he's a man, so ultimately if anything *had* happened, if he hadn't been such an absolute hero, everyone would think he was a scummy paedo.'

'But I'm eighteen!'

'THAT ISN'T THE POINT, YOU MENTAL, FUCK-ING BITCH!' Beth storms out of the room.

I am shaking.

When Mum comes in, I'm sort of in shock. Suddenly the answer is obvious.

'Mum,' I blurt out, 'I'll come to Germany with you.'

That will make things OK, I think, I plead, with desperation in my gut. 'That's what you wanted in the first place, isn't it? I'll come to Germany, I'll defer my A levels, look after Katie and improve my German, like Alan said.'

But it's not going to happen. It's too late for this. Mum's not having it.

'So you're going to stick me in rehab? Very middle-class of you.' I put on a stupid posh voice. 'My daughter is a problem, so we are going to shove her somewhere so other people can deal with her.'

'Nina, you have to wake up!'

'No, YOU need to fucking wake up!' I wish I could put the brakes on but I can't.

'I've really tried my best . . . I've always looked after you.'

'You're my mum. You're *supposed* to look after me. It's the minimum requirement. I can't believe you want a medal for it.'

'You're being a brat!' Mum shouts.

'*You're* being a cunt!' I shout back.

Mum slaps me. Hard across the face. She looks horrified, hateful, angry and sorry all at the same time.

I run out of the room and lock myself in the bathroom and stand there sort of panting with rage. I hate her, I hate her, I actually hate her.

Mum is outside the bathroom door.

'Nina, I won't let you be like your dad. I will NOT have you end up like him, I WILL NOT!' She screams this and pounds her fist on the bathroom door until Max comes back and goes to her, calms her down with, 'That's enough now,' as Mum sobs, and 'What good does this do?' and 'Leave her be, come on, come downstairs, Sandra. Leave her a while.'

And I am alone upstairs in the bathroom. Mum is downstairs, seething that I, the residue of a life that made her miserable, am dragging her down again.

CHAPTER TEN

We're quiet in the car. Nothing has been this big a deal since Dad died. She's got Radio Four on but it's so quiet all we hear is murmurs and neither of us bother to turn it off or turn it up.

I think the rehab people are going to laugh at us, say we are being melodramatic and that 'You're too young to be an alcoholic! Of course you drink!' But they might agree with Mum and everyone else that I'm a mess that needs to be cleared up.

The journey takes more than an hour. Mum hates driving across London but we do, she stays calm and we have gone well past Richmond and Kingston. We are somewhere in Surrey now.

Mum doesn't like sat navs – she's all about proper map-reading – but she's content with being a sheep today, letting the smooth voice guide her every step of the way. She's not leaving anything to chance getting me to this place.

We pull up in front of a gigantic house with a huge front lawn. Bloody hell, this must be costing Alan a fortune.

I see a mum with a pram and her two other little kids riding down the road on scooters.

'Mum, please, I miss Katie, *please*. Please can I go back with you for a bit, then come here?'

Mum doesn't answer me.

'What about with Auntie Jean? I could stay with her . . .'

Mum breathes out in her 'I'm not dignifying that with a response' way.

The inside of the huge house is quite shabby. There's a big wide staircase like in *Gone with the Wind*.

It's got threadbare rugs and a funny smell: musty, mixed with rancid tomato soup.

The fire extinguishers and the metal signs saying 'Reception' and 'Room 12' give it away as an institution, rather than a home.

Mum strides into the reception with fake confidence. I shuffle behind her.

The receptionist is an old-school rockabilly. She's wrinkled from too much sun and fags. She's got bright-red lippy on, heavy eye make-up, a 1950s hairdo and a tight polka-dot dress. She doesn't bat an eyelash at me and Mum coming in to get me treatment.

She looks up, smiles, and gives us forms to fill in. I can't work out if it's a good thing or not. On the one hand, it's good she's not going, 'What? You're only eighteen! What's the matter with you, you silly tart?' But on the other hand, I don't want her to think I'm just another fuck-up coming through their doors. I mean, obviously, I *am* another fuck-up coming through their doors, but I want everyone to know I'm not just any old fuck-up. I'm Nina, I'm all right, I'm quite funny and I write poetry that's 'promising'.

'If you wait here, Jerry, the manager, will be with you in a minute.'

We sit on these little chairs against the wall and she goes back to clack-clack-clacking on her computer. Probably playing Candy Crush.

Me and Mum make dumb conversation.

'It's very peaceful here,' Mum says.

'Yeah,' I say.

I've known this woman all my life – she grew me in her belly – and still, under these intense, surreal circumstances, we make small talk like we're strangers at a bus stop.

My tears come suddenly. My chest swells with misery. I feel like the kid at school who has wet herself and come to the Welfare Room to get a spare pair of pants from the jumble. I don't want my mum to leave me here.

Mum looks at me and closes her eyes. She's saying, 'Stop it, Nina, don't make this harder.'

After a bit a woman comes in – she's dead short and fat but quite smiley and nice – and announces she's a 'clinician'. She takes me into Room 12. Mum is not allowed to come and waits outside. This woman breathalyses me, weighs me, takes notes, asks me about my drinking, how much do I drink, when do I drink, why do I drink, and she writes it all down in a notebook and tells me to go and sit back down in reception.

Then a man walks in with his hand outstretched to shake mine.

'I'm Jerry,' he says with a smile. 'You must be Nina?'

I tell him 'yeah' and then stay sitting like a melon.

'Would you like to follow me? We'll go into the office . . . it's more private.'

Jerry's desk is messy. Really messy, with three empty tea mugs on it.

Jerry hands me tissues and it's only then that I realise my tears are still falling.

I'm pretty sure he's gay; he's definitely Scottish and has longish brown hair and a goatee.

'More boring forms for you to fill in, in a moment. But we'll have a little chat first, shall we? Mum?' My mum is lurking in the doorway, ready to spring into action. 'I'll need to speak to Nina on her own?'

Mum gives a tight smile and goes back outside.

Jerry makes me a cup of tea. 'Have you been in rehab before, Nina?'

I shake my head. Of course I haven't, I've only just turned eighteen.

'Hate the fact you're here or OK with the fact you're here?'

'I don't know.'

'Do you want to tell me a little bit about why you are here?'

Everything has become a swirling, painful mess. It's calm in Jerry's office, though. Totally unfamiliar, but nothing of my chaos is here.

I really want a drink. Jerry has my notes from the clinician. 'Why are you here, Nina?'

I'm here because my mum freaks out when I drink. I'm here because I fuck forty-year-old men in parks. I'm here because I get thrown out of nightclubs because I go down on strangers by the bar. I'm here because nobody wants me and I can't stop drinking and doing things that make me feel like utter shit.

'I got drunk and tried to get off with my best mate's dad.' It seems fitting to start with my latest shameful act.

'OK,' Jerry says.

'A while back, I went to a club with my friends and I got so drunk I got thrown out for giving this guy a blow job in the bar. He followed me out and I don't know, to this day, whether or not I, you know, did more stuff with him.'

Stupid, I know, but for a second I think he might high-five me, all camp, and say, 'You go girl!' But he doesn't. He stays quiet and keeps listening.

'I drink and do this crazy stuff and I can't help it, I can't help drinking as much as I do.'

'Do you want to stop drinking?'

I nod. 'Yes.'

I'm taken aback by how powerfully I mean that.

'Everyone says I should. Mum, Beth, everyone.'

'Who is Beth?'

'My best mate. I live with her and her dad. I *did* anyway. I don't think they will ever have me back after all this.'

Jerry talks to me for a while longer, sitting opposite me on his swing chair. He's not writing anything down or analysing me. It really *is* just a chat. It's quite easy to talk to him. I'd fancy him probably, if he wasn't gay.

He's a recovering addict, he tells me. Cocaine and alcohol. This makes a difference. I was worried I'd be amongst people who say, 'Try alternating your drink with water,' again. I tell Jerry this, and he smiles and says, 'Yeah, that's like telling a coke addict, "Try dabbing icing sugar on your tongue instead!" We are totally honest in here about where we have been and where we are at.'

'You seem so sorted,' I say, smiling finally.

He looks at me sideways with a little smile and lets out an 'mmmmm'. He sighs. 'I wasn't sorted when I first went to rehab. An ex-boyfriend literally threw me out of his car and into the doorway of a rehab centre.'

I knew he was gay.

'That's pretty much what my mum has done.'

'We're the lucky ones, Nina, having people who care enough to risk losing us.'

He asks me why I think Mum brought me here.

I have to think about this. Obviously there's all the stuff I've been doing. Drinking in the day and the crazy stuff with guys. But the main reason is obvious. 'She doesn't want me to end up like my dad.'

And then we talk about my father.

No one knows how much I loved my dad. He was my dad. Whatever he did, whatever he was like, I would do anything to have him back. Even for a day, or just an hour. I wish everything wasn't about how I am like this because of my dad. Dad wouldn't want me to be in the state I'm in now. If he had lived, he might have got help. I might have been a girl like Marcia instead of a girl like me.

I've told so many people the whole 'my dad' story, it feels like a script now that I reel off. I get sick of the sound of my voice droning on about it.

'He was a big drinker, he was fun, he had a crazy temper . . .' blah blah blah blah blah blah. My teachers, my friends, the college counsellor. They are all like, 'Ah! That explains why she is such a fuck-up.' But I might have been a fuck-up anyway, even if my dad had been a Buddhist monk.

Jerry doesn't let me drone on; he interjects, derails me mid-flow when I'm monologuing and asks me questions that I have to think about before answering. Questions like how I felt about my dad's drinking, about his behaviour, about my mum's reaction to his rages.

'From what I understand your alcohol use to be, you need to detox. We will give you lithium to help you through the alcohol withdrawal.'

So I'm having drugs to get me off drink. No booze at all is terrifying.

I have to have therapy and attend 12-step meetings.

'Do you know what a 12-step meeting is?'

No bloody idea.

'Have you heard of AA? Alcoholics Anonymous?'

Of course I have, everyone has.

Jerry gives me a leaflet.

There is a lot of stuff about God. I don't really do 'God'.

Me and Beth went to stay at Caroline Franklin's house once. Caroline is a sweet girl we knew from secondary school. Her family moved to Kent and she invited me and Beth to stay. At dinner, her mum and dad said grace. Me and Beth didn't know where to look. We couldn't look at each other because we were terrified we'd start giggling.

We slept in the spare room and there was a crucifix above the double bed we shared. It freaked us both out.

They were nice and everything, but we had no idea Caroline was like that. We didn't keep in touch after that.

'I'm an atheist,' I tell Jerry.

'So am I,' says Jerry.

Jerry says meetings are a 'crucial part of what we do', how people who go to them recover. 'Go to several meetings and you'll see "God" is not spoken about in the conventional way. It'll become clearer than I can explain if you read the literature and go to meetings.'

I want a beer so badly that I can actually taste it. My heart is racing. This all seems like hard work.

'Are you going to stay? Will you commit to our recovery program and get better? No one else can decide that for you, Nina. It's your choice.'

Choice? I'm eighteen, I'm an adult, but I'm not sure I have any more choice now than when I was eight. Mum decides what is for the best. I still have to do what my mother tells me to do. I can't go to Max and Beth's. Mum doesn't want me in Germany until I'm 'clean'.

'I've got nowhere else to go.'

'Then that's a good reason to stay.'

'Can I still call people while I'm in here, chat to my mates?'

'It's not a prison.' He smiles. 'Although, we do say that while you are detoxing at least, it's useful to be fully focused on yourself and your program in here. Perhaps talk to people who aren't in here with you when you've given yourself a bit of distance, a bit of a chance.'

And that's where they are going to put me, in detox, with other people who are detoxing.

It soothes me, being in here, being forced away from my own life and mayhem and all the things that make me want to run away from my own head, from my own body. I've found a burrow to dive into. All the craziness is going on up above but I'm down here. I'm Down the Rabbit Hole, drinking tea in a messy office.

Jerry talks with Mum about practical stuff. Money, basically. She gives the receptionist her credit card details and goes. She has a flight back to Germany booked this evening. Mum tells me she'll call me, she tells me she will come and visit, she tells me she loves me. We hug and when I cry she says this is for my own good. She gets back into her car and leaves me here. One of those bloody elephants sits on my chest as I watch her go.

I have to share a room. With someone called Isla. Apart from when Katie has stayed with me for a 'cuddly sleepover', I've never ever shared a room.

We go up two flights of stairs. The room is big, with two beds in it. There is a rolled-up pair of socks on the floor by Isla's bed, which is made, but badly. She's got a half-drunk Cherry Coke on the bedside table and a couple of books. The wardrobe is open just a crack and I can see a few bits and pieces of clothes hanging up.

'I can't share a room!' I blurt out.

'Why's that then?' Jerry asks like he's just curious to know.

She's a complete stranger; she's an alcoholic.

I tell Jerry, 'I've never a shared a room before.'

'Give it a try for a couple of nights and, if you hate it, we can talk about it.'

This answer sounds like it totally sorts my problem out, but actually it doesn't at all.

He leaves me in the room alone to unpack and I just sit on the bed. I don't open my suitcase.

This suddenly feels less cosy. Down in Jerry's office was OK. Now I'm in a stranger's bedroom. I'm supposed to sleep here. If I snore, fart, wank, then she will hear.

I tell myself that this is what celebrities do. Or perhaps celebrity rehab is better, posher, with private rooms overlooking the ocean and puppies to play with.

Ordinary people share shabby rooms in shabby houses with earnest people like Jerry looking after them.

There is an AA meeting starting in a bit downstairs in Room 9. I have to go to it.

AA is so famous, you hear about it all the time. I feel the same as when I went to see the Mona Lisa with Jamie. We went to Paris for the weekend. I know it's weird comparing an AA meeting to a painting but they are both something you've always heard about but never experienced, so when you do, it's daunting but exciting.

I go downstairs. AA is in a draughty room with lots of splintery chairs arranged in a circle. There are no Hollywood stars.

People are milling about. All sorts of different people. Smart people, scruffy people, one guy looks like an actual tramp and he takes a seat next to a really glamorous woman about Mum's age.

In the middle there is a table with A4 notices saying: 'ONE DAY AT A TIME' 'THIS TOO SHALL PASS' and 'WHO YOU SEE HERE, WHAT YOU HEAR HERE, WHEN YOU LEAVE HERE, LET IT STAY HERE'.

I'm early. I sit down and more people arrive. I recognise someone from a daytime TV show. I try not to stare.

One woman, I notice, has a Mulberry Bag just like the one Alan bought Mum last Christmas. It was a big surprise to Mum; she was so happy she jumped up and down. 'I have *always* wanted the Mulberry Roxanne! Did you know?' He *did* know, because I told him. I never thought he'd get it, though, because they cost close to a grand, and he'd said, 'It's clearly for people with more money than sense,' but he did it, he went and got it. I was quite proud of Alan that day.

By the time we start, about forty people have crammed into the room. There aren't enough chairs so some sit cross-legged on the floor and others stand at the back, too cramped to be able to take their coats off without jabbing elbows and flapping sleeves.

I'm finding it hard to look at anyone, but from a quick glance I can see there isn't anyone as young as me, although not everyone is old. It's a mixture of smart and trampy, young and old, and smelly and not smelly. The bloke next to me is smelly.

The meeting starts. 'Can we have a minute's silence for those still suffering?' There is no leader, just a chairperson who takes the meeting, reading off an A4 sheet.

A book is passed round and passages read from it, like, 'We are powerless over alcohol and our lives have become unmanageable.'

Unmanageable. Am I 'managing' my life? It's a total mess so maybe I'm not. It wasn't like this a year ago. A year ago I had Jamie. When I had Jamie things weren't like this. The two of us hung out all the time. I liked drinking but when I got into a state, Jamie was there to look after me, giggle with me in the street, take me home safe, hold my hair back while

I puked. A year ago me and Jamie made plans, we took Katie out, we studied together. We had a tight gang of mates. They were mostly his; I only really started to see more of Beth and Zoe since me and Jamie split. He was the really popular one.

Now everything is mad. I'm not even sure where I'm meant to be half the time with college stuff. I don't talk to Mum about anything much. I'd be amazed if Beth was ever my friend again. I drink and get with guys. That's pretty much all I've been doing. Drinking, getting with guys, then cringing about it. Yeah, I'd say my life's got pretty unmanageable.

'We are going to know a new freedom, a new happiness. We will not regret the past or shut the door on it . . . we will know a new peace.'

'Fridge magnet philosophy,' Beth would call this.

But she doesn't know. Beth doesn't know what it's like to fuck things up over and over again. Beth doesn't know that all this is actually blowing my mind a bit because for the first time I'm sitting with people who have done the same sort of things as me, and worse. For the first time I'm with people who have boozed in a way that normal drinkers don't understand. Those who say getting wasted is a 'rite of passage' don't get it. We are not 'hard-core'. We are not 'party animals'. We are ill.

Then the part of the meeting comes that everyone knows about. I've seen it in films and TV shows when people sit in a circle and talk about their feelings. The 'shares' and there's no such thing as 'over-sharing' here.

A timekeeper is appointed and raises their hand when three minutes is up so as many people as possible get to talk.

'In this meeting we allow three minutes' sharing time with fifteen minutes at the end for newcomers and shy-sharers. This is a raised-voice meeting.'

Then it starts. Hungry Hippos. Everyone is desperate to come in and grab what they need from the circle. One after the other, these people trip over themselves to talk.

I listen to all the shares. Some cry during theirs and some people seem so fine that I'm not sure why they come here still. People share about how much they drink, or used to drink. They talk about affairs and passing out and hurting their family. Secrets as shameful as my own come tumbling out.

'My name is blah blah, and I'm an alcoholic.' They actually say this. It's not just something you see on TV. Now I get the joke with the sharks in *Finding Nemo*, Katie's favourite film. The sharks are addicted to fish and have these meetings to support each other in stopping eating fish. Mum always laughs at that part and I have never got it.

There is a man with a bump on his head, a huge lump with straggly grey hair growing around it. He listens to all the shares and nods emphatically. I feel sorry for him because he's old and he's still trying to get away from booze. There is no 'rite of passage' to get *out* of booze. Booze sits its arse down in your life, pretends to be your friend, then trips you up, kicks you and throws rocks at you. You push it away; it runs back at you harder and knocks you over. You barricade your door against it, and it'll climb in through the window. If you promise yourself you won't drink, it'll laugh at your promise, drag you screaming to the ground and batter you unconscious.

I hear a new voice, a new sharer who says something which suddenly shines a sliver of light, a longed-for clarity into the cave of anxiety my life has become. People always go on to me about needing 'willpower' to stop drinking. This person is talking about the huge amount of willpower you need to *keep on* drinking when you know you're wrecking yourself. It's an effort to feel *that* shit and carry on doing the thing that makes you feel shit. Not everyone can do it. We are actually very hard workers. Addicts, it seems, have incredibly strong willpower. Not everyone can feel the crucifying shame I did after giving a stranger a blow job in a club, yet still go on and do more stuff like that. I actually raised my game: I went on to fuck a forty-year-old in a park while I was puking. I fucked two guys I hardly know on the same night and one found his flatmate's condom inside me. I've stolen money from my baby sister's piggy bank to buy booze. I tried to fuck my best mate's dad. Not everyone can do these things. To drink to this level, to stay this fucked up, you need focus and determination and *stacks* of willpower. If it wasn't so awful, I'd insist on a medal.

Everyone in Room 9 understands, or is trying to understand, that acting on our own will is wrecking us. We have to let go of it because, frankly, it's bad for us.

The energy in the room changes with each different voice that pipes up.

A woman tells us she pissed herself on the Piccadilly line.

A man talks about how often he has cheated on his wife.

People say out loud the things that bring them shame and pain.

Being with other alcoholics is a relief I did not know existed.

Drinking on my own, the humiliation and chaos, it was like the end of *me*. I was nothing, a piece of dog shit on someone's shoe. Some rancid old whore. I couldn't cuddle my baby sister because I felt too dirty.

Here, 'shame' is not who you are.

A woman with a sweet round face jumps in. She looks thirty-something and is dressed quite smartly. She's been trying to get in and talk for ages. 'Hello,' she says, 'I'm Isla and I'm an alcoholic.' My new room-mate is not a tramp with missing teeth as I'd feared. She seems really sweet, softly spoken and gentle. She cries and the bloke next to her in motorcycle leathers reaches out and gives her shoulder a squeeze.

Near the end of the hour, the chairperson says, 'The last few minutes are reserved for newcomers. If you're a newcomer or a shy-sharer, we invite you to share.'

Now there is utter silence. I'm the newcomer. The silence gets louder. I am the only one allowed to speak. It seems weird and rude if I don't. But what do I say? My cheeks burn, my eyes sting but at last I hear my own voice admit the truth to a room full of strangers.

'Hi, I'm Nina, and I'm an alcoholic.'

CHAPTER ELEVEN

There is a little kitchen in the house and we are allowed to help ourselves. I go in to make tea and toast.

I'm glad to get out of my room because when Isla wakes up, she kneels by her bed and bows her head. She is like that for a while just praying or meditating. Whichever it is, it's awkward as hell to be in the room while she does it, so I go.

It's Isla's second time in detox.

The old man with a massive bump on his head is in the kitchen too. It's more of a lump than a bump. His long, stringy, greasy hair falls into his face as he shuffles to an old sofa and sits down. I smile, awkwardly, and he nods back. He has a grey raincoat on, which, I later find, he never takes off.

Stuart is very tall and skinny, really spotty and about thirty. His share in yesterday's meeting was funny. But he's quiet now. He is so shy that I feel bad being around him in case it makes him uncomfortable.

Maggie is up too. Maggie is about fifty with very short thick, grey hair and quite fat. She has a rasping voice and her accent doesn't sound quite English.

'Would anyone else like tea?' I ask, hoping they'll all say no, because I can't handle making tea for other people in a strange kitchen. They all want one. Pete, with the bump-lump who I've not yet heard speak, says, in the poshest accent I've ever heard, 'I most certainly would, young lady. Delightful of you to offer.'

Making tea for the first time in an unfamiliar kitchen for strangers who sit and watch makes me feel like a gorilla ballet dancing: clumsy and cack-handed. I open every cupboard door before I find the tea bags, then it's another round of stupidly opening and closing before I find the mugs. There don't seem to be any. 'Dishwasher,' says Pete eventually.

I open the dishwasher and get some clean mugs.

Maggie says, 'Can you make mine strong, please, darling? I cannot stand weak tea.'

I'm flustered. Does strong tea mean it's got less milk in or does it mean you've squeezed the tea bag?

I sort out the 'sugar/no sugar' debacle and I get Maggie's tea wrong. 'UGH!' she says so everyone can hear. 'That's too strong!'

'Oh, sorry,' I stammer, all panicked, even though it's her being rude about tea someone has made for her. I grab more milk.

'No, no,' Maggie says, irritated. 'Leave it, I'll sort it out myself.' She takes the cup off in a huff, pours it away and starts again, making sure I understand that I have failed to please her.

Maggie, I decide, is a total arse.

They don't know me in here. They just think I'm a twat who can't make tea.

I sit and I stare down at an old magazine, not reading a word. My cheeks are burning and I am trying not to cry.

At dinner time, Jerry finds me and takes me to the dining room; it's the biggest room downstairs, adjoined to another kitchen. The tables have jam jars in the middle with a carnation in each. I sit down with Isla, Maggie, Stuart and Pete. Then there is Yvonne who has pink hair and a nose ring. She is chirpy and calls everyone 'sweets': 'all right, sweets?'; 'nice to meet you, sweets'; 'pass us me fags, sweets'. It's a good way of covering when you can't remember someone's name.

This bloke, Sasha, is covered in tattoos; he's tall and beefy. He's even got them on his neck. I tell him my mum has a tattoo of a butterfly on her ankle, to make conversation, but he doesn't seem interested in Mum's delicate purple butterfly. You'd have to have tattoos all over your face and on your eyeballs for Sasha to raise an eyebrow.

I turn back to my food, giving up on chitchat, then Sasha suddenly asks, 'How are you feeling, Nina?' His tone is sweet, really sweet.

I'm surprised by the question. 'I'm fine,' I tell him.

'If you were fine you wouldn't be here.' Then he laughs to himself and goes back to ignoring me.

Isla is easy to get on with. She tells me that after her first stint in rehab she went back to live with her girlfriend but relapsed. 'Claire's an alcoholic too and it's hard for us to be around one another.'

I ask if they are still together. I am kind of excited that she's gay.

'Nope. I came back in here and my brothers went to her house and moved out all my stuff. Claire's in a bad place. Things got . . .' She trails off. '. . . really mental. I'm stopping with my older brother when I get out of here until I sort myself out.'

We have a 'house meeting' tonight. Good, I thought at first: this is what I imagine being at uni is like, deciding who does the dishes, who buys the bread. But no. It's more recovery stuff but without the sweet assurances of AA. Brutal, honest sharing. We have to talk about our day, what's made us happy, what's pissed us off.

Maggie starts. 'I wish to apologise to Nina for saying the tea she made was no good. I mean, it *was* no good, but you don't know my way, you're new. I think I upset you.'

Totally and utterly mortifying.

Later, when we are back in our room, I tell Isla, 'I wish more than anything I could have a drink. With a drink, all this would be bearable.'

'That thinking is how we all got here.' Isla smiles.

It's a shock how much I want booze. I've always had it to hand. A quick walk to the shops or sneaking a drink from Alan's cabinet was all it took.

People talk about every little thing that's bothered them.

'No one knocked on my door to watch the DVD last night.'

'I wasn't thanked for doing the washing up.'

'I don't like being disturbed when I'm reading my book.'

Little bits of paranoia, little feelings of being hurt, no whinge is too small at the house meetings.

I need a drink so badly I seriously consider just leaving. But I don't know where I would go. Who would have me? I have done some pretty major bridge burning.

I can't go to Max's or Derrick's or anyone from college. Besides, there would be *such* a fuss if I left. If they find out you've had a drink, they kick you out. 'Non-negotiable,' Jerry had said at our very first meeting. 'And you can't come back until you're sober.' I have no money and, even though I've started to hate it, this is where I need to be.

I'd got ready for bed in the bathroom; in the bedroom Isla strides around naked.

'You don't mind nakedness, do you?' She'd asked after she took off her clothes that first night.

I only mind because it's hard not to stare. I've seen more naked men than naked women. She has really big nipples. Bright pink. Mine are brown. She has pubes too, like a mega bush. Me and Mum both wax everything off. Mum said it was a fashion thing; everyone started by getting Brazilian waxes where you just have a little 'landing strip' down the middle. Beth won't wax or shave because she's a feminist and she says porn has infantilised women. I asked her why she shaves her underarms then, and she said that's different because underarm hair is just gross.

'You're young . . . you missing school or college or what being in here?' Isla asks me.

I tell her I just turned eighteen and I've had to defer my A levels. She doesn't ask me any more questions. She is totally preoccupied with whatever it is she is thinking.

Isla falls asleep quickly. I stare at her from my bed and feel like a perv. She's quite beautiful. A delicate little nose and full lips and her eyes, shut now, are a really bright blue. I snuggle deeper under the covers and put my hand in my knickers. I fall asleep like that, thinking of kissing Isla.

I have a horrible hangover that first morning. I haven't drunk, not a drop, and yet my head is full of an awful, heavy fog. I even have hangover paranoia: I panic that Isla knew the thoughts I had about her last night and thinks I'm a total pervert. Then I have to remind myself that I didn't drink and Isla can't read minds. Well, being sober seems the same as being drunk. Isla tells me this is normal. 'The bastard messes with your mind,' she says.

I drink loads and loads of water and they give me painkillers, and after breakfast I have a one-to-one session with a woman called Jane. Jane is nothing like Gwen the college counsellor. I'm talking to her and suddenly I am sobbing and hiccupping and have so many words pouring out I don't know if they'll ever stop. Jane draws thoughts and feelings out of me that were buried deep.

Here's what I learn in detox:

> *I really like custard creams.*
>
> *I am angry with my mum.*
>
> *People with tattoos aren't more interesting than people without tattoos.*
>
> *I don't hate Alan.*
>
> *I don't express my emotions.*
>
> *I don't have to just rely on myself, I can ask for help.*
>
> *There is no need to explain any of this to anyone on the outside.*
>
> *I'm not cool, I'm sick.*
>
> *It's OK to ask 'What do you mean by strong tea? Less milk or shall I squeeze the tea bag?'*

I have feelings.

I'm not bad at sharing a room.

I'm an addict.

I will be a better big sister if I stay sober.

Casual sex isn't going to help me get over Jamie.

You can't catch anything by holding hands with a tramp.

I am bisexual.

I am not 'over' my dad dying.

Having one-night stands all the time does not mean I'm a feminist.

It's OK to not want to hang around with someone who makes me feel uncomfortable.

I can learn to stop turning into a werewolf.

'Werewolf' is how I describe my drinking to Jane. 'Have you seen *American Werewolf in London*?'

She hasn't.

'Well, when this guy David changes into The Wolf, at first he's hyper, happy, bouncy, full of energy, then it starts to happen, the awful change. At first he's totally aware of it, he sees the hairs sprouting on his arms, he can't stop it, he's scared. His hand stretches into a hideous paw. He screams in agony as he grows fangs and his face elongates into a monster's. Then that's it. He's a werewolf, a full-on snarling werewolf standing in the flat. Nothing and no one could have stopped it. He goes out and does awful, mental things. Hours later he wakes up in a zoo, naked but normal again with no recollection of the awful things he did as The Wolf. He just sees the carnage and there's nothing he can do to fix it.

'That's what it feels like for me. Obviously, I haven't woken up in a zoo, but I've ended up naked and doing things I would never have done sober. I have woken up with shame so crippling that I'd wished I was dead. People tell me to stop, to drink less, but once I start, I can't stop it. I can't "come out for one" or have just "one for the road" without turning into a werewolf.'

Two weeks in rehab feels like two months. Time goes slowly when you don't drink. They say to take each day as it comes but I'm taking each hour as it comes. There is a lot of talking. There is a lot of TV watching and reading and discussing what to have for tea. It's soothing to talk about and arrange the very simple things. 'Do we need more toilet paper?' Yes, we do. 'I'll write it on the list.' That list is important. Every little detail to make the day run smoothly is taken seriously.

Phone calls with Mum mostly go like this:

'Are you OK?'

'Yeah, Mum, I've never been better. Being here is my dream come true.'

Mum's silences are loud. She is not rising to the crap I'm giving her, which makes me more sarcastic and rude. I annoy myself sometimes, when I'm being a dick. I am horrible to Mum.

Sometimes I can be strong for her, like the night she went into labour and Alan got into a flap. It's been the only time I've seen him lose his cool. Mum's contractions came quick, long ones, way before we got to the hospital. I thought Katie might arrive on our kitchen floor.

I calmed Mum down. *I* was the one, even though I was only twelve, who got her to breathe. She wouldn't let go of my hand

and Alan just stood there flapping about not finding his car keys. I said, 'Alan, your car keys are on the kitchen table, Mum's hospital bag is under your bed. Get it, please.' Alan followed my instructions and was relieved, I know, to have me there.

At the hospital, I became invisible. All the information about what was going on was given to Alan, and once he was in the hospital environment, he collected himself and was the perfect, supportive father-to-be and I was sent off to buy tea. Mum forgets this stuff.

She has told Katie I'm on holiday, which is fine because I don't want to talk to Katie from in here. She'll ask me a million questions about where I am, whether it has a park, if I've seen any squirrels, and I would have to lie about squirrels I've seen, dogs I've met. I hate lying to Katie.

I call Beth. I'm nervous.

'You OK?'

'Yes, I'm OK.'

Talking to Beth from in here is like talking to her from the moon.

She tells me a few bits and pieces of college gossip.

'Zoe's worried Alex has gone cold on her. She says he's been a bit weird since the party. I'm worried about her. You know she's found out he's got two phones? She's obsessed about finding what's on his second one. He's said it's for work, so then how come he won't let her look at it?'

'I dunno.'

'You know he's got one of those two-seater convertible cars? He smacks of having a very small penis.'

'He doesn't.'

'Oh, yeah, forgot about that.'

'Wish *I* could.'

'Can we just pretend it's small to make ourselves laugh?'

'Sure. He has the kind of penis you'd need some peanut butter and a Labrador to find.'

'Eh?'

'That's what they do to get dogs to lick people in films. They smear peanut butter on the actor and the dog licks them.'

'Oh, right. I get it. Gross.'

We laugh slightly awkward laughs. We're trying to find our old ground but we are both a bit off the mark.

'Of course we're not at all jealous our mate is going out with a rich, sophisticated sex god.'

I need a subject change. 'What's going on with you and Steve?'

'He's all right.'

'All right? Beth, from you that means "he's amazing, I'm in love with him".'

'He's pretty cool.'

'How many times have you seen him since the party?'

'Just every day.'

'No way!'

'Yeah way.'

So Beth has a boyfriend. Beth never has boyfriends; I'm the one who has boyfriends. I'm supposed to say, 'I'm happy for you.' But I have no idea if I am or not. It's strange talking about people at home when I'm locked away from them, surrounded by charts on the walls and pills and meeting rooms with people crying and hugging and sometimes shouting in them.

Beth asks me what it's like in here. There's no way she would understand what it's like so I just say, 'It's OK.'

Then Beth says, 'Sorry I was so horrible about everything. I didn't know how serious things were for you.'

I almost cry. I almost cry because I behaved so awfully, yet she's apologising to *me*.

'You know the whole thing with my dad?' she asks.

'Beth don't, please don't. I can't bear to think about it.'

'So . . . too soon to talk about how you tried to become my stepmum?' There is a giggle in her voice.

'I can't laugh about it yet, Beth.'

'OK.' She pauses. 'How about now?'

'No.'

Another pause. 'Now?'

'No!'

She sighs. 'Mummy?'

'No, Beth! We will never ever laugh about the night I tried to seduce your dad!'

And we both laugh. We are back.

'OK,' Beth says, 'but Dad's cool, OK? And so am I. You weren't yourself. You weren't well. You were nuts.'

I was upside down, inside out and back to front. I *was* myself, just the worst 'version' of myself. But I don't say this to Beth. She might not get it and right now I don't want to explain anything. I know that if someone banged on about 'versions' of themselves before I came in here I'd gag.

Isla and me talk a lot. She comes to find me at meal times and we lie in our twin beds and talk and talk. She's sweet and quite funny. No way as pretty as Isabelle, but nice. I think about sex with her a lot. I think about it so much it's hard for any other thoughts to come in. While we chat and I see her mouth move I wonder what it would be like to kiss her, put my hands all over her. I hate it when I talk to guys and you can tell that all they are thinking is how they can get to fuck you. But here I am doing exactly that: chatting to Isla all about our feelings and our families while I'm wishing we could just get drunk and tear each other's clothes off.

The therapy sessions I have in here are intense. Jane sits there while I weep and shake. I say things I didn't know I had in me to say. I hate it, sometimes. I get angry that I have to talk about painful stuff that makes me cry and Jane listens until our time is up.

The most amazing part of rehab is the AA meetings. When I listen to other people, this magic thing happens: someone will suddenly put something *I* feel into words.

Booze gave me the illusion that I wasn't alone but once it wore off I was adrift and sinking. In rehab, I have not yet reached the shore but I am learning ways to keep afloat. I've become like one of those sharks in *Finding Nemo*.

CHAPTER TWELVE

I stay in rehab for five weeks. It's meant to be six but I don't want to have to retake my final year of college. My life is waiting for me and I need to get back to it. I'm strong and clear-headed and ready.

'Pretty fucking arrogant to think you're cured!' says Maggie.

I have brought it up at a house meeting.

'Nina, you can't see past the end of your own fucking nose.'

'Spoilt, middle-class kid that has no fucking idea how lucky she is.'

'I'm happy for you, Nina, you know what feels right for you.'

Jerry asks me if I think leaving right now is the best thing.

'When I came here you said it isn't a prison.'

'I did indeed.'

'So, I'm going. I feel OK. I feel strong enough.'

I surprise myself, how urgently I want to get back to studying; all of that slid far down in my mind after Jamie. I want to grab my A levels. I want to do well.

I haven't had a drink for five whole weeks; I've done it, I've stopped drinking. A whole year out of my studies seems mad. It's one thing to have a gap year, adventures abroad to see waterfalls, go to the jungle, not be stuck in rehab making tea and eating biscuits. I want to run around in my own life again, sober and awake.

I want to see Beth and Max, Trish even, make things up with Zoe. I want to read my books, go back to college and catch up. There was a time when I was as much of a swot as Beth; we were neck and neck in our marks.

Skipping dinner, I go to my room to pack, ready to go in the morning. The idea that I'm going to walk out, by myself, and sort out the mess I left behind excites me and terrifies me.

Isla comes in. 'Are you all right, chick?' She sees my bag. 'You definitely going?'

'Yeah. Do you think I'm mad?'

'If you weren't mad you wouldn't be in here, but I don't think you're mad for leaving a bit early. Wish I could fucking leave.'

'You can leave.'

'I meant I wish I felt well enough to leave. I don't. Not yet.'

I sit on my bed next to her, she takes off her shoes and puts her arms around me and we cuddle. It's a good cuddle, close and warm. She smells of chips but it's nice. Neither of us let go, we stay like that, holding each other. I put my hand up to the back of her neck and I stroke it. She does the same to me. We draw back, look at each other, then I kiss her. On the mouth. She kisses me back. We are sober and this is sweet. This feels OK and even though it's not *actually* OK, there is nothing I can do because kissing Isla feels completely and utterly delicious and I am not going to stop.

I'm kissing a woman. And I am doing this sober. I'm doing what I've fantasised about doing for ages. It's exciting. My head spins and whirls. We hold each other tight before we lie on the bed, on top of the covers. I pull her close; we are kissing necks, chins, eyes and noses. We struggle out of our jeans, almost falling off my narrow single bed. There are hands inside tops and in between legs. She keeps kissing me as one hand cups my breast and the other creeps softly into my knickers and gently touches my vagina lips. I try to do the same to her but the position is awkward and I am too cack-handed with nerves and an unfamiliar body, so I just leave her to it. I let her unbutton my shirt and take off my bra. She puts my boob in her mouth. I didn't know my nipples were so sensitive. I want to giggle because it tickles and I want to shout, 'HA! This is brilliant!'

But of course, I can't. She puts her fingers inside me and I'm wet. I get heavenly waves of tingling pleasure. I close my eyes and pretend she's Isabelle. Then she goes right down; she kisses me all the way down until her head is between my legs. I have no idea where she puts her own legs; they disappear as she does amazing things with her lips and tongue. So soft. So much softer than a boy. I pray there is no lingering bit of toilet paper stuck down there or some other horror. I try to relax but it's too intense. I try to move away but she holds my hips and keeps me there until I come so deep and hard, I think I might pass out. She comes back up, panting gently, and kisses my face. 'Is that better?' she whispers, then kisses my mouth and we fall asleep.

We drift off without drawing the curtains until sunlight streams in and wakes us up.

We lay, holding each other for a while.

Then Isla asks, 'Are you OK?'

'Yeah, I just need to get out of here.'

'Are you OK about last night?'

I shove a few remaining things quickly in my suitcase.

'Oh, God. Sure, it was lovely. Amazing. But I want to go now.'

She is sitting up in bed. I feel a tingle because she is a girl, in my bed, that I've had sex with. I have finally had sex with a girl and it was utterly delicious.

'Stay, Nina. Stay these last few days. Your parents have paid for it, you might as well.'

'No. No. I don't want to.' I want out of this bubble. This is not my life. My life is someplace else, hurtling ahead without me. I need to jump back on.

Walking out of that place, holding my suitcase out in the drizzle, with no idea where I'm going, is, for the first half an hour, bliss. England's grey has never looked more beautiful.

I'm not sure where I am. I find a coffee shop called Rosy's Teapot. It has gingham tablecloths and smells slightly of damp carpets. The waiter is about fifty, with greasy long curly hair tied back in a ponytail. He tuts when I knock into a table with my suitcase as I come in and doesn't smile when I sit down. 'What can I get you?' he demands. He is not very 'Rosy'.

I order a cup of tea and a slice of marble cake and call Alan. I just feel like calling him, so I do.

Mum picks up the phone but I actually say, 'Hi, Mum. Can I speak to Alan?'

Mum is surprised and confused but hands Alan the phone.

'Alan, thanks for paying for all the rehab stuff.'

'That's OK, Nina,' he says after a few beats, because my 'thank you' has thrown him. I don't think I have ever said thank you to him for anything.

'As long as we get you well, that's the main thing.'

'I've left there, Alan. I'm in a coffee shop called Rosy's Teapot.'

Usually, Alan would be the last person I'd tell anything to, but he's the first family member I tell my news to.

'Oh,' Alan says, 'is that wise? I thought you only had a week to go . . . Where will you go?'

I've been sober for five weeks and I feel sort of high, high on being in the normal, outside world again. Apart from the waiter, everything in Rosy's Teapot makes me so relieved I am on the outside. The red on the gingham, the little pot of bright-blue fabric flowers. Even the little tea stain that wasn't from my pot of tea looks cheerful.

'Alan, I want to say sorry about how rude I've been to you over the years.'

I can picture Alan at the kitchen table in their flat in Düsseldorf, looking slightly baffled and uncomfortable. Bracing himself for whatever game he thinks I might be playing next. I can see him standing there not quite knowing if his stepdaughter who hates him is OK, if this was part of some kind of breakdown.

'Er, Nina, that's all right.'

'Thank you, Alan, but it's not all right. I have been unkind and if you have time I have a few more things I want to apologise for. Is that cool?'

Alan assures me it is cool. I take a sip of my tea, cut my cake in half with my fork, and start.

'Alan. I'm sorry I've been a pig to you since you got together with my mum. I thought Mum turned into a proper bore once she met you but now I realise how secure you make her feel and how lonely she must have been with just me and her, and I really appreciate how you never retaliated when I was a total arsehole. And also I'm really sorry for swearing. I know you don't like it but this is the only way I can express myself right now.'

He coughs. 'I see . . .'

'I think you're a brilliant dad to Katie and I'm so sorry for all the times I've been disrespectful to you. I tried to write them all down in rehab, but there were too many.'

'Ah, well, I always understood you were very young and needed time to get used to a new home situation.'

'Yes, but I didn't want to get used to it.'

'Was it me personally that you didn't like?'

Now this question takes *me* by surprise. *Was* it personal? If Mum had got together with a cooler guy would things have been different? With someone like Max, perhaps?

'I don't think so, Alan. I missed my dad. You just weren't my dad, that's all.'

'And that must have been very hard. I knew that.'

'Yes, but you made my mum happy. You took me on with all my kicking and screaming and, like I said, you're a lovely dad to Katie. I'm pretty sure Katie won't end up in rehab!'

The last bit is a clumsy attempt at a joke and, typically with Alan, it falls flat and the silence is awkward.

'I just wanted my dad back and I couldn't have him back so I wanted Mum to myself.'

'Do you still feel like that?'

'Well, no, because Katie wouldn't be here without you.'

'She adores you, you know.'

'I know, she's the best kid in the world.'

'Your mother, I mean. I don't think you understand just how much your mother loves you, how hurt she is by this . . .'

I resist the urge to shout, 'I didn't do all this deliberately!' which is what I would have done five weeks ago. It's OK if people don't get it. Not everyone has to get it.

'Yeah.'

'What are you going to do now?'

'I'm going to finish my cup of tea and find somewhere to stay.'

'Would you like me to hand you over to your mum?'

'Nope. Tell her not to worry. I'll call her later.'

I don't feel like explaining to Mum that I've left. I'll let Alan deal with that.

We hang up. That was surprisingly OK.

I call Trish. Not Beth.

'MUM!' Trish shouts, 'CAN NINA COME TO STAY?' There is a pause. I hear:

'WHO'S NINA?'

Trish shouts again. 'NINA! MY FRIEND IN REHAB, SHE'S OUT NOW. CAN SHE STAY HERE?'

'REHAB? IS SHE CLEAN?'

'You still boozing?' Trish puts the phone back to her mouth and asks.

'No.'

'YEAH, MUM, SHE'S CLEAN.'

'ALL RIGHT, SHE CAN COME. TELL HER TO BRING HER OWN TOWELS.'

'Yeah, that's cool. Come over, and bring your own towels.'

And that is that. I still have Mum's credit card so I get the train back to London.

Mum calls and flips out.

It is very difficult to pacify a flipped-out mum when you have done so much to justify her concerns.

'You haven't finished the program, you couldn't do this one thing? Please go back, Nina, go back. It's just for a week . . .'

There is no way I am going back.

The plan was that after six weeks, I would go to Germany and stay with Mum, Alan and Katie for the rest of the academic year. But I'm not going to do that. I'm going back to college.

'Where will you stay? You CAN'T expect Max to take you in again.'

'I'm staying with Trish.'

'Trish? The one with blue hair? Mumbles?'

'Yes.'

Mum sighs. Mum thinks Trish is a bit of a layabout, which she is, but that's why she's also the sort of person who will have you to stay at the drop of a hat.

'What about all the work you've missed?'

'I'll catch up.'

Mum carries on with fussing and questions. What will I do for money, will I be allowed back to college, how long will Trish put me up for, but the whole time, we both know what she *really* wants to ask is, 'Are you going to go back to drinking? To ruin your life, exactly like your dad did?'

I am *not* going to do that.

I *am* going to carry on with AA meetings; there are loads in London. They say in London you're never more than three feet away from a rat. You're never more than three feet away from an AA meeting either. Little rooms scattered around the city, where lawyers, doctors, homeless people and plumbers sit on plastic chairs and share their most private feelings with total strangers, clutching on to them for understanding.

Mum says she will pay Trish's mum board on the condition that I find a part-time job.

Then Max calls. I think about not answering but I know I have to. Mum will have got off the phone to me and immediately got on to Max and told him what's happened and begged him to keep tabs on me. Mum does not change.

Sure enough Max says, 'Look, Nina, your mum is really worried about you.'

Poor Max, this isn't his problem.

'If you'd like, you can stay here but just until you find somewhere else.'

So awkward. I let him know he's off the hook.

'I already have, Max. I'm staying with Trish.'

Max's voice lightens. Palpable relief. 'Come and have your old job back then?'

'Really?'

'Yes, really. You're missed at the shop. The kids always ask where you are, they want Story Time back.'

I grin. 'That's amazing. I'd love to. Thanks, Max.'

The grumpy Rosy's Teapot waiter comes back to my table. 'Are you going to order something else? This is a business, you know, not just a place for nattering to your mates.' He picks up my plate. I ask for the bill.

As I go to leave he mutters, 'One day at a time, love.'

I'm taken aback. 'Sorry?'

'One day at a time. They all come in here, after they've been in there. Trick is, staying off the stuff once you're out.'

CHAPTER THIRTEEN

Trish's mum opens the front door with a cigarette hanging out of her mouth. She's got short, cropped hair in rainbow colours. She doesn't smile but she is nice and takes my bag.

'C'mon in, darling. Let's get you settled in. Trish is at work.'

Trish did not mention she had a job, which is typical of Trish.

'Really? Where's she working?'

'Dunno. Some law firm in town. Receptionist or summink.'

Trish's mum is called Belle. She pulls a face when she says 'or summink' to show she has no idea of the corporate world and it is beyond her to try and understand.

They live on the Manor Estate which is a council estate but an all right one. Half the flats are privately owned and the rest is mostly families. There's no trouble there apart from the gang of teenagers who sometimes shout 'Oi! My Little Pony!' at Trish when she walks by. That's pretty much as rough as it gets and they never shout it at Belle. Trish loves telling people she's from an estate though. She likes them to think she grew up amongst gangsters.

Their spare room is bigger than Beth's. It's a maisonette, so Trish and her mum are on the top floor and I'm in the bedroom downstairs, by the kitchen.

I'll have to get to Beth's and get the rest of my stuff, but for now, I'm OK. I unpack what I have, then nip out to an AA meeting. There's one just across the road in the church hall. Every Tuesday. Sorted.

When I get back, Trish is home. Only it's not the old Trish. The dreads and the blue dye have gone. Gone too are the dreamcatcher earrings and lip-ring. This Trish has sleek, shiny, straightened, deep plum hair, almost-natural-coloured. She's lost a bit of weight and is wearing normal clothes, like office clothes. No Aztec poncho or purple tasselled skirt. She has on a navy knee-length skirt and a white blouse, for God's sake.

'Oh, hi, Nina.' Her voice is the same. I half expected that to have changed from her monotone drone but it hasn't. A relief.

Her personality is the same too. She says 'Oh, hi, Nina' as though it hasn't been over a month since I saw her at my catastrophic party. She acts like we just saw each other yesterday and I've happened to wander into her house with my suitcase.

'You know what I was saying about the King's Head starting an open mic night? Turns out it's not bands doing open mics, it's comedians. It's a bloody comedy night.'

This is a conversation started before my rehab, and for a moment I don't know what to say. 'Was it good?'

'Dunno. I don't really get stand-up comedy. It's someone on a stage saying stuff, then everyone laughing.'

'So it was funny?'

'Yeah.'

'But you didn't like it?'

'Nah.'

I have missed these maddening 'Trish' conversations.

'You look different,' I tell her.

'Yeah?' she says. 'I had my hair trimmed.'

'She means you've gone all corporate, darlin',' her mum says, lighting a fag and going to stick on the kettle.

'Oh, yeah. I thought I'd better get a job, you know. After what happened to you, I sort of shifted gear in my head. I thought, I don't wanna end up like her, d'you know what I mean?'

'Jesus Christ, Trish,' Belle says, 'you ever thought of being a Samaritan?'

'It's OK,' I say. And weirdly it is. Trish's bluntness is a relief.

Belle is gay. Trish has never met her dad, doesn't know who he is. 'Some bloke Mum met while off her tits at Glastonbury,' she told me once when I asked.

Belle is a proper lesbian. I'm not an idiot, I know 'proper' lesbians can have long hair and wear make-up and dresses, but Belle is an old-school lesbian hippy. She buys her trousers from DIY stores, cuts her hair herself and if a shopkeeper or taxi driver calls her 'love' she says, 'I don't believe we've had sex. I'd have remembered.' She's very on the ball compared to Trish.

Isla has been texting me. Loads. Other than one text back to say 'hi', I haven't replied. I'm not sorry about what happened, not at all, but I don't know where Isla fits out here in my real life, in my real world.

There are people to face. Beth, Max, Zoe. I haven't been in touch with Zoe at all. Beth had said Zoe has gone a bit mad because she is so insecure about Alex. She adores him, she's fallen head over heels, but Beth doesn't reckon he has. 'It's so one-sided. He'll go off for whole weekends and not call her, or he'll chat other girls up right in front of her.'

Fair play to Jamie. Seriously, fair play for being honest. I mean he was an insensitive prick about it and totally broke my heart, but there are people who behave worse than that. People who will string you along until something better comes up. I told Beth this and she said, 'But babe, that's exactly what Jamie did.'

It wasn't as black and white. It can't have been. Maybe Jamie didn't know our relationship wasn't right for him until he met someone who made him feel like he couldn't *not* be apart from them. That pain rises up in my chest again and I use everything I have learned in rehab and recovery to deal with it. I meditate, I run a nice hot bath, I lie in it reading a book. 'Feel the pain, don't drink the pain,' I say out loud in my bath. For ages, the only real feeling I possessed to deal with crappy things was anger. Now I discover I have a whole range of other feelings. Sadness, loneliness, shame, loss; they all have an impromptu party inside me and thrive now I'm not drowning them in booze.

I go back to college. My teachers are all supportive and give me notes and offers of lunchtime catch-up lessons. Isabelle tells me I'm 'very brave'. I don't know if I'm brave. I am calm. I am quieter, and I get my head down and study.

When I go back to Beth's for the first time to say 'hi' and get my things, the house itself seems standoffish with me as I walk to the front door. The windows and bricks are saying, 'Look who's back! You caused an awful lot of trouble here last time, I hope we don't have a repeat performance.'

Steve is there in his dressing gown, sitting on Max's chair in the corner of the kitchen with a cup of tea, reading a book. Beth has said that he practically lives with them now, but even so, I wasn't expecting him to be quite so at home. He looks up when I come in, then up at Beth, who gives him a look to reassure him that his presence here with us is fine.

'All right, Nina?' he says. Bless him, he gets up, then isn't sure what to do so he sits back down again. 'How's it going?'

'Fine. How's it going with you?'

'Yeah, fine.' He holds up his book. 'Chaucer. Total bastard.'

'Yeah,' I agree, 'but we do get to say "cunt" out loud in class though.'

'That's always nice.'

'Yeah.'

I wouldn't have put him and Beth together, but then what do I actually know about the 'right' fit? Beth is whizzing around the kitchen, sorting me out a cup of tea and telling me all the latest gossip. She doesn't stop for breath. Is Beth nervous? I have never seen her nervous around me before. Steve absorbs himself in his book and doesn't look up once or join in our chat.

The house is clear of all of the evidence of our party. Of course it would be; it's been weeks. Still, I stiffen when I go upstairs to pack my stuff. I glance across the hall at Max's bedroom door and I shudder at the ghostly image of myself staggering in there in my underwear and throwing myself at him. God, I want to grab that ghost and stop her going in Max's room. I wish I could go back in time and be my own guardian angel. 'There, there, hon, you don't want to be behaving like a total whore. Come with me and I'll put you to bed with some water and paracetamol.'

Later, at Trish's, I unpack my things and start working on my short story. I know I have a lot of college work to catch up on but I'm confident I will do it, fairly easily, so I'm going back to Isabelle's creative writing class. I wrote every day in rehab. I wrote a diary, which helps in recovery, and I made a start on a short story. We're all submitting an entry for a competition.

My laptop purrs; it's Katie, Skyping me. I grin and answer her call. She's got her hair in two plaits quite high on either side of her head and her face is painted like a lion.

'Rawwww!' says Katie, putting up her hands clenched into claws and scrunching up her face to look fierce.

'ARGH!' I scream, and duck for cover. We play like that for a bit, then Katie says (in German), 'I went to a party.'

'A party!' I reply (in German). 'Was the party at your friend's house?'

'Nina, can we speak English again now? I don't know what you said. Where are you? You're not at Beth's.'

'I'm staying with my friend Trish now.'

'I like Trish; her hair's all pretty colours. What are you doing?'

'Well, before you called I was writing a story.'

Katie the Lion's eyes light up. 'For me?'

'Oh no, not this time, I'm afraid.'

Katie dramatically folds her arms up and sticks out her bottom lip.

'Come on now, Katie, lions don't sulk.'

'Is it for grown-ups, your story?'

'Yes, it's for a competition.'

'What's it about?'

My story is about a woman who can't stop ordering stuff she doesn't need on the Internet and ends up having a houseful of taxidermy animals and useless trinkets cluttering her house. Pretty much every room is full to the brim, up to the ceiling with junk, and she ends up having to pitch a tent up in the garden. I may have been thinking of my Auntie Jean when I came up with the idea.

I tell Katie about the woman who can't stop buying stuff.

'But I'm a bit stuck,' I tell her.

'Why?' she asks.

'Well, because something else has to happen apart from her buying stuff, otherwise it just gets boring.'

Katie doesn't need to think about my problem. She instantly shrugs and says, 'Put a dragon in it.'

'What?'

'Put. A. Dragon. In it,' she says slowly. 'Whenever someone reads me a story and it gets boring I imagine a dragon coming in and making everyone go ARGHGHGHGH!' She raises her thin little arms in the air, closes her eyes and does a full-on impression of a rampaging dragon.

After a while we say goodbye and I go back to my story and think about my own dragon.

Not drinking means I have more time. I have hours and hours when I'm not hungover and can actually do stuff. It's productive, calm and wildly boring. But then I sit in AA meetings and listen to people talk about what boozing has done to their lives and remember that boredom is not the worst thing.

I see the drama lot prancing about and squealing in the canteen. They exhaust me.

I catch up on college work. I shut myself in my little room at Trish's and work on my English, history and philosophy. I read like a demon. Studying is, to my surprise, hugely enjoyable.

I have dinner with Trish and her mum every evening. Trish sometimes goes out with people she's met at work and it'll just be me and Belle. Belle never goes out: 'Done all that, darling. I can't be arsed with it now.' Belle is very cool. Mum sends her money each week for my food and board. Belle told me off when I bought a load of groceries. 'Oi you, your mum gives me money so just write what you want on the shopping list. Don't use your weekend money on food, else I'll be making a profit and I'm not running a bleedin' business, I'm helping out my daughter's mate.'

She's not like a 'mummy' sort of mum. Like, if I tell her stuff she doesn't just half listen and give me advice, and she isn't always understanding. If I say something she thinks is a load of bollocks, she'll say, 'Well, that's a load of bollocks,' which – once you get used to it – is refreshing.

After dinner Trish usually watches trash TV and Belle sits at her laptop and sells stuff she buys from car boot sales.

Belle 'upcycles' furniture. 'You buy a load of junk and tart it up,' she tells me. 'Posh people love it.' She shows me a picture of an old drinks cabinet before and after she painted it. 'Cost me twelve quid that. I sold it for two hundred and twenty pounds. People are mental, eh?'

I don't think they are. Belle spends hours and hours 'tarting up' the things she buys and making them look beautiful. She doesn't just paint them; she gets rid of mould, she mends and sands. She puts a lot of love into her junk.

I go to AA and I hang out with Beth but things are very weird with me and Zoe.

I have gone further up the 'cool' ladder as far as Phoebe is concerned, though, and she treats me to her company more than she used to.

'God, babe,' Phoebe tells me, 'I know exactly what you went through.' Well, actually, she tells pretty much the whole canteen in her concerned foghorn voice.

'*We* have alcoholism in *our* family and it's *so* not a joke, like it's a proper disease, you know. You can talk to me about it any time, hon. I will, like, totally understand.'

I just smile at her, grateful for the one or two 'what is she like?!' glances from other people thrown my way.

Robbie finds me as I walk back home. I haven't sought him out. I hadn't known how to play it.

'It must have been a good party . . . I mean if you had to go to rehab after.' He grins and makes me laugh.

Even when I'm sober he is very, very cute.

'Most people are happy with a hangover and pizza in front of the TV but not our Nina, she goes ALL the way home!'

I elbow him in the belly and we walk to the high street.

'Cheers, Robbie. You're the first person who's been able to make me laugh about this.'

'Seriously, though, you OK?'

'Yeah. I think so.'

'And you can't drink ever again?'

'I can, but you saw the state I was in, right? I don't want to get in those states again.'

'Bit rough your mum not being here. My mum is up my arse when I sneeze in front of her. Something like this she'd pack her bags, climb in my ear and camp in my head. I wouldn't hear the end of it.'

People have said it must be cool, not living with your parents . . . that you have freedom. No one texting you demanding to know where you are at any point, no one laying down rules and curfews. And yeah, it is like that at first, but after a while, you notice other things. There's no one to care if you've not had your dinner. No one to fuss if you've not got a coat. No one to notice if you haven't come home or if you're not quite yourself. No Mum rushing around, gathering her things, filling the hallway with her perfume as she clatters out with far too much stuff in her arms. No little sister to fling her arms around you and tell you the crazy thoughts in her head.

No Katie to snuggle into my bed and pretend it's a boat on the high seas.

'Yeah,' I say to Robbie, 'I miss my mum and sister.' I pause. 'And my stepdad.' The latter surprises me by being true.

'Your real dad's dead, isn't he? Sorry, do you mind me asking?'

I don't mind. I tell him yeah, and I tell him I was nine.

'That's intense. I can't imagine that.'

We say bye at the bus stop, but he doesn't go straight away.

'Nina, can I have your phone number?'

This hasn't happened for a long time. I'm not sure if it's ever happened. A boy asking for my number and we haven't even kissed. I give it to him.

Zoe, me and Beth go for a coffee like we often used to after the bookshop closed for the day. Trish meets us too. I am pretty much obliged to take her everywhere with me now that I live with her. Zoe thinks Trish is a freak. Beth once asked me if Trish is 'a bit slow'. She's not slow, she's just on another planet to most people.

I remember Zoe was bitchy to me at the party. She said something to Alex about me being 'attention seeking'. There was an edge to her and a bad vibe between us. I hate that. It stresses me out. It's not obvious what the problem is. Was it jealousy? Had she been jealous that Alex had shown me concern? That he, despite our party being a little beneath him, had insisted they look for me, stay and help Max. He *did* do that. I didn't know why.

Zoe looks really skinny. Even more so than usual. She used to be the coolest, most chilled girl ever but I hardly know her now, she's so drawn and jumpy. She doesn't concentrate on anything but her phone. She *constantly* checks it.

'Are we cool, Zoe?'

'Oh my God, yes, why wouldn't we be?' she says, not looking up.

Trish is picking the cream from her hot chocolate off with her finger and not really joining in our conversation, but she suddenly looks up at me and says, 'Didn't you get off with the bloke she's seeing? Didn't you get thrown out of a club for going down on him?'

Beth and I both freeze. Trish looks at us for a second, then, not getting an answer, goes back to decimating her hot chocolate.

Zoe stares down. I literally can't speak, and Beth says, 'Have you ever thought about being a politician, Trish? Your tact is amazing. You shouldn't waste that talent.'

Zoe pushes her chair back and blinks away tears. She hadn't known. She hadn't known the full story of what happened. I go to follow her but Beth says, 'Honestly, hon, I think it's best I go,' and she does.

I sit in silence with Trish. The silence is broken by her slurping hot chocolate from her spoon. Sometimes *I* wonder if she's a bit slow.

There's no point getting pissed off with her. She wouldn't get why you're pissed off. Actually, she wouldn't *notice* you were pissed off.

Beth comes back after a bit. 'She's gone home. Trish, what were you thinking? She thought they'd just kissed.'

'You don't get thrown out for just kissing. Didn't she know there was lewd conduct?'

'No, she bloody didn't, Trish,' I can't help but snap. 'She thinks I was just drunk and being an arse.'

I text Zoe. *Babe, I was so drunk, I don't even remember it. I can't even be sure what happened.'*

'Look, I've got to go,' Beth says, 'I'm meeting Steve.'

My heart sinks. This is it now. She will leave me in a cafe with just Trish for company when we are in the middle of a crisis. For a boy.

I can't demand she drop everything for me anymore. Steve is her priority. For the first time ever, I feel anxious about our friendship. Is she going to ditch me? Do I still mean to her what she means to me? Is she just hanging out with me because she's a good person and feels a sense of duty? It's miserable. I feel miserable about how things have changed, how I've fucked things up . . .

'Are you and Steve doing anything fun?' I say, sounding totally needy.

'Just pub. Wanna come? I didn't ask because I don't know if you can. Would it be weird?'

I can do it, I think; I can sit in a pub with my friends and just enjoy myself, and not get shit-faced.

'No, I'll come with you.'

'Can I come?' Trish asks. She has been chomping on a chocolate muffin and shows us bits of it mashed in her mouth as she speaks.

Beth's face falls ever so slightly. This was not the evening she'd been looking forward to, but she's far too nice to say no or let it show that she would rather stick pins in her eyes than have Trish around all evening.

'Er, yeah, if you want.'

To most people, 'if you want' is not an invitation it's a brush-off, but it's good enough for Trish. She goes, 'Cool. I'll go home for my tea, then come down.'

She looks at Zoe's untouched hot chocolate and says, 'D'you reckon it's OK for me to have that then?' and pulls it towards her.

We will go to The Mash Tun later, after tea, though Mum and Alan never call it 'tea'. We have 'supper'.

Trish moans about the choice of pub. 'It's all wankers that drink in there.'

'Oi! I go there!' Or I used to.

I get what she means though. Trish isn't part of the college crowd; she's slightly older than everyone and although she pretends she just finds everyone immature, I think she's self-conscious that she's almost twenty and still hangs out with seventeen- and eighteen-year-olds. She doesn't seem to have any other friends besides me. I'm not sure who could put up with her. I like her because she is always the same. She's always in exactly the same mood. Nothing shocks her, nothing much upsets her; you always know where you are with Trish. She's like a comfy old sofa.

I'm getting ready to go out. Zoe didn't return my text, but now she turns up at Trish's house. Trish lets her in and they both come into my room. Trish sits on the bed. I don't know why Zoe is here. I'm caught off guard.

She is clearly very upset, very angry and nervous. She doesn't know how to handle this either.

'So tell me exactly what you did with my boyfriend?' Her voice is cold yet still shaky. Neither of us is the type of girl who will usually fight over a guy. This is alien territory for us both.

'He wasn't your boyfriend then, Zoe. You hadn't got together. You hadn't met! He was just some bloke in a club.'

'Yes, but why lie?'

'I didn't lie. I just didn't tell you.'

'I called you up to see if you were OK. You knew I'd got off with him, you could have told me then.'

'Zoe, you have no idea how bad I felt getting thrown out. It wasn't just a bit of gossip I didn't want anyone to know . . . I wanted to forget it happened.'

'Did you tell Beth?'

'Yes, I told Beth.'

'And she told me,' Trish chips in.

'So you DID tell people.'

'Just Beth, Zoe – she's my best friend! Of course I told Beth, and I told Trish because Trish is just Trish.'

'I am, yeah,' confirms Trish.

Zoe looks stung.

I am standing there with my hair straighteners in my hand in my little room, staring at Zoe who has tears in her eyes, from anger, not sadness.

'So, all of you, the whole time I've been going out with Alex, knew what happened and didn't tell me.'

She's being an idiot. Suddenly I'm angry. It was an incident in *my* life, nothing to do with Zoe. Why am I having to explain myself to her?

'Don't act like I owe you something, Zoe!' Now I'm trying hard to keep *my* cool.

'You *could* have told me! Do you have any idea what it's like finding out your friend has got with your boyfriend?'

OK, now I *am* going to lose it.

'Got with? I didn't "get" with him, Zoe. It wasn't a romantic kiss in the fucking park . . . I was so drunk that I couldn't stand up and I did something disgusting. Go and have it out with him. *He* was driving, *he* wasn't drunk . . . go and ask your boyfriend why he finds paralytic girls and sticks his cock in their mouth.'

I've lost it. I've lost my temper now. I'm shouting.

'Go and ask your flash fucking boyfriend why he is such a fucking perv. *I couldn't stand up by myself.* You *saw* what state I was in that night.'

'Have you stayed in touch with him, have you seen him again?'

'NO!'

'You're a fucking liar! You're a LYING FUCKING SLAG!'

I think Zoe might hit me. She is so angry her face is bright red, and she's shaking and shouting.

She's screaming 'You WHORE!!' at me, and then she loses control and goes for me. Her long thin arms lash out and Trish shouts something, I don't know what, I think it's just a sound.

I have never been hit before. I hit back at Zoe with the hair straighteners. Just once, and I strike her with the hot edge across her head. I don't mean to, I really don't, it was just a flash, a second, and she screams and flies at me again, then Trish jumps up and grabs Zoe's arm, twists it round behind her back and trips her so she is face down on the floor.

Belle comes in and sees Trish restraining a screaming Zoe. I am standing with my top torn, hair ripped out, holding the straighteners, flushed and snarling.

'Everything OK, girls?' Belle asks with her eyebrows raised. 'Trish, you know your karate is just for self-defence, yeah?'

'Yeah, Mum, I'm using reasonable force.'

'OK, well, you'd better let her go now.'

Beth releases Zoe. Zoe gets up, sobbing, and runs out of the house.

'I don't know what's going on,' Belle says, 'and I don't want to know, but any more fighting in my house and you leave, Nina.'

And she goes back upstairs to her room.

Trish, it turns out, has a black belt in karate. Trish has never ever mentioned this, even when occasionally we've had conversations about karate.

I put my shoes on, crying and panting with rage. I need to get out. My feet take me to an AA meeting. I have to wait an hour and a half for it to start but I don't care. I sit inside this church. I can't go out, not in this state. I am still shaking with shock when I get there. There are texts from Beth: *'Where are you?'* and *'Call me, babe, I'm worried.'*

I have made it to a meeting. This is the only place I want to be right now. I've got hot blood pumping around my head so fast that I can't really hear people properly in the meeting. But slowly, as the meeting goes on, I calm down. The relief is incredible. My head is one of those snowstorm ornaments, all shaken up with stuff flying everywhere, but gradually it settles and I am not angry with Zoe anymore. Zoe is not the enemy. Alex has harmed us both.

Whatever Jamie did, I know he's a good guy, he would never hurt anyone, but Alex hurt me. When you see someone that drunk, you look after them, or you find their mates and get *them* to look after them. That's what most people are like. When he came to my party he acted like it was a game of ping-pong we had that night instead of something I found so humiliating that the rest of my year was spent totally and utterly fucked up.

I next see Zoe again at college in English; she blanks me. She stops coming to creative writing class.

Beth tries to talk to her but Zoe doesn't want to hear my side of things. She doesn't want to talk to me or fix what happened.

'She's totally changed,' Beth says later in the bookshop. 'I can't talk to her about anything other than Alex. She's always stressing about him not calling or that he's been out and not said who he was with. Do you know she actually went round to his house in the middle of the night and waited in the car for him to come home? He came back at, like, one in the morning and she just drove away, relieved he was on his own.'

'That is madness. Why is she with him? He's not making her happy.'

Me and Beth talk endlessly about Zoe and Alex.

Beth works with me every Saturday in the bookshop now. I love it, I get her all to myself for a day. Max has increased my wages a bit and appointed me 'assistant manager'. I joke with Beth that this makes me her boss but really all it means is that Max trusts me with deliveries and to be alone in the shop. Strangely, for all her brains, Beth isn't reliable with keys.

Max has started seeing a woman called Juliette. She's another artist like Sandy and has a house by the sea in East Sussex somewhere, and he goes there pretty much every weekend. Beth has met her. She's got a little kid, Tommy, who's only two. Beth says Tommy is super-cute and that Juliette is sweet and impossibly pretty. The most stupid thing ever is the sudden pang of jealousy I feel. Again someone else gets the actual respect and affection of a guy I threw myself at. Ridiculous because it's not like I want to be Max's girlfriend, that would be so wrong in all kinds of ways. I'm jealous because I don't know how to be the girl that guys want to love and protect. What is wrong with me?

'*Is* there something about me that just says "slapper"?' I ask Beth. 'Be honest.'

Beth says, 'Nah. "Dickhead" maybe, not "slapper".'

I smile and she says, 'Babe, you've been through a really rough time. Give yourself a break. Look after yourself, which you *are* doing and I'm *so* proud of you. Everything else will fall into place.'

Beth is wise and says stuff like this without ever having even been in therapy.

She has the house to herself with Steve most weekends and we have little dinner parties where I cook and everyone gets drunk. As long as I'm there from the beginning when everyone is sober, it's OK. It gets annoying if I go somewhere and everyone is already drunk and not making sense, but if I sort of go through the journey from sober to drunk with them, I'm on their level; I can handle it when someone spends five minutes repeatedly telling me they're drunk or asking me the same question three times.

'What exactly happened with you and Zoe?'

I haven't told Beth the full story. I tell her about the fight.

'That's mental!' she exclaims. 'She attacked you? Why didn't you tell me?'

I didn't tell Beth because I was in shock and, also, too ashamed, and in that moment I had needed AA more than I'd needed to talk to Beth. Also, I whacked Zoe with hair straighteners. Not cool. I think me *and* Zoe wanted it kept between us. And Trish. Trish of course might mention it randomly at some point, somewhere inappropriate, but it wouldn't occur to her to gossip about it.

Trish has got a promotion in her job. She is now a Personal Assistant and it baffles me. Surely her colleagues can tell how weird she is? She invites me to her work Christmas do. I go because I have to, she doesn't have anyone else to take, and I find out she is a totally different person with her work colleagues. They are all older, in their thirties and forties and not remotely curious about my not drinking. Trish sits and chats with them all completely normally. Trish is full of surprises.

CHAPTER FOURTEEN

I have actually been horrible to guys. This is something I've learned in AA. I used Derrick and his flatmates. I even used Dave. I laughed at him with Beth and thought he was 'lucky' to have got with me. I have been an arse.

I don't know how to be normal with guys. I either fancy them or I ignore them. I don't have guys who are just mates. I knew Jamie's mates, but they drifted out of my life after Jamie left.

I was a bit put out when Beth got together with Steve. I didn't know how she could prefer his company to mine, which I know is selfish and a bit insane. I'd kissed him that time after the pub and thought he was a crap kisser, which is rubbish really, because it's about chemistry. Beth thinks he's an amazing kisser and I should be happy for her, but I'm jealous. I hate being jealous. Jealousy is the one emotion no one gives you any sympathy for having. If you're jealous, you're an arsehole and that's that.

One Friday, after English, Steve mumbles to the class: 'It's sort of my birthday, so if anyone wants to, you know, come to the pub . . .' and we go. Even Isabelle comes for one. It's cold but sunny and one of those times where everyone seems happy; everyone seems to be friends, and the atmosphere is good.

We go to the Mash. Beth joins us, of course. She's bought Steve loads of silly presents like chocolate bars wrapped in fancy packaging and a Superman kids' pencil case. She gives him a baggy jumper and his 'big' present is a night out seeing a band he loves, and I think, 'Steve is cool, I have been a dickhead.'

Derrick is still working behind the bar. My surprised, 'Oh my God! Hi!' was probably a bit much. I've only been away for just over a month; I don't know why I act so surprised to see him here. My life has changed, my world has changed so much that, I don't know, perhaps I expected Derrick to have been replaced behind the bar by a giraffe.

Even though it's a Friday and it's really busy in here, Derrick has a word with the girl he's working with and tells me, 'I can duck out for a couple of minutes and say a proper hello.' He gives me a big hug. 'You OK?'

'Yeah, I'm OK. How are you?'

'Grand. Worried about you though. I had no one to call to see how you were. Your mate's been in and told me what happened. I'm glad you got help. You were in bad way.'

I pull a cringe face, then smile.

He gets me a pint of blackcurrant and soda and doesn't charge me.

And here I am, in the pub, on a Friday night, not drinking but having fun.

Trish shuffles in later.

She starts chatting to an old man who has come in by himself, which is the sort of thing Trish likes to do.

Beth and Steve hold hands and kiss a lot. I think about Isla. She has sent me a text asking if I want to meet up when she's out from rehab next week. I haven't replied yet. I feel bad but I don't know what will happen if I see her. The sex I had with her was great, like a parachute jump, something I never thought I'd get to do, but there I was doing it. But I don't know if I want to do it again. I'm being like a bloke; the woman has only asked if I want to meet for a coffee and I'm acting like she's asked for my hand in marriage.

I decide to reply. *'Sure, babe, just gimme a call.'*

I look at Derrick serving behind the bar again and wish I wasn't so shallow, wished I could really fancy a guy like him who is sweet and nice and sensitive.

I know it's time to leave when the girl I'm chatting to starts to slur. Fewer and fewer people are making sense now. I'm outside of the 'drunk' bubble. That's the thing about being sober: you obey the Home Time call. Trish comes with me. No matter how much she drinks, she never seems drunk. If anything she's more lucid than when she is sober.

We slam into Robbie as we are leaving. Stupid luck! I can't just turn around and stay. Trish says loudly, 'Isn't that the bloke from the party you liked? Do you want to stay now?'

Robbie totally hears and grins. I don't know how Trish has got through her life without being punched. I am mortified and Robbie smiles and says, *'Are* you leaving?'

Damn. If I was drunk I'd shout, 'Er, no! Drinks! Now!' and drag him to the bar, and jump on him soon after that.

But I am sober, and I am shy, and so I say, 'It's all got quite hectic now and I want to go home. Can I see you another time though?' Wow. That was bold of me. I surprised myself.

'Sure. I'll text you.'

And that is that. Why there is ever such a fuss about these things I don't know.

It's busy in Max's shop, Christmas is coming and lots of parents are desperately looking for books to buy that will excite their kids more than a computer screen. 'It's hard,' one mum tells me. 'He won't get the least bit excited about *Wind in the Willows*.'

I tell her to try an Asterix book; kids always love those. So she buys *Asterix and Cleopatra*, crosses her fingers and grins. I love these sorts of mums. They come in and seem to be *all* about their kids. They don't shout at them; they are patient and calm. I imagine their houses are full of books and art and ordered chaos.

Katie has that. I didn't though. Mum didn't stand a chance of giving me that chilled childhood. She makes up for it now with Katie. Her life is amazing. I'm glad she is such a different mum now. Dad took so much of Mum's energy. I think there were times when she couldn't breathe and dashed about clearing up the aftermath of his hurricanes.

Mum carefully chooses books for Katie and reads with her and gives her the sort of childhood where everything is pleasant and calm. Katie has space, she can be herself.

Christmas has come and Mum has bought me a ticket to Düsseldorf as my 'main' present. I'm really happy I am going but, really, a ticket should be something she gets for me any-way. Trish and her mum *and* Beth and Max invite me to have Christmas with them, but though Trish's mum is actually ace, I think they could do with a break from me. Max and Beth have invited Steve and *his* mum and Juliette and her kid for Christmas dinner, and even if I wasn't absolutely desperate to see Katie and my mum, I don't fancy being the third wheel all day.

'Don't bring me too many presents otherwise the plane will get heavy,' Katie warns me on Skype.

'Really? OK, well, I'll have to give the baby elephant I bought you back to the zoo.'

'Good,' she says, not batting an eyelash, 'we don't have a garden at our flat.'

On the last day of term, Isabelle tells us she's engaged. She's got engaged to Sian, the girlfriend I met in the pub. She's going away for Christmas, to Scotland to look at wed-ding venues. I almost tell her about Isla but there is no way I can think of saying it without it sounding like I'm going, 'Hey, I slept with a girl so, y'know, I'm a bit lezz . . . maybe I can be bridesmaid?'

We all chip in and buy her a bottle of champagne and a card.

I tell Mum that Isabelle is getting married to her girl-friend. Mum thinks I've got a 'girl crush' on Isabelle. A girl crush is when you're straight and idolise another woman, not when you fantasise about them tearing your clothes off and shoving their fingers inside you. But I don't say that to Mum.

My short story is called *Heartache and Bric-a-brac*. The lonely woman who orders a load of crap from the Internet dies in the end. She buys so much it smothers her.

Isabelle says it's great – 'fantastically believable character' – and Steve says, 'Yeah, it's dark, man. Nice one.' I don't really get Steve's story, *The Hedonist's Other Head*. 'Surreal' is the word everyone says because they're too polite to say 'bollocks'.

Beth thinks he's a literary genius.

Zoe's mum has called Beth. She is really worried because Zoe isn't eating, doesn't go out and is miserable because she thinks Alex is seeing other girls.

'She basically sits staring at her phone when she's not with him, waiting for him to call. Her mum hadn't gone into work because she was so worried about her,' Beth tells me.

'That's a bit dramatic! She's not a kid.'

'No, she literally doesn't eat and her mum says she's having these mad anxiety attacks where she can't breathe. Anyway, her mum called Alex to ask what was going on and he was all like, "Yeah yeah, I love her, everything is fine," but it's not fine because she's a total wreck and doesn't trust him.'

'Jesus, why doesn't she wake up and realise he's just a fucking sleaze?'

Beth shrugs. 'Same reason you won't wake up and realise Jamie is a fucking flake.'

Ouch.

I go to Germany the day after we break up from college. Katie has grown. She bounds up to me in the airport and I feel how much taller she has got when I pick her up.

'Wow! You're such a big girl now!'

Her face has got older. I can almost see what she will look like when *she*'s eighteen. To both our delight, I can still twirl her around by her arms. Just.

She clings to me for ages, right there in the airport, before I can take my rucksack off and while I'm still in everyone's way. Mum stands and smiles and when she can she leans in and gives me a kiss and a hug.

I've never been to Germany before; Katie is delighted she knows a place, knows some words and facts, that I don't. She doesn't stop telling me things; she will not let go of my hand.

'Great to see you, Nina.' Alan has stood a way back and I give him an awkward-as-fuck hug. He takes my bag from me, relieved at having something to do, and leads us to the car.

It's nice, where they live. It's a smart two-bedroom apartment and it's familiar to me because I've seen most of it on Skype.

Katie and I are sharing her room. I tell her a story that I have made up about a squirrel who has mislaid his hat. Once she is asleep, I go and sit for a while with Mum and Alan. We talk, me and Mum, about college and about my friends. No one mentions rehab; no one mentions all the problems. Alan and I certainly don't mention the talk *we* had, though we both clearly recall it as he stays and listens to our chatter instead of disappearing to get away from my hate vibes.

I stay for a week and although I get some revision for my exams done, I pretty much spend every minute with Katie and Mum. We go shopping at Christmas markets. There is mulled wine and German beer everywhere we go, and Mum gets edgy around it all but I don't and I tell her, 'Mum, chill, please, I'm OK.' I haven't seen any alcohol in their apartment at all – I don't know if it's just well-hidden or they've cleared it all out in anticipation of my visit.

Katie doesn't want me to leave. 'You'll be back in London soon, silly,' I tell her as she clings to me and cries on my last day.

'No, we won't,' she tells me. 'Mummy and Daddy want to stay here and sell our house. We're going to stay here for ever and ever. We're never coming back!' Katie wails.

Mum and Alan look at each other.

'Now, Katie, nothing's set in stone,' Alan says.

I go to an AA meeting near their house. My sponsor said I should try and go to one in Germany and I am so glad I did. I couldn't understand that much, but just being there was soothing and kept me in touch with what I need to do to stay off booze. A couple of German AA members made the effort to speak to me in English once the meeting was over. Doesn't matter where I am, other drunks are drunks and they understand me.

Back at the apartment, I ask, 'What did Katie mean earlier? About you staying here?'

Then come the boring explanations of Alan doing so well at his job here, and offers of a renewed contract. Better money. Much better money. Mum loves working at the school and Katie is settling and making friends. They sit and they tell me how much better their life is here. Better than life in England.

'Except you're not here,' Katie has told me. 'You're not here so it's not better.'

So Mum has dumped me with people in London that she's paid to put me up. I don't shout, I don't scream, I don't grab my purse and run to the pub. I want to, but I don't.

Alan now *does* leave the room.

'Can you understand, Mum? Can you understand that I'm still your child and you're putting money and yourselves before me?'

Mum stands her ground. I know she's torn. I can see she is. On the one hand, I'm her baby, but I'm eighteen now and I'm from the life she used to have, from the life that made her unhappy and insecure. She's worked hard for this normal, boring life. After what she went through with Dad, I get it, I really do, but still, I wouldn't do this if I had a kid; I don't care how old they were, I wouldn't just leave them in the middle of their A levels and bugger off somewhere that my kid could only get to by plane.

I tell her this. Unfair of me, I know. Mum can't stop her life because of me. But I want her to. And so we row. I stomp out of the room. I can't slam the bedroom door because I'm sharing with Katie and she's fast asleep. I close the door gently in a terrible rage.

*

Back home it's New Year's Eve. Loads of people from college have got tickets to go to the Boulevard's New Year's party. Except for me. It's the place I got kicked out of in the summer. I can't ever set foot in there again. I would die if the bouncer recognised me.

Phoebe decides to have a New Year's Eve 'soirée'. Places like the Boulevard aren't for her. She doesn't like being out where people don't know who she is, with 'civilians', as she puts it, like she's a celebrity. Her mum and dad are going out so she's invited a few of us over. I am finally invited to one of her *soirées*. I really want to hang out with Beth on New Year's Eve but she's gone to Devon to a party at Steve's cousin's house. They didn't invite me. Trish and her mum stay home and watch TV on New Year's Eve; it's their tradition, Belle tells me. Zoe is going to some bar in Clapham with Alex. I would rather die than go out with those two and his friends, not that they've invited me either.

So I go to Phoebe's. Robbie will be there. Phoebe makes a fuss of me now that I'm out – 'out' as a drunk.

She thinks it's cool to have a friend who is a recovering alcoholic. She thinks it makes her look more interesting, like the way she tells everyone her cousin Roma is a lesbian. If I told Phoebe I'd got with a girl in rehab, she'd probably appoint me as her lady-in-waiting.

'Oh my God! I so couldn't give up drinking,' Martin Novak shrieks when I ask for a Coke. 'I'd be like, oh my God, kill me now!'

'Ah, if only we could, my friend,' Robbie says once Martin flutters off out of earshot.

I used to think Martin knew the secret to having a good time. I was curious about his and Phoebe's friendship, but bloody hell, when I'm sober, he's exhausting. 'Do you think when he's on his own at home he's all butch and watches football?'

'Wouldn't surprise me. No one can be that hyper the whole time.'

Robbie is drinking Coke 'in solidarity' with me. I tell him there's no need but he says, 'Actually, I'm training for the marathon so I'm not boozing, but I'm blaming you to make myself look like a hero.'

He makes me laugh, Robbie does; he's so smart but not a geek. If I saw him out I'd think he was just a bit of a pretty boy who spends too much time in the gym. But he's so well read, more so than me. Although he's good-looking, he doesn't just chat to hot girls. It's like he doesn't notice if a girl is smoking hot or not; he'll chat to anyone. I don't think he fancies me. I think he likes me. I can feel he likes me and thinks I'm a laugh. We properly get on as mates. It feels good to have this new friend.

The party fills up. There are people here I don't know.

'I'm a friend of the family,' an extremely posh girl barks as she introduces herself to Robbie, not me. He is forced, because he's so polite, to talk to her for a bit.

This time last year, on New Year's Eve, Jamie and me were at his mum's, snuggled up on his bed, listening to a playlist he'd carefully put together that summed up 'us'. We held each other close that night, and I cried a lot. We both did. He told me he would be going to Hong Kong after his A level results in the summer and every minute, every second counting down towards midnight, was an agony of making the most of him. This time last year I was in love; I was one half of a whole. I was 'Jami-na'. I was utterly incapable of imagining my life without him.

The posh girl swans off, and Robbie and I return to chatting and laughing, but that ache, that dreadful heaviness in my heart, is back.

'Are you OK?' Robbie asks. 'You look like you're about to cry.'

I can't answer him because all the air is suddenly gone from inside me. I stare past his shoulder, I stare hard, because what I'm seeing must be a trick my mind is playing.

He's standing in the doorway for a moment, a second or two, before he's noticed and someone thrusts a hand in his and pats him on the shoulder. A few more people notice him, a few girls squeal his name and he's kissed and hugged and play-punched by familiar old faces. It's Jamie. My Jamie. My Jamie has walked into the room.

It spins. I stare and it's like staring at the sun; I can't quite do it.

'JAMIE!' Phoebe swirls over to him in a gust of air-kissing and hair swishing. It's really him. Jamie – who I've pined for, longed for, dreamed of, torn myself apart thinking about – is here, in this room, right in front of my eyes.

Robbie turns around. 'Who's that?'

Jamie has never been friends with Phoebe. Jamie could never stand her and her drama friends. I need to speak, say something, because at the moment I'm just standing next to Robbie, who has no idea who Jamie is, gawping. Eventually 'Jamie' is the word that drops out of my mouth.

Jamie catches my eye. I know he saw me the moment he walked in. He stretches out his arms and hugs me. We hug each other. He smells the same. He is wearing a shirt he bought from Camden market. He's wearing his old clothes. Perhaps I expected a T-shirt with Marcia's face on or something.

Then, me and Jamie natter. We natter like we did, like we always did, straight in there, not pausing for breath, but not about 'us' or Hong Kong or rehab; we don't exchange news, me and Jamie. We natter about the vodka jelly and why people think it's a good idea at parties when no one actually likes to *eat* jelly, they just like wobbling it. People should neck vodka and just wobble plain jelly. Then we talk about all the things people eat because it's fun and not because it tastes good, like candyfloss and stringy cheese. We laugh about the pressure we are all under to have THE best night EVER just because it's New Year's Eve. He doesn't talk about his life in Hong Kong, and I don't mention it.

Eventually I ask him what on earth he's doing here. I hadn't heard he was back in London; I had no idea.

'I promised Mum I'd have Christmas with her again this year. So, I had a nice time with Mum and then I came looking for you. Beth told me you were here.'

I know why Beth didn't mention it. She didn't mention it in case he didn't turn up and I would've been miserable and disappointed and hurt. I love Beth. I totally forgive her for falling in love and putting me second, because, actually, she is still an absolute hero and never ever shirks when it comes to being the best friend ever.

'Why didn't you just get in touch with me?'

'Because you've unfriended me everywhere, changed your identity . . .'

'I did, yes, fair enough,' I say, grinning.

'And you blocked my number.'

'Yup,' I say, nodding. 'And the Voodoo doll, don't forget the Voodoo doll I made of you.'

'Indeed. So, given the whole "fuck-off-Jamie vibe" I wasn't sure if you'd see me, but I just had to find you and Beth said you were coming here and . . .'

'And Phoebe has always fancied you so she jumped at the chance to invite you over and show off her house.'

'Ex-actly . . .'

I vaguely notice Robbie isn't here anymore; he had been next to me.

Jamie says, 'There is no point staying here is there? Shall we bounce?'

I grin and we go.

We go to Jamie's mum's house. I don't mention Marcia; he doesn't either. His mum is out, and we sit on his bed eating nachos and watching the crappest TV ever and at midnight we do a little dance around the room, collapse back on the bed, giggle our heads off, then eventually fall asleep covered in nacho dust and happiness.

CHAPTER FIFTEEN

My phone is bulging with text messages. It's eight o'clock in the morning, New Year's Day. Jet-lagged Jamie is already up and making breakfast. I can hear him singing along to the radio. I smile. This is real, this is really happening. I'm here with my Jamie.

Mum has texted me *'Happy New Year darling!'* with loads of emojis that I know are Katie's work.

Beth has texted, and several other friends, generic, pissed midnight messages, some funny, some really cringy like *'May all your dreams come true'* stuff.

Then a text from Zoe that freezes my blood.

'You dirty fucking bitch.'

There's a video. It's only a few seconds long, and it's dark, but you can tell it's me, outside, bent over a wall, skirt around my waist, knickers pulled down. And Alex – Alex, Zoe's boyfriend – holding my upper arms, standing behind me and fucking me. 'Legend, mate!' cackles a voice, not Alex's; his mate . . . his mate who was with him outside.

I watch it again. In the film, I am limp, I stagger and Alex holds me still, and he's fucking me. I throw my phone down on the bed. I pull my knees up to me, I let out a really low howl from deep inside me, a sound I have only heard myself make once before.

I pick up my phone again, like it's an unexploded bomb. I look. There are more pictures. I'm on my knees, on the ground, in the dark. Alex has his cock in my mouth. My eyes are closed. Then there's me, just lying on the ground, exposed, this weird smile on my face which I'm not sure is an *actual* smile, with Alex crouched beside me, looking straight into the camera, giving a thumbs up, like those hunters you see with their big game prey on the Internet.

"Neenaneennaaaa!' Jamie calls up to me. 'Brekkie! Come on!'

I can't move. I haven't told him about that night. We haven't talked *about* anything. His Nina wouldn't do that. His Nina, the one he left behind when he went to Hong Kong, the Nina who liked arthouse films, who liked indie music and who would spend hours in the library with him. *That* Nina had only ever slept with him.

He is coming up the stairs; I can't breathe.

He is holding a tray and struggles with the door. 'A hand, lady, please!'

I get up and hold the door open for him. Then I grab my phone and rush to the bathroom. I wash my face, I use Jamie's toothbrush to clean my teeth, then I tell him, 'I have to go, I have to go home.' Where the fuck is my home? I can't take this to Trish's. I need Beth.

'I need to go to Beth's house.' I do not sound like myself.

'Nina, what's wrong?'

Jamie won't understand. Jamie is going back to Hong Kong tonight. What's the use of Jamie?

'Can you drive me to Beth's?' She lives on the other side of town. I am not crying. This is too big for crying.

'Sure, but Nina, what's wrong?'

I can't open my mouth to say the words. My phone rings. It's Zoe. I pick up.

'Zoe?'

She screams and cries down the phone.

She calls me an ugly bitch and a slag and tells me I've ruined her life. She shouts that I'm a whore, a dirty slag. I can hear Alex in the background saying, 'Zoe, stop . . .' And she screams 'FUCK OFF!' at him and 'YOU BASTARD' at the top of her voice. Then the phone goes dead.

We get into Jamie's car. He's baffled.

'I don't know what's going on, Nina, but I'm here for you.'

'You're not. You're going back, aren't you?'

Then I say it, because suddenly I can, 'You're going back to Marcia.'

And he quietly says, 'Yup.'

'So you came back to London and got bored so you came to find me?'

'No, I promised Marcia I wouldn't contact you, but I heard everything that's happened and I wanted to see if you are OK.'

We get to Max's and Jamie goes to get out of the car.

'You're not coming in,' I tell him. I'm in shock, but I know, very clearly, that I don't want Jamie to know anything about any of this.

'Nina, what's wrong? What's happened?'

Then, with every bit of willpower I can gather, I tell him, 'You're not my boyfriend. You're not my friend anymore. You dropped me from a huge height and I don't think you being in my life in any way is helpful.'

And I shut the car door and go to Max and Beth's front door.

I knock. Max opens the door, in his dressing gown, sleepy-eyed.

I see the look on his face and quickly say, 'I'm not drunk.' Then I start to cry.

Max sits me down, makes me tea. I cannot tell him what is wrong. I wail.

'Has someone died, Nina?'

Me, I want to say. I have died. I can never live again.

'Shall I call your mum?' asks Max.

No. No. Oh God, no.

I can't speak but I need help; I need help to know what to do.

Then this woman comes in. Tall with long curly red hair.

'Nina, this is Juliette.'

Behind her totters an incredibly cute toddler with crois-sant crumbs all over his face.

'And this is Tommy.'

I smile but I'm panicking so wildly inside that it shows on my face and Juliette takes Tommy's hand and says, 'Come on, poppet, let's have a look at your Christmas books. Nice to meet you, Nina,' and off she goes.

She *is* really pretty and seems so nice. I hope Max hasn't told her what I did at my party. I don't want her to feel sorry for me.

'Are you OK?' Max asks. 'You look like you've been crying.'

'I need Beth.'

'She's away, in Devon with Steve.'

Shit. I forgot. How could I forget?

'Oh yeah. It's OK. I'll go and see Trish.'

'Do you want a lift?'

'No, no, I'm fine!' I smile at Max and leave.

I practically run to Trish's house. Belle is up; Trish is still in bed.

'Hello, love! Happy New Year!' Belle says. 'Your mum just called, said she couldn't get hold of you on your mobile. You might want to give her a ring.'

I start to cry. I just stand in the hall and cry until Belle says, 'Flipping heck! You OK? You been drinking?'

I shake my head and wail. She puts her arms around me as best she can – she is holding a cigarette – and leads me into the front room.

'Sit down, what's up? You look like you've seen a ghost.'

But, I don't want to sit in the front room. 'Belle, I need to go upstairs,' I croak. I run to my room and shut the door.

Beth calls. I can't pick up.

Beth texts: *'Have you seen what Zoe has put on Facebook? CALL ME!!!!!'*

I fumble urgently with my phone. What has Zoe done? What has she done to me?

Zoe has put the photo of me going down on Alex on Facebook. She has put the caption: 'Stay classy, Nina Swanson.'

It's got sixty-seven 'likes'.

I read the comments.

'Er, why you shaming your friend like this?'

'Whoa! That's a worst blow job ever! She needs lessons!'

'Is that the alley by the Boulevard?????'

This is not happening. Some people have shared the post already. I look and see I've got messages from strangers.

'You're such a slag!'

I don't know any of the people writing to me.

I call Zoe. She doesn't pick up. I call Beth.

'What am I going to do?'

Belle knocks on my door. Trish has been on Facebook. She has seen and told Belle. Belle comes in.

'You tell me this girl's address now, please!'

I tell her where Zoe lives.

'Right. I think I need to have a word with this girl's mother.'

Belle and Trish get in the car and go to Zoe's house. Half an hour after they leave, the post is taken down.

'It's nine in the morning on New Year's Day,' Belle says. 'Hardly anyone would have seen it.'

'It was shared by tons of people,' Trish says, 'so it doesn't really matter that she took it down. Heaps of people will have seen it, and some of them may have even copied it onto other sites. Nothing really disappears off the Internet.'

Belle tuts and says, 'For God's sake, Trish.'

I want to shrink until I'm so small I can jump down a plug-hole and drown in a sewer.

Maybe if I just stop breathing I'll pass out and die. Perhaps I can go into town and jump out of a window at the Shard, or throw myself in the Thames.

There *should* be an instant way to kill yourself if you're so humiliated that you can't go on.

A picture of me, off my face, with a guy's cock in my mouth is going around the Internet. People from college will have seen it, their friends, some teachers. I'm burning alive with shame.

'No one will know it's you unless they know you,' Trish says. 'It's quite dark. Though Nina Swanson is not that common a name, I suppose . . .'

'It'll fizzle out in no time,' Belle says. 'There are much weirder things on the Internet.'

'So many people saw it!'

'You did nothing wrong. Zoe is the bastard here. This is Zoe's shame, not yours.' Belle is firm.

I start getting texts from people from college, some of them people I hardly know.

'Did you see what was on Facebook?'

'Oh my God, you need to check out what's on Facebook about you!'

The photograph may have been removed but the comments remain.

Derrick calls me, of course; we're friends on Facebook. 'Nina, it's fucking awful what your mate's done. You OK? You want me to come over?'

No, I do not want him to come over; I do not want to see anyone at all. I want to throw my phone into a river and stay in bed for ever. Maybe I should go to an AA meeting? Call some-one from AA? Talk to someone who can tell me everything is going to be OK. But I can't leave the house and I can't pick up my phone. I can barely speak.

Belle and Trish have had to go and see Trish's gran. The doorbell goes. I hope in vain it might be Beth.

I go downstairs. It's Jamie.

I'm surprised, and just say, 'Oh.'

'Now that's twice I've had to hunt you down,' he says, smiling. He knows.

'Have you seen . . .?' I ask.

'Yes, and I wanted to see if you're OK.'

'Aren't you meant to be at the airport?'

'Not till tonight.'

I make us tea, then tell Jamie exactly what went on that night and exactly how I had been feeling.

'And some animal took a photo of you? Who does that?'

'That's not the worst thing, Jamie, even her putting that photo on Facebook wasn't the worst thing.'

I can't tell him what the worst thing is, so I show him Zoe's message, the film with Alex fucking me. I show it to Jamie who watches it in shocked silence.

'And there's another picture.'

I show him the 'thumbs up' photo.

Jamie looks and gives me back my phone. He leans against the kitchen counter with his head down, not saying anything.

I panic. 'What? What?' Does he hate me? Is he so disgusted he can't look at me? Does he think I'm a total slag?

'You don't remember that, Nina?'

I shake my head.

'You don't remember the sex? The blow job in the alley?'

'No.'

'Nothing?'

'NO! I just remember the cab ride home but only bits of it . . .'

Jamie's face looks dark, really dark. I don't know if he's angry or upset or what.

Then Jamie says, quietly, 'I've just watched a film of you being raped.'

'Jamie, don't say that!' I cry. I go to him for a hug, a cuddle, but he steps away.

'You've been raped, Nina,' he says again.

'Fuck off. I have not.'

Jamie gets out his phone. Now it gets really dramatic because Jamie is calling the police.

'You have, Nina, and we need to report it.'

I try to grab his phone off him. He's much taller than me and easily holds it away. I'm in a panic, a frenzy, I grab my own phone and threaten to delete Zoe's texts.

'No!' Jamie says. 'Don't, don't! I won't call, I won't call.'

'Do you promise me?'

Jamie promises me and holds me and cries and says, 'How could they do that to you?' and I cry and I tell him I love him and I miss him and that it's been so awful without him and he rocks me and strokes my hair and tells me I'm special and that he has missed me too. Then we kiss and we go up to my room and we have the most incredible, intense sex I have ever had in my life, then his mum picks him up and takes him to the airport.

CHAPTER SIXTEEN

Beth and Steve have spent all of New Year's Day arguing with trolls on the Internet who are calling me a slag.

The photo had been shared more than forty thousand times and because Zoe tagged my name to it I'm still getting loads of awful, horrible messages.

> *'The girl must be a walking STD.'*
> *'Bet her mum and dad are so proud.'*
> *'Total whore. She should kill herself.'*
> *'She deserves to be gang raped.'*

I shut down every social media account I have as well as email. I'm too scared to leave the house. I think the entire world knows what a slag I am, knows what happened that night.

No one can get hold of Zoe. Beth reckons she's gone away to stay with her gran in Cornwall.

I don't know who she has shown the video and other pictures to. I just thank fuck she didn't put those on the Internet too. Jamie said I was raped. Was I raped? I don't remember consenting. Is it rape if I was so drunk that I couldn't be totally clear about not wanting to have sex in the alleyway with a stranger? Is it rape if you later invite him to your eighteenth birthday party? Is it rape if you can't be a hundred per cent sure you hadn't bent over and said, 'Fuck me, fuck me now,' like a total whore because it's all a blank to you?

I'm not an idiot; I know that boys who fuck girls when they are unconscious are rapists. I know that. I can't remember anything from when they came out of the club to when they put me in a taxi. So was I unconscious? The video is dark and he is holding me up, over a wall.

Why would he keep the video for Zoe to find? Was he proud of it?

I stay indoors for the whole of New Year's Day, and on January the 2nd, I text Isla.

We go out. She wants to go to a bar. I say, 'Let's go for a coffee,' but I know she will persuade me to go to a pub, that is why I got in touch.

'Oh, come on! Let's sit in a pub and have one tiny drink.'

We sit in quite a nice little bar near where her brother lives in Balham. It's got a strawberry beer I love.

I get a Coke. Isla orders two strawberry beers.

'I don't want one.'

Isla shrugs. 'Well, don't have it then.' She puts it in front of me when we find a table and sit down.

I take a sip. It tastes of mighty heaven.

'You know,' Isla says, 'people put you in a fucking box, they tell you you're an alcoholic, that you need help, when sometimes, you just need a pint and a natter with someone who gives a shit about you.'

I am lightheaded after just one pint. Isla gets more drinks, beers and then shots. We have a laugh. I tell myself I'm young, and I can't be an alcoholic if I haven't drunk for all these weeks. I can be a normal teenager, I say, and Isla agrees.

'Though stop saying you're a teenager,' she says, giggling, 'cos you make me feel like a fucking pervert.'

We get totally and utterly shit-faced around bars in Balham. In the corner of one, we find each other's mouths and kiss. We are drunk. The kissing is hard, fast, with hands wandering all over each other's faces and bodies, right there in the pub. There is a group of guys at the bar. I hope they can see us.

We go back to her brother's and we neck vodka, then have fast and loud sex in his living room.

In the morning, he finds us passed out naked on his sofa.

'Get the fuck out of my house!' he screams at her.

I dress, quickly, even though I can barely see through my hangover. I leave them screeching and shouting. The first trains are just starting on the Tube. I am sick on the north-bound platform. An old black lady gives me her entire packet of tissues. I make my way back to Ealing.

Mum, Alan and Katie are all sitting in Trish's front room when I get in. I feel so rough I think I'm dreaming. I'm sick in the hallway and collapse as I try to get upstairs. They can't see me like this; Katie can't see me like this. But they have all just seen me like this.

Alan, surprisingly, is the one who helps me upstairs. I hear Mum telling Katie: 'Nina isn't feeling very well.'

Belle is a genius with Katie, and gets her to help her decorate an old chair.

This is surreal. I have relapsed and Mum, Alan and Katie have appeared out of the blue to witness it. Belle will throw me out for sure; she made it clear that she would only take me in if I was clean. I can't think anymore; I'm lost in the putrid, heavy fog of a hangover.

Alan waits patiently outside the toilet while I puke my guts up.

When I come out he says, 'Nina, I need you to know that your mother and I are back now for good. I need to give our tenants notice and find temporary accommodation.'

Alan usually makes an excuse and shuffles off to another room when I am in trouble with Mum. But this time he sits me down on my bed, while I stink of booze and puke, and says, awkwardly, of course, but sincerely, 'Your mother is dreadfully upset, as I'm sure you are. Please, can we pull together, as a family, to help each other through this? I'll leave you to rest.' He goes out, then comes back in when I'm lying very still on the bed and puts a glass of water and two paracetamol on the bedside table for me.

A little while later, when Mum comes into my bedroom, I say, 'If you had told me you were coming then I wouldn't have relapsed.' I'm spiteful, mean and unfair.

'Please, Nina, please let's not fight. You have no idea what a sacrifice we've made to come back and look after you.'

On the one hand, she's always telling me you sacrifice everything for your children; on the other hand, she moans when she actually *does* make a sacrifice.

Alan has had to forfeit his job in Düsseldorf. Their little dream of a new life in Germany is finished because Mum is stuck with an obligation to take care of me. She does not look happy about it as she gathers kitchen towels and disinfectant spray to clear my puke off Belle's floor. All of this is a lot to take when you are hungover.

'When you feel better, then we'll talk,' Mum tells me.

Belle doesn't seem cross with me; she hasn't asked me to move out. In fact, she's offered to put my family up.

'It'll be a squeeze but we will manage,' she tells them.

Alan insists they don't want to be in the way and I don't think Mum can stand Belle. They arrange for us all to stay with Alan's brother until the tenants vacate. He doesn't live too far.

To be fair to Mum, she *is* back. Although she's making me feel terrible about it, making sure I know what a hindrance I am. I remind myself that I'm hungover and not seeing anything in the kindest light. I remember it is brilliant to have her and Katie physically back in my life. I have a family again.

Before Mum has a chance to talk to me, Katie, when she is finally allowed to come into my room and see me, fills me in on as much as she knows.

'Jamie called Mum and said you weren't very well and then Mum called Max. I miss Jamie,' Katie says suddenly. 'Why isn't he your boyfriend anymore? Were you horrible to him?

Why are you so ill? Have you got a cold? When I get a cold Mum makes me toast and honey.'

Mum brings me a cup of tea and sends Katie downstairs.

'Mum, what's going on? What did Jamie tell you? Why did you call Max? What is everyone saying about me?'

Mum starts to cry. She puts her hand over her face and really lets go. Her hand looks old. Her face looks tired.

'I'm so sorry,' she says. 'No help really, am I?'

I drink the Lucozade Belle had got me.

'Jamie called me because he was worried about you and thinks, rightly, that this is too big a deal for you to cope with on your own, or for you to rely on friends to help you through.'

What friends? I want to ask. At this precise moment I don't feel like I have any friends.

'Darling, you need to tell me what happened that night. What Jamie said was . . . Well, what he said didn't bear thinking about. Tell me what happened that night when you came home in that taxi.'

'I have no idea.'

'You do. I believe you have video evidence of what happened.'

This is horrific. This is not something I want my mum to know about. Jamie didn't stick around to help me; he dumped me in it with my mum. This *is* serious. This isn't just about me getting too drunk and making a fool of myself. This is about how one minute you are safe inside a nightclub with your mates and the next a stranger is having sex with you in an alley and you can't remember it. What's worse is that he cares so little about you as a human being that he lets his mate take a trophy shot while you're passed out and half-naked on the ground. This is not all down to me. *They* made decisions, *they* had choices.

All these months I've been destroying myself over this. They did this to me. Just two blokes on a night out. They hurt me.

Mum is saying the same as Jamie, that I should go to the police. But what will they say? What can they do? All they would need to know is that I fucked that forty-year-old in the park and I tried to fuck my best mate's dad and they will say, 'Well, this is what she does! Big deal.'

'Mum, there is no way I am going to the police.'

'Can I see the film?'

'No.' She cannot see the film. My mother must never see the film.

She tells me I'm her baby. Even more reason for her not to see a picture of me giving a blow job.

'Nina, these sorts of guys need to learn. They need to be pulled up on this or they will do it again and again, to other girls. I doubt you would've been the first. Think about other girls they might do this to.'

Other girls are not my concern right now.

'Mum, please. Let me sleep. I just want to sleep. Let me sleep.'

She does, and I do, for sixteen hours. By the time I wake up, everything in my world has changed. The room is bare, except for a clean pair of knickers and an outfit laid out neatly for me on a chair, and my wash bag. My phone isn't by my bed.

*

She is waiting in the kitchen for me. She has my phone.

'Hello, love,' Belle says, 'can I make you a cooked breakfast? You've been out for a while, you need a good feed. You look terrible.' Sometimes, you *can* see where Trish gets it from.

For some reason, Belle's offer to make breakfast annoys Mum. She puts on her tight-lipped, fake smile. Belle and Trish are not her type of people. They are too unconventional, too upfront and too ill-fitting in the ordered world she has worked so hard to create. Mum thinks she's very open-minded; she makes all the right politically correct noises when injustice is done, she supports all the right human rights causes and criticises all the government policies which create social injustice. She is, though, when all is said and done, a total snob.

'We have no time, Belle,' my mum says, 'thank you.'

'All due respect, love, I was asking Nina. *Do* you want breakfast, darling?'

Mum needs us out of here. She probably thinks Belle and Trish know too much already.

'My phone, Mum, you've got my phone?'

'Yes, Nina, I have. Let's not talk about it here.'

'You had no right to take my phone.'

'Please, darling, not here!' she says sharply.

'Listen,' Belle says, 'I don't know what's gone on here, and I don't want to know unless you want to tell me. But your mum coming back, you falling off the wagon . . . it doesn't take a genius to work out this is serious. Is this still about what that Zoe did to you?'

I look down, not knowing what to say. Mum has a look about her I've never seen before. She's not angry, I don't think, but she looks like she's seen a ghost. Actually, she looks like she *is* a ghost. She's hovering at the kitchen door, aching to leave.

'Alan and Katie are already at Uncle Pete's house,' she tells me.

'He's not *my* Uncle Pete.'

'Nina, please love, come on, say "thank you for having me" to Belle.'

Like I'm five and have just come to Belle and Trish's house for tea.

I hug Belle, tight. She hugs me back; she's got tears in her eyes. 'You're always welcome here, my darling, you know that? Me and Trish will always look after you.'

Katie is already back in school. Mum and Alan have worked fast. They are moving to Pete's in Greenford and waiting for their tenants, who Alan informs me 'have been remarkably understanding of the fact we've had a family emergency', to find another place and move out.

So now I am on a camp bed, sharing with Katie, wondering what is going to happen. Mum hasn't said a word.

Alan hasn't either.

Pete is a 'confirmed bachelor' and for someone of his generation that means he's totally gay but never felt able to come out. I've always liked him; he comes for Christmas and for Alan's birthdays but that's pretty much it. Katie likes him because he makes a fuss of her and, as well as Oscar the cat, has a Great Dane called Ludo that she adores playing with. He and Alan aren't that close, though I suppose they must be a bit close if Pete has put us all up. When Mum thanks him for all the trouble, he says 'Family is family', which is a polite way of saying, 'Well, I had no bloody choice, did I?'

Mum gives me time to unpack, have breakfast, then she sits me down in Pete's study.

'I've seen the film, Nina.'

'I wish you hadn't, Mum.'

'I had to, Nina, after what Jamie told me.'

'Jamie gave you the code to unlock my phone, didn't he?'

Jamie and I have always had the same code on our phone: 1209. Twelfth of September, the day we first ever spoke to each other. He will know now that I never changed mine. He will have changed his, I'm sure, to Marcia's bra size probably.

'Yes, he did. Jamie had no choice.'

Mum isn't cuddling me or anything. She is businesslike, quite cold.

'You were paralytically drunk in that video.'

'I tend not to do stuff like that when I'm sober, Mum.'

'Nina, what happened that night was rape.'

I don't say anything.

'I saw the state you were in when you got home. If I had known then that you'd had sex that night, I would have known it could only have been rape. Do you understand how serious this is?'

It happened to *me*. I know how serious it is. I'm the one who has had to live in this head, live in this body since it happened. I'm the one that has made a million excuses, like, 'I was having a laugh, it was a bit of fun, everyone gets that pissed, right? Everyone does stupid things like that, right?' But actually, everyone doesn't.

Since I saw the film, a million other excuses for *him* have come to my head: *he couldn't have realised how pissed I was; it was my own fault for getting that bladdered; no one forced me to give him the blow job in the club, I did it all by myself so obviously he thought I was up for it.*

All these thoughts have been crashing in as I try to find a way to live with this, try to find a way not to throw myself off a cliff. I mean it; I'm not being dramatic. I don't know how two people could do that to me. I'm a person. I'm a nice person.

'Mum, I am not going to the police, I AM NOT!'

Then I hear this screaming and it takes a good few seconds before I realise it's coming from me.

Finally Mum holds me, quite forcefully because my arms are flying everywhere, and eventually I succumb to just normal sobbing.

'Your dad would have killed those boys.' She holds my face in her hands and wipes tears away with her whole palm.

'Now,' she says, 'Alan isn't going to kill them, is he?' She smiles and I laugh through tears. Then she grabs me and hugs me and doesn't let go for ages.

I can't go to college the next day. How can I face anyone?

I beg Mum, really beg her, not to go to the police. She promises that she won't but I know she's not going to let this go. For now, though, she leaves me to think.

Beth comes to see me. So does Trish. Thankfully not at the same time.

'I finally got through to Zoe. She's not at her nan's, she's at Alex's. She's totally forgiven him. She sounds mad, hon.

He's told her all sorts of rubbish and she can't see through him.'

He's told Zoe that he feels really bad about not deleting the pictures and video; he just forgot he had them. He told her he was so in love with her that it scared him.

Zoe, it turns out, has shit for brains after all.

Beth asks to see the video. I let her, and I let her see the other photos too. She starts to cry, proper hand-to-mouth 'oh my God' sobbing. I need people to stop freaking out because there is nothing I can do about what happened. Beth cuddles me and tells me she loves me. We don't normally do stuff like that, me and Beth, but she is really upset.

'Zoe has seen this and thinks it's OK?'

That baffles me too, if I'm honest.

'It's obvious you're out of it. There's no way you would have done that if you were sober.'

'I don't remember it.'

'And he just walked back into the club, after doing that, and hooked up with Zoe?'

I nod. Having everyone upset on my behalf has made me numb and dumb. All my feelings are being felt for me.

Trish texts me with a link to a news website. A pixelated version of what happened is plastered on their site. There are loads of comments already. I can't leave the house ever again.

Alex's mate Spencer had taken these pictures.

Beth says he's every bit as disgusting and she agrees with Mum and Jamie; this is rape.

Beth is still with me when Trish comes round. I don't want to see Trish because she is the voice of doom.

'Some of the debate forums have been interesting. It's raised the issue of slut-shaming and some people are really defending you. Most are calling you a slag though.'

Beth glares at her. 'Don't hold back, will you, Trish?'

'Beth, it's OK, honestly. This can't get worse.'

Jamie has been calling me and messaging me, asking me how I am, asking me if I've called the police yet. I wonder how Marcia feels about his sudden concern for me. Beth says she probably doesn't know.

I haven't been to the police. I haven't done anything. I have just had everyone else telling me what I should do.

But I know where Alex works so I get dressed and go to Clapham.

CHAPTER SEVENTEEN

It's a swanky estate agents. A small fridge holds cans of soft drinks so you can refresh yourself while buying a million-pound one-bedroom shoebox.

Alex is at his desk, on the phone. His face locks into a freeze when he sees me. It's recognition, surprise and then irritation all in one split second. His colleague comes up to me. A very pretty girl, not much older than me, she says, 'Can I help you?' chirpily.

'I want to speak to Alex, please.'

The girl's smile fades awkwardly.

This is Lottie. I know this is Lottie. Zoe – when she was talking to me – has told me and Beth about a pretty girl called Lottie that Alex worked with. She was upset when she'd found out he'd been for after-work drink with her and had been with her again when she'd texted him on a Sunday afternoon.

She can tell that this is a personal visit and it's giving her discomfort. I can guess that Zoe's fears were not paranoia.

'He's on the phone just now.' Her smile was still fixed but her face defiant.

'I'll wait.' I sit down on a chair. I feel sick with nerves but wildly confident at the same time. Alex hangs up; Lottie speaks to him. By the way they talk to each other I can tell they have definitely fucked.

He says something to Lottie, touches her forearm, then puts on his jacket, glancing at me briefly, with mild irritation. He strides over, unsmiling, and says, 'Come on, let's go somewhere more private, shall we?'

My confidence shakes. This was *my* intrusion; this was *my* decision. I walked into his place of work to pull the rug from under his feet, a brave thing to do, some would say, but he has taken control; his feathers remain unruffled.

We are sitting in a smart bar across the road and he has ordered two Diet Cokes. Without asking me what I would like.

'Nina, I think I know why you are here, why you've waltzed into my office . . .'

He is totally unfazed and talking to me like I'm a kid.

Suddenly my mouth is dry and all the sassy things I was going to say to him have left my head and I just manage to mutter that I needed to say a few things, the photo having got out.

He interrupts me. 'Zoe was not in a good place. I'm sorry you're bearing the brunt of it, but she and I are working things through. I love her very much.'

He's so posh and so handsome as he tilts his head to say 'I love her very much'. A perfectly glossy strand of his dark hair falls into his eyes and he sweeps it away.

'The whole thing with the photo, it'll blow over. You shouldn't be ashamed – you had fun . . . we both did.' He smirks at me as he says this.

'What about the videos? And the other pictures?'

'Ah,' he says. 'Zoe didn't want to post those because you can see my face.'

She was protecting him, even in her rage, but had no concern for me, no concern about what this would do to me, to my mum, to my baby sister if she ever found out, which, let's face it, she will, at some point.

I'm finding it hard to get some words out. 'I didn't know that we had . . .'

'What?'

'I didn't know we had sex.'

He laughs. 'Really? You were gagging for it.'

I think about running out. But actually my legs are lead and I can't.

'I don't remember it.'

'Wow, don't spare my feelings, will you?' He's laughing. He's actually laughing.

'I mean, if I was so out of it that I don't remember it, then you shouldn't have done it.'

He stops laughing. 'Are you being serious?'

I nod.

'You don't remember anything about it at all?'

'No.'

He laughs again. 'Christ, I must have lost my touch.'

'Who was the guy with you?'

'Who filmed us? Spencer, mate of mine from uni. Really great bloke actually but total nut job.'

'Did he, did anything happen . . .'

'With you and him? No, God no, he's not like that. Look, Nina, you were totally up for what happened. You were all over me. It was very enjoyable and afterwards, you said, "I want to go home," and like the gentlemen we are, we checked you had money to pay for it and we put you in a cab.'

He glances at his watch. 'Look, I've got to get back to work. I'm not quite sure what you needed to get off your chest, but please don't come into my work like that again. I don't like mixing personal stuff and work, OK?'

'OK. Sorry,' I say. I'm apologising. Why am I apologising?

'Also, I don't know if this is a jealousy thing with Zoe or whatever, but you might want to remember who was with us that night. Spencer has more videos that show you *really* enjoying yourself, which thankfully I deleted from my phone before Zoe saw. I'm just letting you know that he still has them, just in case you think about getting silly with this.'

Silly? Why is he calling me silly? Blood rushes to my cheeks. I wasn't prepared for this, I thought he might understand. My voice comes out in a squeak: 'You *raped* me!'

He pulls a face as he laughs. He laughs at me. He actually throws his head back and laughs, then he gets up. He looks down at me and says, 'You need to look that word up. I don't think you know what it means. Regret is not rape, darling. And if I found your friend more beguiling than you, then take it on the chin and move on.'

He kisses the top of my head before I have the chance to recoil. Still laughing, he goes back to his office.

CHAPTER EIGHTEEN

I can't get out of bed. I can't eat. I can't talk to anyone. I lie in a ball on my camp bed at Uncle Pete's and sleep, and when I wake I immediately try to sleep again. I can't go to AA, I can't do anything. I can barely even speak. I think about a week goes by.

Katie is baffled and asks me if I'm ill. I can't answer her; I just wave my arm towards the door, making her go.

Mum lets the college know what's been going on, even though she's not sure what's going on. I haven't told anyone that I met up with Alex.

I don't think the college admin staff are surprised by anything to do with me now: 'The alkie girl, you know, whatsername . . . yeah, that's the one . . . she's all over the Internet giving some fella a blow job outside the Boulevard. Can we have her tutors email the work she's missing again? She's too ashamed to come in just now.'

Mum brings me toast and tea and in the evening makes my favourite meals, which I hardly touch. After a few days my tummy feels noticeably thinner, which is satisfying. I want to disappear altogether. I don't read the emails from college. My phone battery dies and I don't recharge it.

I see what happened in my mind over and over again. Spencer laughing at me while Alex used me like I was nothing. He couldn't care less who I am, how loved I am, how hard I work. He couldn't care less that I have a little sister called Katie, that I am a good writer, that I make Beth laugh until she almost wets herself.

Other guys I know would never do that to a girl. Jamie, Derrick, Robbie, Max, Alan, they would have looked after me, or any girl in that state. They wouldn't have fucked her; they wouldn't have.

Trish comes to see me. She tells me she's going to change her degree to law. I don't answer; I don't care. I pull the covers over my head. She pulls up a chair and sits by my bed eating crisps and reading magazines.

'Do you want me to open a window?' she asks. 'Smells a bit in here.'

I burrow further down the mattress.

'Shall I read you your horoscope?' She rustles the magazine to the right page and says, 'Leo. Taking matters into your own hands is a risky business. Now is not the time for self-pity. You will come out of this stronger.'

Wow. Anyone would think they write some generic crap that is bound to relate to your life if you took it a certain way. 'Taking matters into your own hands' *could* mean trying to have it out with your rapist on your own. *Or* it could mean taking a soufflé out of the oven when you think it's ready and not when the recipe says you should.

She reads her own. 'Your sunny nature is more irresistible than usual so expect a fiesta of fun coming your way.'

Deep down under my duvet, I smile. Despite everything, Trish's monotone about her 'sunny nature' tickles me.

I pull the duvet away from my face and actually sit up.

'Read mine again.' I haven't spoken for such a long time my voice croaks.

'Leo. Your actions did not have the desired effect. Do not be defeated . . .'

'Am I being defeated?' I ask her.

'Yeah,' she says, chewing her thumbnail. 'You're wallowing in self-pity, which is fair enough, I suppose.'

I'm not actually Leo, I'm Cancer, but it doesn't matter. Trish is right, I am wallowing in self-pity. And I am beginning to smell.

Trish carries on with her own one. 'Be wary of friends who lean on you. Will they be there when *you* need a shoulder.' She looks at me. 'What do you think that means?'

I think she's joking for a minute and then I realise she's not.

'Well, it means be wary of friends who are, you know, users.'

She nods her head knowingly. 'You get used to being used.'

I sense a weird 'Trish' conversation but for once I'm in the mood for it.

'What do you mean? Who uses you?'

Trish looks at me. She's got a crisp crumb at the corner of her mouth. She looks up like she's thinking. 'You use me sometimes.'

I wasn't expecting it to be *this* weird.

'Do I?'

'Yeah,' she says, 'like, not so much now, but for ages I was like your "plan B". Like, if "plan A" with Beth or whoever didn't work out, you'd call me and know that I'd hang out with you.'

I never realised she saw through that.

'Then like, we'd go out and you wouldn't talk to me. You'd look around for better people to talk to and go off with them and you'd know I'd just hang around and walk home with you.'

She says all this like she's describing what she's had for dinner. She's not upset, not angry, not hurt – they are just facts. I suddenly feel incredibly sad. And a total bastard.

She carries on eating her crisps. 'Shall I read Sagittarius? My mum's Sagittarius.'

Out of all my friends, who is here right now? Trish is. Who has been the one person not telling me what to do, how to think and how to feel? Trish. I have been annoyed at people for taking her for granted, taking the piss out of her, but I've done it more than anyone, yet here she is, spending her weekend reading trashy horoscopes to me and keeping me company. True, she hasn't got anything better to do, but that's not why she's here; she's here because Trish is a friend, a proper friend who doesn't care who you know, what parties you go to. She just cares that you're around, that you'll hang out with her and listen to her read her mum's horoscope.

'Trish, if I have ever made you feel used, I'm truly sorry. It says way more about me than it does about you. Yeah, you're right, I've been a crap friend when actually what I think of you is that you're one of the kindest, sweetest people I know, and I've taken advantage of that sweetness and I am really, *really* sorry.'

Trish looks at me for a bit, blinks, then says, 'It's all right. Shall I read Sagittarius?'

I pull the covers back. 'No. Let's go downstairs and have a cup of tea.'

Trish puts her magazines down, and we go into the kitchen and find Mum who's so happy I'm up and about that she plonks down a heap of chocolate digestives on the table. Trish eats each and every one.

I shower and have dinner that evening with my family.

'Are you feeling better, Nina?' Katie asks.

'Yep, I feel fine now, Katie.'

'You didn't have a cold, did you?'

'Erm. No,' I answer truthfully.

'Mummy said you wouldn't get out of bed because you were too sad.'

'I was sad, but I'm OK now.'

'That's good to hear, Nina,' Alan says. 'Very good to hear. Would you mind passing the potatoes?'

Mum gives me a lift to an AA meeting. She is so scared I'll change my mind about going to meetings and instead wander into a pub that she says, 'Do you know what, Nina, I think I'll stay here and wait for you. I'll read my book until you get back, save you getting the bus home.'

Mum, who is always talking about how she has 'a million things to do' and who can barely sit still for a moment, sits in the car for a whole hour while I'm in my meeting. Miraculously, this doesn't annoy me. I missed being cared for like this while she was away.

In the meeting I have company in the huge pit of helplessness and despair. With his slick hair, posh accent and expensive clothes, Alex picked me up and threw me down this well. I have been trying to crawl back out ever since that night and again and again slipping back down on my arse. AA is my leg up.

How many men have I seen unconscious at a club or party or in a doorway? I wouldn't dream of stealing from them or attacking them. But that's what Alex did. He stole from me; he battered me.

Mum drives me back home. She resists asking me how the meeting went. I just sense her desperate desire to know that it's working, that I'm getting the help I need. There's nothing I can do to reassure Mum. She just has to hope. She has to hope I won't slip and I won't end up hopeless like my dad.

Alan has 'struck a deal' with our tenants. He has waived the last month's rent in return for letting us move back in now. Alan is not usually one for 'deals' – Alan does everything by the book – but it's crowded at Uncle Pete's.

I return to my old room. I have thrown a lot of my junk out, old posters, books, things I feel too old for now. I get a box and put in it all the letters, cards and sentimental presents I got from Jamie. Framed photos, framed gig tickets, cute little notes we sent each other. I put them all in a box, secure it with packaging tape and Alan gets the loft ladder out, climbs into the loft and dumps it there for me amongst all the other junk we haven't the heart to throw away.

Mum goes back to her job teaching refugees. She's made a fuss of and feels really needed there. I think, secretly, she's pleased they've come back. Mum will make the best of anything. She's so focused on herself and Alan and Katie that there is no way she would have admitted that trotting about in Düsseldorf while Alan became Mr Big Potatoes IT Man wasn't all it was cracked up to be.

I tell Beth this, and Beth says, 'You might *want* to think that, Nina, but I think your mum and Alan made a bigger sacrifice than you imagine.' Trust Beth to shove the truth into my face. She can't ever let me think what I feel most comfortable thinking.

I have banned Mum from mentioning all the *stuff*. I can't go to the police. I can't tell them what happened because they can get lawyers to find out exactly what *I* have been like this past year and I can't bear it.

I meet Beth and Steve and we get the bus to college together.

Steve is even more awkward than usual. What's he supposed to say? Poor guy. All he did was fall in love with Beth and now he has *my* life as part of the package.

They are here to give me moral support. It's strange, lonely and frightening knowing people have heard something so intimate about you, have seen you doing something that should have been totally private. There are some sniggers. Not many, just a few. Beth says I'm imagining them. Then someone amidst a group of lads trooping off to the canteen shouts: 'SLAPPER!'

'You didn't imagine *that*,' Steve says.

Beth shouts back: 'Judgemental CUNT.'

'Jesus, Beth!' Steve says, shocked, knowing he'll have to protect her if it kicks off.

Steve stands protectively next to her, in case the blokes 'start'. Not sure what Steve would actually do if they did but it's still very sweet.

'Beth, I think I want to go home.' I can't be as brave as she wants me to be.

'Forget about those idiots, Nina,' Steve tells me. 'Beth's right, they're judgemental wankers and you've got nothing to hide or be ashamed of.'

Beth rubs his forearm supportively.

I've been trying hard to believe that myself. But these people staring or smiling awkwardly, what if I told them I'd been raped? Would I be cocooned in concern and become one of those girls we all feel so sorry for when we see their story in a magazine article, or would they laugh at me and say, 'You were raped? When you went down on him in the club out of your own free will? You were so drunk you let him pull your knickers down and bend you over a wall? How was he meant to know you didn't want it? Generally when a girl unzips your fly in a public place and sucks you off, it means she's up for it.' That's what they would think. I know that because even though I have tried not to, sometimes, it's what *I* think too, maybe.

I can't look anyone in the eye and the thought of bumping into Zoe is beyond uncomfortable. The only thing stopping me from being really angry with her – the thing that makes me tolerate this situation and not move colleges or something – is that I know, for her to have done this, things must be bad for her. There is no way someone normal would do what she did, humiliate a friend like that, when previously she's never showed any meanness or bitchiness. She must have gone a bit mental. She doesn't talk to anyone at college anymore. She's cut herself off.

More people think that she's an arsehole than they think I'm a slag, according to Beth.

Of course I DO see her; she's in my English class. She avoids me and I want to shout, 'What did I do to you?' but I don't. I don't want to cause any more drama. Zoe doesn't look at me or speak to me during our lesson and afterwards she dashes out.

Isabelle gives me a sweet little smile at the end of the class, and I go off to meet Beth. We go to a cafe around the corner from college because I can't face the canteen. A few people we know go here, but not many.

My Mum texts. *'How is it going?'*

'Fine.' Mum and me have agreed to have this strained *'everything is FINE!'* text exchange.

Beth says that hardly anyone is re-posting the picture now and the comments have all but died out. 'You can't let this get you down. After everything you have been through, how brilliant you've been with giving up booze.'

'I relapsed.'

'So what?' Beth's been reading up on this stuff. 'It's normal to relapse a few times after rehab, with or without all this stuff.'

Isla's been calling me. She's left so many messages, pissed, begging to see me, telling me she's homeless now. I call her back; she's so drunk when she picks up that I can't manage to hear what she's saying. I'm not even sure she knows who's calling her. She hangs up, or drops the phone, or something. I don't call back.

I look at Beth. 'Beth, I need to talk to you . . .'

Beth pulls her chair in close. I must look very serious because she's put on her most sincere 'listening face'.

'I went to see Alex.'

Beth gasps. 'No! When? Nina, you need to report him, not hang out with him.'

'I needed to have it out with him.'

'Oh my God, Nina, this is serious. He . . .' she whispers '. . . *raped you*.' She mouths the word 'raped'.

'Regret,' I say, 'is not rape.'

Beth looks shocked. 'I can't even believe you said that.'

'It's what he said to me,' I admit.

'Nina, I regret having a chocolate éclair for breakfast. I know what regret is. This, what you've been through . . . you're a victim of a violent crime.'

She taps the table forcefully with her finger as she insists I have been raped, that I'm a victim, that I should do what she and Mum want which is march into a police station and say: 'Hi, I'm Nina, and I'm an alcoholic. I fuck strangers in parks and leave condoms up my chuff when I fuck two flat-mates in the same night. However, I would like to bring to your attention that I feel this particular time when I fucked someone whose name I wasn't sure of, *this* particular time, it was rape. I'd like him arrested now, please, and put in prison. Thanks.'

'Beth, I can't know that for sure. He said I wanted it.' He'd actually said 'you were gagging for it' but I can't repeat his words.

'Of course he said that! He's not going to say, "Oh yeah, sorry, you were paralytic and I just couldn't help raping you."'

I need Beth to shut up. I look at her and even though she usually gets things, she usually understands, or at least tries to, she doesn't get this. She doesn't get this at all.

'Can you please stop saying I was raped, Beth? You're not helping. If *you* want to go on some mad feminist crusade – "No means no!" . . . "Drunk consent is not consent" – then fucking do it, but don't use me as a fucking poster girl.'

Beth looks stunned, then upset. Suddenly her eyes are full of tears and I'm up and out of my seat and sitting next to her, with my arm around her shoulder as she cries.

She rarely cries, so she stops pretty quickly and laughs, surprised at herself. She wipes her eyes and grins. 'Yeah, cos, y'know, this is *all* about me.'

'Absolutely. I mean, I have no idea how you're coping.'

She puts her hand on her heart and does her best awful American accent. 'I know. I'm just like, y'know, so brave.'

We giggle and it's gone, the anger is gone. Beth can drop things. Some people can't. An argument becomes about how well they can defend their point of view instead of listening to yours and realising they were talking out of their arse. It's OK to admit when you've been talking out of your arse. I respect someone more for it.

'Beth, he said he has more film of me from that night.'

'Oh my God.'

'His mate took more. He said he's got stuff where I'm consenting, more or less.'

'He's bluffing.'

'How do you know?'

'Because he's a slimy, manipulative, public school wanker. He'll have thought of every way he can to get out of this. Even if he has got more stuff, it still doesn't change the fact that you were out of it, he wasn't, and that his mate and him did something terrible.'

'But I can't go to the police and say, "Can you arrest this guy because he's a bastard?"'

Me and Beth talk some more and she stops going on about me going to the police and says, 'It's your path, you go down it your way.'

'Don't go all Buddhist on me.'

'I'm not! I like burgers too much. I just mean I respect that you know what's best for *you*. And I'll stop interfering. Even though I *really* want to.'

I smile at my ridiculous friend.

Beth thinks Zoe is in an emotionally abusive relationship. She is. Alex is a disease she has caught. There is no point hating her or being angry with her. She doesn't talk to Beth anymore now either. She's moved into Alex's flat and has unfriended both of us on Facebook.

Beth and Mum both suffer the fact that I haven't gone to the police. Each of them has tried to persuade me, but screeching 'You've been raped!' in my face hasn't helped. I thought talking to Alex might have put me in control. I thought Alex might be horrified. I thought he might say sorry, say he had no idea how I had been feeling. I thought he might have a clue that not remembering being fucked is a pretty huge fucking deal for anyone. I thought Mum and Beth might understand that telling the police what happened that night, going through it all with a policeman who would have seen loads of girls getting drunk and doing things they regretted, was not something I could do.

I have read lots of articles with women talking about when they were raped. They are in every trashy magazine and in Mum's weekend supplements. How they couldn't have sex with their partner afterwards, how they had nightmares. I don't know how to measure what happened to me. Yes, I felt dirty at the time and again months later when I found out more of what happened. But I *could* have sex afterwards with other people, too many other people.

After lunch I go back to college and to the library. Robbie comes in. I smile. Sort of. Well, I make a face. It's strange seeing him. He comes over to talk to me except we can't talk in the library so we go and have a cup of tea in the canteen.

'I thought either I ignore you for ever out of sheer awkwardness, or I come over and ask how you are.'

'I'm OK. Well, I'm not OK, but better than I was.'

I don't know if Robbie still fancies me. I don't know if he ever did. Phoebe said he did but Phoebe talks all sorts of bollocks. Even if he did, I doubt he does now. He'll have seen what's online. Who would like a girl after that?

And then he asks me out.

'That bloke who stole you away from me on New Year's Eve?'

I smile. 'Jamie.'

'That's it. Is he your boyfriend?'

'Ex,' I tell him. 'Very ex.'

Robbie looks shy. 'So, if I asked you out on a date, would you come?'

'Why, do you think I'd be easy?' are the words that shoot immediately out of my mouth.

His face falls. 'Erm, no, I like you and think you're pretty and I want to spend lots of time getting to know you.'

I don't know where to put my face. We're sober. Who asks someone out when they're sober? Normal people. Nice people. So he should ask someone out who's normal and nice.

'I don't know if I could handle a date with you,' I blurt out.

'Nina, most girls just say they're washing their hair. I'll be honest, yours *could* do with a wash.'

He is grinning at me.

I carry on being weird. Perhaps I'm turning into Trish.

'I don't mean I can't handle a date with you, there's nothing wrong with you.'

He knows I'm waffling because I'm nervous, and he smiles gently, humouring me. 'Thank you,' he says with mock seriousness, putting his hand on his heart. 'I'm touched.'

'I don't know if I can handle a date with anyone. Everything has been awful.'

I should have stopped there, but I don't. I add, 'Plus, I fancy girls. I'm not a lesbian but I'm definitely bisexual.' I am definitely a twat.

'Well.' He exhales, eyebrows raised. 'That's all very interesting. For what it's worth, as long as you're a tiny bit interested in blokes, then I'd still like to take you out.'

'OK,' I say. What about Jamie? I think. What if Jamie comes back to be with me again? Jamie isn't going to come back and be with me again, I'm being mad.

'Great,' he says, 'I thought dinner with my mum and dad, then we'll all play Trivial Pursuit? Girls against boys? I know Mum will be dying to show you pictures of me when I was a baby.'

It takes an embarrassing amount of seconds before I realise he's joking.

'Idiot!' I try to give him a playful punch but he's sitting slightly too far away and I miss and my hand clumsily punches the air. I thought I was all right at flirting, but sober, I'm rubbish.

'Well, I'm guessing you don't want to sit in a pub, so will you trust me to plan something fun and meet me at the appointed hour?'

That sounds great. 'OK,' I say, and that's that. I've got a date.

CHAPTER NINETEEN

Mum is not letting any of this Alex stuff go. She makes it clear to me again and again that all this trouble is the reason they came back from Germany.

She says loudly on the phone to her friends, 'Well, obviously it was a missed opportunity for Alan, but Nina needed us. Not that she's helping herself at all.' And it seems like she's saying, 'And the very least she could do is lodge a complaint against this boy who raped her.'

Mum's very upset that I'm not going to the police. She hardly speaks to me.

'My going to the police doesn't make me less of a slapper.'

This upsets her, which is why I say it, thinking of all the other things I have done. The fact is Alex isn't 'nice' like Dave, the older bloke from the pub, and Derrick. Those guys at least checked I was OK. Alex didn't. Alex didn't care.

'The police won't be able to do anything. They'll say they can't arrest someone for being horrible to me.'

Mum doesn't see it that way.

'You have to accept what happened to you,' she shouts.

'No,' I shout back, 'YOU have to accept what happened to me!'

After one of these rows, a huge one where Mum started crying, Alan asked me if I'd like to go to lunch with him.

Alan has never asked me to go to lunch with him. In fact, the only times I've been on my own with Alan is in the car when Mum has run out to grab Katie from ballet or something.

We go to a nice cafe near us that does amazing pancakes and I go to order a Nutella and banana one but feel too guilty because that's Katie's favourite and we haven't brought her. Before we left, Alan gently told her, 'I'd like you to stay at home with Mummy this time, darling. Your sister and I will bring you back a lovely treat from the cafe, OK?'

Katie pouted but she's such a clever kid, she knew there was something more serious going on than she could understand or question, so she gave Alan a big kiss on the cheek and said, 'Can you bring me back a double chocolate muffin, Daddy?' and off we went.

I order a ham and cheese pancake. Alan and I both draw out the process of ordering our food because once all that is done, Alan will have to start the awkward business of talking to me about whatever it is he brought me here to say.

'Nina, I wanted to speak with you privately because . . .' He looks at his fork for a moment before continuing '. . . because your mother has told me what happened.'

I'm sure Mum tells Alan stuff that's going on for me, but Alan is thoroughly committed to never admitting he knows anything at all about my private life. He takes pride in 'staying out of it'; even though those pictures were all over the

Internet and in the bloody paper, for God's sake, Alan didn't crack. But here he is now, taking me to lunch and clearly needing to talk.

'Oh,' I say, 'has she told you everything?'

'I think so. She's told me beyond what has sadly been public.'

I stare down at my plate. Alan knows what a slag I am. Great.

'You've done nothing to be ashamed of,' he says calmly, surprising me.

Then why, I want to ask him, do I feel like I want to crawl out of my own skin into someone else's?

'You're a very young, very kind, very intelligent young woman who has been through an awful lot.'

Miraculously, I don't take this prime opportunity to bite his head off for being patronising.

'What happened to you is sadly what many women go through. The fault is entirely with that—' A look of anger and disgust comes over Alan's usually utterly neutral face as he has to mention Alex. 'That excuse for a man.'

Alan does not 'do' angry very often. His hand shakes a little as he picks up a napkin.

'I'm sorry, Nina, but this is very upsetting.'

I'm touched and embarrassed, very embarrassed. I wonder for a moment if I should pat his shoulder or something, but I don't and the moment passes.

Alan soldiers on.

'I know a lot of women prefer to put this kind of thing down to experience, even though they have the option, traumatic though it may be, of going to the police. I want you to know that whichever you choose to do, it's your decision, and yours only. I will support you one hundred per cent either way.'

'That's not how Mum feels.'

'I know. But it isn't your mother's business, it's yours.'

That's the first time ever, in the History of Alan, that he has said anything even remotely derogatory about Mum.

We finish our pancakes and both hastily decline when the waitress comes up and asks us if we want anything else.

Before we get back into the car, I almost go for a 'Disney Moment' with Alan. It's on the tip of my tongue to say, 'Thanks for this, it meant a lot,' but I don't. Instead, Alan says, 'It's getting very nippy again, isn't it?'

Once we are home, Alan disappears into his study and I read to Katie in the living room while she carefully eats her muffin. The atmosphere in the house is post-calamity calm. Mum is like a lioness after an unsuccessful hunt. She is resigned. She is defeated. She quietly gets on with re-potting her orchids, her face full of questions.

Beth, Trish, Steve and I sit and write down all the awful Internet shaming stuff that has happened to famous people who have all got over it and none of them have died. We can't think of that many, which Beth says proves the point that no one cares or remembers.

Then comes big news. Steve – Beth's Steve, Steve who can barely string a sentence together and whose writing makes no sense whatsoever – wins the short story competition.

Isabelle is beside herself with pride and gets all teary saying she was 'impossibly proud', then quickly adds 'of all of you, of course'.

Beth acts like he's won a Pulitzer Prize and not just some local talent contest.

I get my story back with a really nice letter, telling me to keep writing and that it had been 'very tough for the judges'.

It is obvious the letter is a generic one to everyone. Just to make me feel even more of a loser, my letter was addressed to 'Dear 65 Madeley Crescent', which made Robbie laugh until he cried.

We go on our date, me and Robbie.

'It's a daytime date with an option of going on through to the evening if I decide I like you enough,' he texted, adding a 'wink' emoji in case I thought he was serious which, I'll admit, I thought he was for a split second.

He tells me to meet him on the Southbank. I don't know what to wear. I try on different dresses, put on a load of make-up, then I decide that's all stupid because he's seen me a million times looking normal, and turning up all glam in the middle of the afternoon looked desperate.

In the end I wear my favourite jeans (they make my bum look great) and a cute gypsy top with boots. I wear neutral make-up. I put a calming treatment on my hair, blow dry and straighten it. I look good, but I don't look like I've taken four hours to get ready. Though if you include having a bath and doing my hair, taking clothes on and off and back on again a hundred times, it *has* actually been about four hours.

Robbie hasn't made an effort at all, except he has: he's bought me a rose.

'This could go either way . . . you could either find it funny, or so cringy you'll run away,' is the first thing he says to me.

I take the rose.

'Hmm, it's cringy AND funny,' I tell him. 'I will give this date a go . . .'

He grins at me. 'Don't build up your part, love. I've got Taylor Swift on standby if I get bored of you.'

I smack his arm with the rose and the head falls off. We laugh, a little too hard. Nerves. He says, 'Bah! Cheap rose!' and I toss the stalk away. It hits a suited middle-aged man on the arm. He looks round, and glares.

'I'm sorry about my friend,' Robbie says. 'She's a total savage.'

We scuttle off giggling.

He has tickets for the London Dungeon and I actually squeal because I have ALWAYS wanted to go there.

It's dark in the dungeons, really dark, and our group is taken round by actors dressed in olden days costumes with wigs and black teeth. They stay in character as they walk round. We go in a huddle of tourists through dark corridors and creepy rooms. At the Jack the Ripper exhibit, Robbie stands behind me and puts his hands on my hips. There is something so subtle but insanely sexy about a boy doing a simple, protective gesture. Like when they take your hand to jump down from somewhere, a wall or something, when you don't really need them to. Here, in the dark, Robbie's hands on my hips feels like the nicest thing a boy has done to me for ages. The group moves on. He only lets go as we turn a corner and then he catches my hand. Robbie holds my hand for the entire time around the rest of our tour of the London Dungeon.

We fool around in the gift shop and he buys the cheesy photo they took of us, him in stocks, me holding an axe. We leave and walk down by the river. The sun is out. I want him to hold my hand again, but daylight brings shyness.

'So, miss. What would you like to do? Hang out some more? Or go home?'

What I would like to do is go to the pub. I want to sit and get drunk with him. But we can't, we don't.

We find a little Italian restaurant near the station and have pizza.

He won't let me pay for a thing.

'But the tickets were so expensive!'

'Where I come from, if you invite a girl out on a date, she's your guest for the duration of that day.'

I grin. Jamie once made me go halves with him on my birthday.

What I can do now, which I couldn't do before rehab, is have conversations when I'm sober. Proper conversations, about stuff that's more than having a laugh chitchatting.

Robbie talks about his family; they sound lovely. His big brother is in the army. He shows me pictures. It's a bit weird because me and Beth are both pacifists. If I was drinking, I'd start going on about soldiers being 'cannon fodder' for self-serving politicians and I'd have ruined our time together. But now I just listen because his big brother, Jacob, is his hero, and my opinions about war, in this moment, don't matter.

After we eat we catch the Tube home.

Back in Ealing, he walks me all the way to my door. It's only eight o'clock. We sit on the wall and chat for a bit longer. It's dark now. He leans in and we kiss. Oh my God, he's a good kisser. Our living-room curtains are drawn and the light is on. I bet Mum and Alan have heard us outside; Mum will be wondering when on earth I'll come in.

My hand is on the back of his neck, one of my favourite parts of a boy, and his hand is, excruciatingly, on the flab spilling over the waistband of my jeans.

'Can we go out again soon?'

'Yup,' I manage, between kisses.

'Friday?'

It's Sunday today. Why Friday? That's ages away. I can't bear not to kiss him again until Friday.

'Fine,' I say. We hug, and I go inside. I am high as a kite.

Katie is still up when I get home.

'She's dying to tell you a story she's thought of,' Mum tells me.

I go to her room straight away. My lips are still buzzing deliciously from Robbie's kisses. Katie sits up in bed and excitedly tells me her story and I have to force myself to listen because my head keeps flying back to Robbie and the way he held my hand, the way he makes me laugh, and his beautiful, fluttery, not-too-wet kisses.

'You're not listening properly!' Katie scolds. 'Can you please concentrate?'

So I do, and she tells me a story about a boy who's in the park with his mum. He goes too fast on a roundabout, and when he comes off he can't stop spinning. He spins out of the park. He sees his friend spinning towards him. His friend can't stop either.

'Did you come off a roundabout too fast as well?' his friend shouts.

'Yeah,' says the boy. 'I'm so dizzy and I can't see my mum.'

'Neither can I,' says the other boy.

When they eventually stop spinning, each has reached the other one's mum. Each mum knows where the other boy lives and returns them to the right houses.

'The End,' says Katie proudly when she's finished.

'That's a great story.'

'Yes,' she says, 'I WAS going to make it so that each of them goes to the wrong mum and they actually swap lives, but that was too sad. They needed to be with the right mum.'

I think about Katie's story as I lie in bed. I think about spinning out of control and just hoping good people, kind people, will stop you and direct you back to where you're safe.

CHAPTER TWENTY

I see Robbie a couple of times in the canteen that week and he just waves at me. He doesn't come over to chat. The week is torture. No text, nothing! Beth forbids me to text him.

'You made an arrangement for Friday. Wait till Thursday and if he hasn't texted by then text him!'

'But we kissed! Why won't he just text to say "hi"?'

'Because he's a bloke. You've had one kiss. He doesn't need to tell you about his day and it's too soon to text you to tell you you're beautiful. I know you . . . you'd run a mile if he did.'

This is true, but I still say, 'But why won't he say "hi" in college?'

Beth slams her book shut. I'm supposed to have come over to revise. 'Because he has a life! Because he wants to take things slow. It's awkward when you get together with some-one from college. You don't how it's going to go, you don't want to announce it to everyone in case it ends up not going anywhere.'

'Is that what it was like with you and Steve?'

Beth looks slightly apologetic and says, 'Nope. We were told off in the canteen by a dinner lady. We were snogging and holding up the queue. It was the Monday straight after the party.'

'Yuk!'

'Nina, the man knows what you have been through. He doesn't want to push it. He's being perfectly reasonable and sensible so you do the same. Now. Please, can we revise? I don't want to fail and go to a shit uni because *you're* neurotic.'

I try to focus on my work but I look at my phone so often that Beth confiscates it and doesn't give it back until we've finished revising for the day.

Of course, I missed a lot of work while I was in rehab, but I stay behind at college most days in the library working. If nothing else, it stops me from obsessing about Robbie, about whether or not he will call me on Thursday.

Thursday morning I get a text.

'We still on for tomorrow? x'

'Yup. When? Where? xxx'

Far too many kisses. I should have just stuck to one like he did.

Then nothing. Nothing! No text for hours!

Beth reassures me this is normal. 'Guys aren't slaves to their phones like we are.'

I call Trish who says, 'It's been a week. Maybe he's changed his mind.' Trish is not helpful in these circumstances.

I sit in AA that evening and go on about how crap I feel that he hasn't texted me. I feel a twat. Such a stupid thing to be bothered by but, really, the anxiety is making me want a drink. After everything I have been through, it would be so stupid to relapse because some boy hasn't texted me back.

I tell Beth that I feel better after talking to my new sponsor Julie.

Beth is a bit jealous of Julie. 'So what do you tell her that you can't tell me?'

It's not like talking to a normal mate. For a start, sponsors are addicts who have done all the twelve steps. They're addicts who support other addicts as part of their own recovery.

I'd been to lots of AA meetings before I was brave enough to ask someone to be my sponsor. It feels like you're asking them out. I was scared she'd say 'No, I'm taken' or 'I don't think it would work with us' and I'd feel rejected. Feeling rejected is how most of us got here in the first place. No one says in a meeting, 'I've always felt like I belong! Now, if I could just sort out this silly drinking habit I could skip back off to my perfect life!' AA is not for those people.

We had a coffee, and a chat, me and Julie, and she said 'yes', which was a relief.

Julie is thirty-six and so sorted. Well, she's not, because she's an alcoholic, but she hasn't drunk for eight years and she has two little kids who've never known her drunk. I tell her I feel lucky I found AA while I'm still so young.

'People find it when they are ready to,' Julie says. 'It's lucky you understood how ill you were; loads don't.'

So Julie will now be the one I call and meet with to talk about anything that might affect my drinking. She's my 'break glass in case of emergency' friend. She's the only one I talk to about the steps. Julie says, 'Early recovery is this fragile, beautiful thing that you don't want to let every person in your life gawp at and give you their opinion about.'

I feel better after the meeting, hopeful, but I am still so glued to my phone that I almost walk in front of a van.

The van driver does an emergency stop and then shouts 'YOU FUCKING IDIOT' at me through his window, and he's absolutely right, I am a fucking idiot.

Then Robbie texts. *'Is it too boring to come to my place? The old folk are up north and if you're willing to risk my cooking, dinner is served at 8p.m. See you at 7? 79 Ashby Road W5.'*

Oh my God. Straight in there with 'come to my place'. I don't know why I'm so nervous. Jesus, it's not as though I haven't gone straight in there with guys before this in the last year. I think about what Julie has said to me about 'owning your actions', and this is owning them, right? I don't want to jump into bed with him. I want to take things slowly. If I'm in his house, with no one else around, I'd have to fuck him, right? This is stupid. I can hear Beth and Julie and everyone I have ever met in rehab and all the magazine articles I have read shouting at me, 'You don't owe any guy sex!' But still I know it's going to be a monumental challenge to not fuck him, even if I really don't want to. But what if I DO want to? What if I do, and we fuck, what then? More agonising waiting for a text? He would be within his rights to not ask for a third date. How would I feel then? You can't call a guy a bastard for not wanting a third date, even if you fucked on the second.

What if he DOES just think I'm easy? What if we fuck, then I see him around college with another girl and I won't have a leg to stand on because we've only been on two dates. Should I make it clear to him that if we fuck, he HAS to want to see me again? How can I do that without sounding totally mental?

I text him back. *'OK, great. See you then. Just to say, though, I won't stay the night, I'm not ready to start a sexual relationship.'*

And like a total dickhead, I press send. I send this really nice guy a text that makes me sound like a total freak.

My phone vibrates as it rings. It's Robbie. I jump. I almost drop it. I can't answer. I should answer. What if he's mad at me? What if he's calling to say he thinks I'm batshit crazy and doesn't want to see me at all?

I answer with an overly cheery 'Hi!' as though I hadn't just texted him and practically called him a sex pest.

'Hey, Nina, I just got your text.'

'Oh yeah, sorry, I'm sorry.'

'No, look, it's OK. I just didn't want a big texting to-and-fro about something so important.'

He's being mature about this which makes me feel about two years old.

'Nina, I don't want you to do anything you don't feel comfortable with. I'll be honest, I'm not into casual sex. I just thought it would be nice to cook you a meal and bore you to death with a film. Plus, I'm skint after our last date.'

He is entirely lovely.

'OK, no, that's fine, I just wanted to be clear, before I come over, because . . .' and then a whole lot of words come babbling out of my mouth '. . . because I'm so new at this. I mean, I know I've been with a lot of guys in the last year – actually, not that many and not all of them my fault – but I've always been drunk and got carried along by all that crap and now I just don't know how to behave and I'm scared I'll do or say something that will make you think I'm a freak.'

Robbie smiles. I know he smiles, even though we're on the phone. 'I already know you're a freak because you agreed to go on a date with me. Look, I promise I'll look after you. I just want to spend some time with you.'

He's nice. And sexy. Sexier than Jamie. Too sexy for me. He could get someone much prettier, thinner. I hate myself for thinking like this.

I must stop comparing him to Jamie. Robbie's not my boyfriend, this is just a date, and he knows what I look like, so no wishing I was taller, thinner, hotter, but I still can't help it.

I finally get home. Mum's cross with me because I'm late and she's been texting but I hadn't replied because I was annoyed it was *her* texting and not Robbie and wished she'd chill out and leave me alone.

She's relieved I'm not drunk. When I don't get home at exactly the time I say I will, Mum worries that I'm getting shit-faced somewhere. Poor Mum.

On Friday morning, I bump into Robbie. We're in the canteen, at lunchtime, and it's busy. He's with some friends, three guys I don't know, and I'm with a girl called Susanna from my history class. There's literally no space to sit except at his table so we go and I say 'hi' and we sit and he introduces me to his friends, Pete, Jake and Owen.

'This is Susanna,' I say, and we all have lunch together.

And it's OK, good actually, but then these guys come up. I've seen them around college but I don't know them. They come over, they have football shirts on, and in that moment all of them seem ten feet tall. They have horrible, sneering looks on their faces.

'You're that slag, aren't you? The one that has no idea how to give a decent blow job.' His mates laugh. Pete, Jake and Owen look baffled.

As they walk away, one of them utters, 'Rancid cunt!' and knocks my plastic cup of water all over the table. They walk off laughing, pleased with themselves.

Susanna's really straight. She's a quiet girl who looks like this is the most 'out there' thing that has ever happened in her life. She quickly dabs napkins on the water and doesn't look at anyone.

Robbie gets up. His face is thunder. He goes up to one of the boys, the one who called me a cunt, I think, and grabs him by his shirt, yanks him around and punches him in the face, knocking him to the floor. There's blood everywhere. People gasp and there's a scream, from where or who, I don't know.

Suddenly all I see are the other two on Robbie. They're huge, they've got bigger. They set on him and punch him to the floor and he's not able to fight them both.

The third one gets up, his face full of blood and fury, and joins in, kicking and punching Robbie. I don't know what to do.

There's another scream; this time it's me. I tug uselessly at someone's shirt. Pete, Jake and Owen look like they're wondering if their friendship with Robbie is worth getting a broken nose for. To his credit, Owen wades in but is flung back out again. A couple of our male teachers appear. The boys are pulled off and held back.

'He fucking started it,' one of the boys says, and with a final kick, which misses, they're pushed out of the canteen.

The dinner ladies come along then, three women in their fifties, and help Robbie onto a chair. He looks a mess. His nose and his mouth are bleeding, he's clutching his stomach and he's still angry.

'I'm OK, I'm OK . . .' he says.

I stand there like a pillock.

Robbie is taken to hospital by one of the dinner ladies. The college call his mum. He doesn't want me to go with him and he doesn't return my texts for the rest of the day.

The next day Phoebe earnestly tells me, 'It's like, really bad. Me and my mum went to see him. He's got like a black eye and his ribs aren't broken but really bruised. He's in real pain.'

'Why won't he talk to me?' I ask her.

'Babe, he's, like, really upset. He says he doesn't want anyone to see him.'

There is nothing I can do but wait for him to get in touch.

On Sunday, he does.

He calls me and his voice sounds muffled. 'I've got a fat lip and my ego's really bruised, but I'm OK,' he tells me. 'Sorry about our date.'

I'm the one who's sorry. I'm the one who got him dragged into this.

*

Mum puts Katie to bed then steels herself to talk to me. There's been a silence between me and Mum about all this. I reckon she's promised Alan to 'not bring it up' and 'give Nina some space', which means Mum has been seriously passive-aggressive as she tries to control herself. She's horrified people are still talking about what happened to me; she knows about the fight because the Deputy Head at college had to let her know my name was brought up by the people who witnessed the fight and, because of my history, they had to stick their noses in my business and ruin things at home for me.

'Nina, you have to realise that by not going to the police in the first place, you condoned what that lout did to you.'

'What the hell does that even mean?'

'It means you don't understand the severity of what happened to you and now people think it's a stick they can beat you with.'

Why do people feel I don't understand 'the severity' of something when it's *me* it's happened to. They say: 'This is *serious,* Nina'; 'He *raped* you, Nina'; 'What he did was against the *law,* Nina.' Like I'm some idiot who thinks guys are *supposed* to fuck you when you are out for the count.

There's a tension between her and Alan too. It's the first time he hasn't supported her, the first time he's actively disagreed with her.

'She isn't condoning anything,' he says quietly. 'None of this is Nina's doing.'

'She's letting him get away with it. Letting animals like these boys bully her, bully her friends.'

Mum is making me sound weak and pathetic. She's doing it deliberately, to force me to go to the police.

'It happened ages ago, Mum. Women who go to the police, on the night, crying their eyes out, even those women have a really hard time getting the bloke convicted, and you want me to prance in there, months later, and say "I've been . . ."' I can't say 'raped' in front of Alan.

'I feel it's very important that Nina does what's right for her,' Alan says.

Mum glares at Alan. She's outraged he's not supporting her. She doesn't understand that *I* am the one who needs support.

'Since when were you so understanding about Nina's needs? You couldn't wait to get shot of her up until now.'

Ouch. Mum doesn't go below the belt like this usually. There's no new information she can give me about mine and Alan's relationship. I don't need telling, I know I wasn't his favourite person, who can blame him? But here's Mum now, trying to shame him, embarrass him, let me know he hasn't always been on my side because she feels betrayed that he isn't backing her up.

Alan looks hurt and uncomfortable.

Mum looks sorry but she's too angry to *say* she's sorry.

I want to say to him, 'It's all right Alan, I know I've been a nightmare, I don't hold anything against you. In fact if I was you I'd have blasted me off to the moon years ago,' but I don't. I just stand there like a plank.

Mum's crying suddenly.

'You're both as spineless as one another,' she blurts out and leaves the room.

'Spineless?' There goes *my* self-control. I follow her out. 'I wonder where I get that from, Mum,' I snap. 'What did YOU do to protect us from Dad? Fuck all. You made me like this. You made me so wrecked in my head that I put myself in these awful situations, then you try to blame *me* because you can't bear to think how responsible *you* are for all of this.'

This is, of course, absolutely the wrong thing to say. But I'm far from bloody perfect, and I can't be expected to keep my shit together when I am goaded.

She stops on the stairs and hisses at me, 'I'm responsible? *YOU* get yourself into such a state, such a drunken stupor, that you behave like a *whore* and I am so ashamed of you.' She narrows her eyes. 'You have no idea! You have no idea how difficult things were for me.'

'And *you* have no idea how difficult things are for me, are for me *right now.*'

I stomp by her and go to my room. I sit on my bed, snarling and crying, and I kick my dresser, but not very hard because I don't want my jewellery holder to fall and get all jumbled up.

*

By the morning, my self-pity has gone but there's deafening silence between me and Mum. We both said things we wished we could take back but we are both too angry, too hurt. Alan has left the house already and Katie is full of beans. She has a school outing today and she's excited about sitting on the coach next to her friend Marnie. 'Me and Marnie are going to sing songs and play Cat's Cradle.' Katie has string all over her hands and she can make elaborate patterns with the string wrapped around her fingers. She's learnt it all off YouTube and has practised so she can do it even with her little hand.

'Would you like a lift to college?' Mum asks. This is her way of saying she's sorry we fought and that she wants to stop fighting.

'No, thanks. I'm OK,' I say, which is my way of saying, 'I can't just gloss over last night; I'm too angry and you were out of order.'

I go to see Robbie after college. His mum lets me in and she's dead sweet. She doesn't sound as northern as Robbie and she's pretty, young looking, wearing clothes I wish Mum would wear more. She's got on a girlie dress with wedges and a cute cardigan. Mum is strictly jeans and knitted tops.

'It's good to meet you, Nina. I've heard a lot about you, though my Robert would kill me for saying that.' She smiles and I'm relieved. I thought she might hate me, blame me for what they did to Robbie.

'Is he OK?' I ask her.

'I'll be honest, I think it was worse for me. When I saw what they did to my boy, I wanted to kill them. I still do. Do you think I'd stand a chance?'

I smile and shake my head. She's absolutely tiny. I tower over her and I'm not tall.

'I hope they throw the book at them,' she says. She smiles back and hands me a packet of biscuits. 'His favourites. He's upstairs. I'll make a pot of tea, shall I?'

I go up the stairs. Their house is homely; it's not as modern and smart as Mum keeps ours. There are baby pictures of Robbie and his brother lining the walls as I go up the stairs.

'In here, Nina.' I hear his muffled voice and go into his room. He's on the bed and his face is all mashed up and swollen. I put my hands to my own and gasp.

'Oh my God!'

'Honestly, Nina, don't get all upset. It's worse than it looks. I mean better. Look, I'll be honest, it's worse.' He smiles, then winces.

I'm almost in tears. I sit on the edge of his bed, gingerly as though my very presence might hurt him.

'What did the doctors say?'

'That I'll be fine. The swelling will die down. I've had stitches, see?'

They're covered with dried blood but I can see the stitches to his lip and he shows me the few he's had by his ears.

'The worst is my ribs. You can't make me laugh . . . it's agony. I'm having to watch war movies to entertain myself. I can't watch anything funny.'

His mum brings up tea and me and Robbie talk a bit about what happened but not much. He's trying to laugh the whole thing off but I know he's being brave, he's being a bloke. He doesn't want me to know how shitty he feels that they did this to him, how shitty it feels to be scared.

After a while, I help him hobble to the bathroom to have a pee. 'Not quite the date I had in mind, I'll be honest,' he tells me.

An investigation panel is put together at college and Robbie and the other three put forward their version of events. Given that everyone saw exactly what happened, the three boys aren't able to pin the blame on Robbie like they tried. One of them, Marco, who Robbie hit, is expelled from college. Turns out he was already in trouble and was on a final warning. Robbie and the other two are suspended for two weeks, which is massively unfair, but, actually, Robbie needs that sort of time to recover anyway.

I go to see him a few times in that two weeks he's off college. We do coursework together and his mum, Janet, makes a fuss of us and fills us up with biscuits and always insists I 'stay for tea'.

'So are you two going out?' Beth asks me.

'No! We're just friends.'

'Yeah, right!' she scoffs.

'But nothing's happened.'

'Only because he's an invalid.'

Truth is I really don't know what is 'happening' with Robbie. I got him hurt, though Beth says, 'You didn't ask him to go all Knight In Shining Armour.'

Beth thinks that, as a feminist, I should acknowledge that my 'honour' didn't need defending and it was macho 'control' that made Robbie twat that boy in the face.

'I'm not having a go at him – Robbie seems ace – but we should acknowledge that when a man verbally abuses us, having another man fight him physically means he thinks of you as his property.'

I don't tell Beth that I have been secretly delighted that Robbie defended me like that. Obviously I wish he hadn't been hurt, and I hate fights and I am NOT one of those girls who likes guys that get into fights over her. But, his instinct had been, 'Oi, that's my girl you're talking about,' and I liked that.

I wish I could accept a guy just likes me because he says he does. I wish I didn't have to wait until they had themselves hospitalised and suspended before I think, 'Hey, maybe he does fancy me.'

My name's all over Facebook again. Seems this Marco guy has friends as vile as he is and again I'm being called a 'whore' and a 'slut', with people acting like the fight was my fault.

There's a gang of girls who hang around the refectory on the other side of the canteen. They're loud and rough, and they stand outside smoking and deliberately eyeballing me. One afternoon, one of them actually comes up to me.

'Why do you fink you're so special?'

'I don't,' I say.

'Yeah, you do. If you weren't all middle class, you'd never have got away with stitching Marco up like that.'

'Do you know what happened? He came over and verbally assaulted me.'

'So you get him kicked out of college? You better watch yourself. Someone'll teach you a lesson.'

That was a threat, a definite threat, I decide, as they shoulder-barge me when they pass.

I can't handle this.

The next day Isabelle asks me if she can take me to lunch. 'I wonder if you could do with a chat?' she says.

I could. I could do with a chat because right now I want to go to another college, another city. Perhaps even another planet.

Miraculously, I'm doing well in essays and stuff.

'I hate you,' Beth told me the other day. 'You go nuts, do fuck all work, then swan back in and get all As anyway. It's not fair!'

'Beth! I'm an alcoholic. I have mental health issues! "Nuts" is politically incorrect!'

'Oh my God!' she says. 'I'm so sorry. I meant "mental".'

'I think you'll find that the correct term is "batshit crazy".'

Robbie isn't returning my texts.

I try flirting.

'I'm guessing hang-gliding is out for our second date. Never mind. Whatever we do, I can't wait.'

I send it and he calls me.

'Definitely not hang-gliding. Wing-walking is more my thing, Nina. Clears your head after it's been kicked in . . .'

I can't joke about that.

'How are you, you OK?'

'Yup,' he says. 'Of course my mother now wants to move back up north because she doesn't think London is safe. Like *no one* gets a kicking in the north.'

'I really am so sorry, Robbie.'

'You have nothing to be sorry about. Although you *are* a walking soap opera.'

Then we talk about uni stuff. I'm not sure about Warwick. It's got the course I want to do, but I don't know if Jamie is still going and how hard that will be.

'There are twenty-three thousand students there,' Robbie says. 'You COULD avoid him. Or you could trust that by then you'll be OK, maybe even be good enough friends by then to support each other there.'

I don't tell Robbie I would rather rip my eyeballs out and roll them down a hill than be 'friends' with Jamie and hang out with him and Marcia.

Jamie has started messaging me quite a lot. He's gone from totally ignoring me to *'You OK?'* on a daily basis, and if I don't reply straight away he'll write, *'I'm worried about you, reply, dammit.'*

Mum is not happy about Jamie being in touch. 'Be careful, Nina. He's a nice boy, Jamie, but he's someone else's boyfriend now and it's not fair of him to play with your feelings.'

I've thought about the sex me and Jamie had when he came over at Christmas. It wasn't just that it was good sex. It felt good because he knows me, he knows my body. He knew me before all the awful stuff. When I had sex with him it was like being back in a place before that awful night and every bad thing that's happened since. My body was still unharmed.

I tell him this. Well, I write. He calls instead and says the way I'm feeling about myself made him cry. He also says he had no idea how much pain he'd caused me. Though he then adds, 'Please don't ever put in writing that I slept with you. I feel guilty enough about it and I'm terrified Marcia will find out.'

'Insensitive arsehole.' Beth is disgusted when I tell her about the phone call. Has Jamie always been this careless with my feelings? He must have been. Why didn't I see it?

I thought the sex we had might change things. Being so close again, I thought it would make him think about what he has lost. Make him question whether Marcia really is for him. Nope. He's just scared Marcia will find out.

Isabelle's car is a Mini, as cute and sweet-smelling as she is. I feel like a heifer getting in with my clumpy boots. I immediately get a bit of mud on the floor and she brushes away my apologies. I had to wait for her outside the staff room for a bit after English and I felt good; I felt special being taken to lunch by my teacher. She drives us to a pizza place on the high street.

'I wanted to check in with you properly, Nina,' she says when we're seated. 'You've been going through an awful lot.'

I have. I have indeed.

'I just wanted you to know that support is here, from me and the college, if you need to have a little objectivity. Sometimes it helps to talk to someone who isn't one of your mates, or your mum, or a counsellor. I'm here.'

I tell her that I sometimes wish I was dead. This is true. I don't get all dramatic about it but I do keep thinking that things would be easier if I just dropped dead. I try very hard to not think about it but I don't feel like 'me' anymore.

I tell her about the video that Zoe found on Alex's phone, separate to the photo on Facebook. Isabelle is horrified. She's being very professional, though. As a teacher, she knows she can't throw her pizza off the table and scream, 'OH MY GOD YOU'VE BEEN RAPED' but I sense she wants to.

I feel bad telling people what Alex and his mate did. It upsets them and they want me to 'do' something about it, but

I can't go to the police. Everything I have ever read about rape says how difficult it is to get a conviction. I wish it wasn't like that. I wish I was brave and could do it anyway. But I can't. It's difficult enough getting through the day as it is. Everything I do is about college and not drinking. These things take up all my energy. I'm also helping Katie make a book: *The Adventures of a Kitten Called Mittens*. She's got me to cut pages out of card and bind them together. The first story is about Mittens climbing a tree and getting stuck. She's rescued by a little girl called Katie; no surprise there.

When I say 'helping' I mean Katie's giving me her orders and I'm following them. She tells me to draw a car under the tree for Katie to climb on so she can rescue the cat. She tells me she wants the story to rhyme so she tells me the plot and I have to come up with the rhymes. She also wants each line to be in a different colour felt-tip and I get into trouble when I muddle up the purple pen with a dark-blue pen, but Katie is compassionate enough as a boss to forgive me and not give me the sack. Katie has no idea of any of the other things going on in the mad adult world around her. My world with Katie is sweet and fun and she overwhelms me with love. The thought 'I'd be better off dead' melts away when I'm with Katie.

All this is hard to explain to Isabelle and Mum and everyone else who thinks I just need to go to the police then everything will be OK.

Isabelle says that if I go to the police, she will come with me. 'I will be there every step of the way if you feel your mum is too close to this.' I'd told her how Mum has been doing my head in.

I tell her I will think about it. I won't think about it. I don't want to think about it. I want to forget about it. Everyone is talking like the advice pages of Mum's 'guilty pleasure' magazines, the ones where women with badly dyed hair look into the camera under headlines like: 'I HAD MY BROTHER'S BABY.'

Alex, I imagine, is strutting about thinking he can do whatever he wants, knowing he has gotten away with it. I hate it. It makes me want to scream. But how can I prove that he raped me when I don't remember it? It wasn't like I'd been knocked out in an accident and he had sex with me; I got *myself* into that state. I put *myself* in danger. Can I really expect a guy to take the blame? I mean, yeah, I can, because he *was* to blame, but the police will just think I'm a slag. They'll talk to the bouncer in the club who was disgusted by me, they'll talk to the cab driver, and they will all say: 'Oh my God, that slag is crying "rape".' That's what everyone will say, that I'm 'crying rape'.

I think of Alex's cocky sneer when he said 'Regret is not rape' and a bit of me crumbles. He humiliated me. And he'll get away with it.

In AA all this doesn't become a conversation or a debate. No one tells me 'you must go to the police'. They just listen and some of them, the women, give me a hug when we have coffee afterwards. I'm tired of hearing everyone's opinions. I need to say what I'm feeling and just let it hang there. Just let those words and those thoughts dangle without anyone saying they're the wrong words, or the wrong thoughts. Or offer me more opinions about how I could be better at handling all of this. In AA I don't have to 'handle' anything.

I have been working really hard with Julie, my sponsor, going through the steps. The steps are private. Me and Julie live in our own little bubble where we only talk about my recovery. I meditate and it soothes me in a way that alcohol promises me it will but then pulls me to the ground and kicks the shit out of me.

As one of the steps, I call Max.

'I need to speak to you, Max. I need to talk to you properly about that awful night. Is that OK?'

He agrees to meet me in the coffee shop by his bookshop one Saturday afternoon. This must be the last thing Max wants to do with his lunchtime, but he's a diamond who knows this is for my own sake so I can move on.

'I'm so sorry about what I did when I was staying at your house.'

I've actually rehearsed this, exactly what I am going to say, but it all comes out in a bit of a jumble.

'You took me into your home and I abused that trust by coming into your room in the state I was in after my party. I was in such a dreadful place and didn't consider the position I put you in.' I force myself to look at him as I speak. What I would really like to do is crawl under the table with paper and a pen and pass him notes.

'I'm truly sorry, Max, for embarrassing you and trying to use you while I was in my chaos.'

Max stands up and hugs me. 'You're one of the bravest people I know.'

His smile and his hug tell me it's going to be all right. We will never need to talk about what happened that night again.

I've been trying not to be angry with Zoe . . . to understand that she's in a hellish place. I'd actually thought that this is all worse for her because she's deluded about Alex and at least I know the truth.

It begins to eat away at me, though, that Zoe has no idea about what she did to me and my family by putting up those pictures. I don't think she has a clue. It bothers me that she thinks that *I* have done something wrong. She treats me like I'm invisible, and as though I have something to be ashamed of.

Julie suggests I write to Zoe, telling her how I feel. She says, 'Write to her, but don't send the letter. Keep it for yourself.'

So I do.

Dear Zoe,

We used to be friends. Me and Beth, when we first met you, we didn't really get you – we thought you were a bit dim. But we got to know you better and realised you were actually really nice and smart, just a bit quieter than us. You became part of our gang and that's not easy because me and Beth have always been such a unit.

I've sometimes been a bit jealous of how pretty you are and how guys always liked you first before they even noticed me or Beth. But you were always so nice and sweet that I forgave you for being so pretty. I guess pretty girls have to be dead nice if they want other girls to like them and not hate them. You can't be a bitch if you're pretty, you'd never be forgiven.

Anyway, I was really drunk that night we went to the Boulevard. You know how heartbroken I was about Jamie.

You saw how I cried and cried and without you and Beth looking after me, I would have handled it all even worse than I did. I DID handle it badly. I got drunk. I drank more and I drank faster than you and Beth. I was wasted that night even before we got to the club.

You went to the loo and I saw Alex. I say 'saw' Alex, but it was a blur. I just saw 'a guy'. I am not proud of what happened.

I had only ever slept with Jamie before then. You know that. I'd never done anything more than kiss a couple of guys before him. You know that too.

I wanted to be liked, I wanted to be fancied, and stupidly, really stupidly, I thought going too far in a club meant I was being 'cool'.

I got thrown out by a bouncer. Did you know that? I don't know where you and Beth were. I think you'd gone to dance. This bouncer threw me out and he thought I was utter scum. I was stood out in the cold without my phone, without you guys.

Alex and his mate came out. I thought they were being nice to me. They held me up as I was so pissed I couldn't stand.

The next thing I remember was them putting me in a taxi. I was more afraid that the cabbie was going to hurt me, not Alex.

I had no recollection of what had happened. I had my knickers in my hand. I honestly don't remember taking them off. I didn't know if I'd had sex. I passed out in the cab and the driver went to the door and got my mum. I puked all over our garden wall and the cabbie didn't charge us for the fare. I was a state. A proper state.

For ages I didn't know if I'd had sex that night. I tried not to think about it, I pushed it out of my mind. It was hard to forget about that night, especially when you started seeing Alex. I know you thought I was being 'weird' with you. I was. I was totally being weird with you because I didn't know whether or not I'd slept with your new boyfriend. It was wrecking my head.

My way of dealing with it was to drink more. So I did. I drank more and got myself into situations where I slept with guys I didn't even know because I wanted to block out what had happened. That didn't work.

I didn't know he'd had sex with me for sure until you texted me the film of it. Then everyone knew. You put that awful photograph up on Facebook. Not the ones that incriminated your boyfriend, just the one that humiliated me. My friends made you take it down but by then the damage had been done.

How can I describe what it felt like for me? I felt broken apart and scattered all over the place then stamped on.

I was with Jamie that night. He'd come to see me. You know how desperately I'd missed him. You'd listened to me going on and on about him enough times.

I don't know why humiliating me was your first instinct. In all the time I've known you, I had never done or said anything to hurt you. I don't know why you didn't give me a chance to have my say.

When I step out of my house, go to college, I feel everyone

has seen that terrible photo you posted and is judging me and thinking awful things of me. I don't believe I deserve that. I'm not sure anyone deserves that.

I know you're hurt because I didn't tell you anything, but he wasn't your boyfriend when it happened, you hadn't even met him!

After he did that to me, he walked back into that club and hooked up with you. I'm not sure why you don't question his behaviour. He took photos of me as 'trophies'. You can see when you look at them and the video I was totally out of it.

Everyone is telling me I should report him but the reality of reliving that awful night to the police and to lawyers is too much for me to bear.

I need you to hear my side of what happened.

Nina x

I know I shouldn't have sent it. I know the whole point of these cathartic sort of letters is that you don't send them, you just use them to get your feelings out.

I know that. I know.

'It's intrusive and potentially damaging because it is unlikely you will ever get the response you want,' Julie had said.

But I did it. I emailed it to Zoe and when I told Julie what I'd done she told me to brace myself for a defensive email back, or, perhaps worse, nothing at all.

Robbie is back at college. Two weeks away has seemed an age and I don't know if we're just friends now or if another date is still on the cards. Getting beaten up because of me seems to have been a real passion killer.

'So what's going on with you two?' Beth asks me, in front of Steve, because pretty much everything is in front of Steve now because they're glued together. I don't know why she lets him in on everything. He's perfected the art of pretending he can't really hear.

'I don't know. Nothing really. We're just friends.' I can't be bothered going into any more detail, especially when Beth has her Oprah face on.

Official uni offers come through. Beth gets an offer from her first choice, Edinburgh. She wants to spend her summer holidays working at the Edinburgh Festival.

I will get into Warwick, on condition that I get two As and a B, which I might. I just might.

Robbie gets into Bristol. Unconditional.

'Right then,' Robbie says, 'you can call it a second date if you want, or we can call it a celebration. So, are we going out?'

We are. Well, actually, we're staying in, at his place and watching a film. His parents are sweet and go to bed early to leave us to it. No matter how cool someone's parents are, it's always awkward when they give you privacy. They might as well cry out, 'Well! It's eight o'clock now! We're banishing ourselves to our room so you two can touch each other up. Night!'

The film is a bore. Some science fiction story I can't get into because just as I've figured out what's going on, someone turns into an alien and kills someone and I'm lost again. Robbie puts his hand around my shoulder and we snuggle up.

He's not into the film either. Or if he is, he can't concentrate because it's hard to ignore the fact that we're in an embrace and this is only our second date. I have a piece of pizza stuck between my back teeth that I'm desperately trying to get out with my tongue without looking like I'm having a fit. I can't take it out with fingers because Robbie is now holding my hand, and I can't let go and yank pizza from out of my mouth then put my hand in his again. My palms are getting sweaty and my shoulder has started to ache from the position it's in.

Finally Robbie just goes for it. He turns to me, puts his hand on my cheek and kisses me. He really IS a lovely kisser. I pray the pizza doesn't dislodge now. We sink deeper into the sofa and Robbie's hand starts to wander over my boobs. Now in these situations, if I was drunk, I would just go for his cock, with my mouth or hand, whatever was nearest. But what I do now is stop him. I gently break away from him and sit up.

'I need to go home,' I tell him. I'm not sure why; I guess I must want to go home.

A second of hurt that he's unable to hide scuttles over his face. 'Is this too much? Should I not have kissed you?'

I've put him in an awkward position. I can hear Julie saying, 'No, you stopped something happening that you weren't comfortable with. His response to that is not your responsibility.' Having Julie in my life is like having a mini-Oprah in my head at all times. Sometimes this 'recovery speak' gets on my nerves. I DO feel bad because I've made him feel like he's done something wrong when actually, stuffing your hand up a girl's jumper when she's got her tongue halfway down your throat, under normal circumstances, is acceptable behaviour. But this isn't normal circumstances for me. I'm not ready to have sex. This thought pirouettes clearly and neatly in my head. It's not buried deep under booze and crazy feelings. It's unmistakable and I'm not going to ignore it. I don't want to touch or see his willy. Not now. Not tonight.

'Robbie, I really like you. You're ace.'

He gives me an embarrassed little smile. 'I *do* know that, Nina. What's the bit you're gonna say that I *don't* know?'

I smile back. 'I need to stay clean.'

'Hey you, I showered just before you came!' He grins. His innate sweetness is making this easier.

'You know what I mean. I'm worried that sex right now is going to confuse me.'

'Nina, I get it, it's fine. Come here.'

Robbie hugs me and I think what a shame it is that it's now, when I have met someone this sexy and this nice, that my stupid head starts getting sensible.

'Take a pause,' Julie always tells me. I need to be on my own. I need to be boring. I'm getting better. It's dull, but sane. I wish things were different and I could dive into a love story with Robbie. He walks me home.

When we get to my door he holds my hand and says, 'Shall we be mates then? Just mates?'

I nod and he hugs me and I think I might cry, but I don't. He waits as I go in and he gives a little wave to Mum who has appeared in the hallway.

I lie on my bed and read the AA Big Book. It's easy to take the piss out of some of the stuff in there. It's not a great work of literature and some of it is proper American schmaltz that would probably be pretty unbearable if you weren't a drunk. But I can pick it up, open it at any page, and read stuff I totally relate to. It's written by people who know exactly what it feels like to be locked in booze and locked in a place where you keep doing things that make you miserable and ashamed.

There are people who think I should just 'get on with it', just be 'strong willed', people who think I should 'pull my socks up'. But in AA whether I'm in a meeting, or with Julie or reading from the Big Book, it doesn't matter. None of what people *don't* understand matters. I don't need the whole bloody world to get all this. I just want me to get it, me to get better. Poor Dad. My poor dad. I think about him so much. If only he'd had the help I've had. He wouldn't have died, probably. He would have been so much happier. What an awful place his head must have been to live in.

Some people just naturally don't do things to fuck themselves up. I find that amazing in people like Alan. I thought he was boring, and to be honest, he is, but he's happy. He doesn't jump up and dance everywhere, but he appreciates his life, Mum, Katie, his job, even me now. He likes himself. He likes the person he is which is why he can put up with me in the calm way he has. You can't put up with other people if you can't put up with yourself.

Even people my age at college. So many of them are happy with the night they've had. They enjoy a film, a party, the company and that's enough. They know when to go home. They don't carry on until the bitter end, drinking and drinking, thinking THE night of their life will happen. Before, I would stay at parties even when I wasn't having a good time. I talked to people who I knew were arseholes. It was exhausting. All the messages I sent to Jamie, knowing he would ignore them, each one was like punching myself in the face.

Sober, I realise that no party, no man, no woman, no fuck is ever going to be the answer. All that shame, all that regret, all that pain, can't be drowned in booze.

I meditate. Not like full-on 'om' but I read a chapter and then sit cross-legged on my bed and breathe in and out, staying 'in the moment'. Katie wants to stay 'in the moment' too and she does this by rushing into my room in her little white nightie, her face full of giggles and mischief as she says, 'I'm not asleep! I woke up!'

She climbs into my bed and puts her face up close to mine, and I smell the sweetness of her breath as she whispers: 'Better not tell Mum! She'll tell me off because I'm not allowed to disturb you –' she presses her hands on each of my cheeks '– because you have *exams!*' She says this in a whisper because her notion of exams is that even when talking about them you must do so with utmost seriousness.

She gets under the covers and I put my arm around her and she snuggles into me and I hold my sister tight trying to push out the thought of how many times have I missed moments like this with Katie because I've been drunk, hungover, or ashamed and just wanted her to go away.

'You never disturb me, Katie. I'll always want you to come into my room for a cuddle.' My little sister and I drift off into the deepest, most wonderful sleep I've had for a long time.

*

These days I go to college early. For a 9a.m. lecture I like to get there at 8.30a.m. so I can go to the canteen and have tea and toast. There's quite a few of us who do that. Yeah, we can all have free tea and toast at home, before we leave, but there's something nice and warming about sitting and chilling together before a class that early, before the scramble and rush of the rest of the day.

So I'm sitting at the bus stop when his shiny white Audi pulls up and stops. Its tinted window is wound down and Alex turns to me, his shades on, and says, 'Hey, beautiful. Are you going to college? Can I give you a lift?'

I'm frozen; I don't know what to say. Suddenly, on this fairly busy road, there doesn't seem to be a soul around.

'Erm, no thanks, I'm OK.'

Why am I being polite? What the fuck is wrong with me?

He takes his glasses off and tilts his head. 'Look, Nina.' He said my name. I hadn't been sure if he even knew my name.

'Nina, I feel bad about our last conversation. Please get in and we'll start again.'

I get into his car. I get in because he catches me by surprise and I'm still hoping he will be sorry for what he did. I sit stiffly, staring ahead. He has a really flash stereo and he asks what music I like and I say 'everything', like we're on a date and I'm too self-conscious that he'll think my taste is lame so I say 'everything' which means, 'I'm happy for you to take control, I'll like what you like.'

I regret getting in. He is not sorry.

He makes a bit of chit-chat and I actually laugh at a joke he makes. He's the kind of guy whose jokes you laugh at not because they're funny, but because he's the author of 'cool' and so his humour must be right. There is another 'me' that's looking at all of this thinking, on what planet was it OK to get in his car? Why, after everything, were you worried about being *rude* to him? Or care if he thinks you are cool?

He doesn't stop at the car park; he stops at the main gate, then drives up to the door. A few of the early crowd see me and wave.

'Nice wheels, Nina!' someone shouts. I go to get out.

He touches my arm and says, 'Hang on, just one sec.'

Then he sits right back in his seat, looks straight at me and says, 'Nina, you have to stop harassing my girlfriend.'

'What?' I say. My letter. Of course he knows about my letter. I shouldn't have sent that letter.

'The nonsense you wrote to her, it has to stop. You've upset her.'

His tone is gentle. So gentle that it gives me no room to recoil from its chill. I could scream, jump out, everyone would see, but his stillness and calm keeps me sat there, forced to listen.

'You have to accept, Nina, that I would never have gone for you, even if you'd been sober. You have to end this jealousy thing. I go for girls like Zoe. *Most* guys go for girls like Zoe. Not girls like you. You're not pretty enough or smart enough. Do you understand that?' He looks at me, his face calm, his cool blue eyes fixed on mine.

I nod. I nod at what he says. I feel incapable of doing anything else.

He smiles at me. 'You're a mess. You tell lies because you're jealous and inadequate.'

I look down.

He continues. 'No amount of rehab or whatever it is you're doing is going to change that. So stop being a pest and save Zoe the embarrassment of asking you herself.'

I make some kind of noise. I'm not sure if it's even a word. I can't hear it because the blood is roaring through my head and blocking my ears. I get out of the car. I shut his door carefully so as not to slam it.

I am set adrift from the part of me that is sober and strong. *That* part of me sprinted off and left me to it the moment he pulled up beside me.

I am left a piece of dirt making my way through the corridors, unable to lift my head up or look anyone in the eye.

I don't go to the canteen to get my toast and tea before the lecture. I go to the loos and lock myself in a cubicle and I dig my nails deep into my palm; I do not let go. I want to draw blood but none comes. I feel I should cry but even my tears have abandoned me. I just pant. My chest seizes up and I make a weird, low whining sound.

I look at my hands and I'm shaking. Did he hit me? I feel like I've been punched in the head and stomach. I now know how those phrases, like 'it was like a kick in the guts', come about because you can *actually* feel kicked in the guts without anyone touching you.

I appear in the off-licence in a numb fog. I stand in front of the bottles of cheap, unbranded vodka. I grab one. The middle-aged Sikh guy quietly asks, 'ID?' I flash my student card. If I wasn't so desperate to get out of there and drink I would've been insolent. What a relief it is to be eighteen at last.

I don't look at the shopkeeper. I want to find somewhere private.

On a bench, in the park, I sit with the vodka on my lap like a bomb. It's drizzling. The sort of weather that makes my hair frizz and my thighs feel fat.

I try breathing in deeply. I can't. I will my racing heart to stop. It doesn't.

My head's screaming what I *should* have done. I *should* have said, 'Why the fuck would I want to get in your car?'

I *should* have called him a dirty pervert. I didn't.

I *should* have said, 'You're no prize, you're every woman's HELL.'

But I didn't. I let him undermine and insult me. I let him see me tongue-tied. My acceptance of a lift was an acceptance of inferiority, of my worthlessness. I handed him all my power.

Finally, tears arrive. I wipe them off my face with my sleeve and undo the top of the vodka. That satisfying 'click click' of a new bottle being unscrewed. All that therapy, rehab, endless AA meetings. What was the fucking point if I'm back here?

Upset and shaken to the core because my rapist has said he doesn't fancy me. This is insanity. Would I have felt better if he'd raped me because he simply couldn't resist my beauty?

He said he doesn't go for girls like me. But he *did* go for me. Not with hearts and roses, but with hate and violence. It was violence, what he did to me. Not just now, in his car, but when I was drunk outside of the club. I did not 'have sex'

310

with him. I was attacked by him. Now he tells me that's all I'm good for. That 'most men' wouldn't think I'm good for anything else.

There is whining now; I have no strength to sob, but there is gasping and whining and more tears and a soreness in my chest from where I am trying so hard to breathe out this agony.

Like a character in a bad soap opera, I stare at the booze. This scene is familiar.

'Insanity is doing the same thing over and over again and expecting different results,' Julie in my head says. In a miraculous moment I remember this is an emergency. I 'break the glass' and call her. It goes to voicemail.

I am in a moment in which recovery can free fall into relapse. I'm on The Tightrope.

Will I drink this? Which way will I fall? Even sat here, with the bottle in my hands, I don't know.

My phone rings. It's Julie calling me back. Julie is the tiny blink-and-you'll-miss-it chink of light in my mind where I can get out of this.

I have a choice, she tells me. 'You either drink it and check out from the sober life you have built, check out from your feelings, disconnect from all the people you love and are present for. Or, you don't. You pour that drink away and we talk about what has brought you here.'

Why isn't *he* in the park on his own in the rain with a bottle of vodka? Why am I the arsehole? I haven't raped anyone. I haven't pretended to be friendly to get someone into my car just to treat them like shit all over again.

I sit and I sob down the phone to Julie. It feels like I've been swallowed up by a whale. I have to hang on and hope that help comes and pushes me out through the blowhole.

As Julie tells me I'm brave to have called, as she tells me I'm loved, I tip the bottle over and watch the liquid splash on the already wet ground and run down the slight incline of the path. The smell of cheap vodka hits me. Using all my might, I close the door in the face of my screaming, clawing disease.

I think about skipping my class – Zoe will be there – but I don't. Reassuring Julie I'm in no immediate danger of a relapse, we make plans to go to a meeting later and I hang up. I scramble around in my messy bag, find powder and lip gloss and some blusher. I brush my hair and sort out my face.

I'm late, but I'm here, in class.

Zoe sits across the room from me. Zoe looks painfully thin. I haven't looked in her direction for a long time; today I do and she looks away. She doesn't look like the girl we went out with, the girl we had a laugh with. She does not look like my friend. She is still impossibly pretty but she's drawn and unsmiling and I know thoughts of him consume her.

The second I'm out of the class I call Mum. She doesn't pick up – she's at work – so I text her.

'Hi Mum. I want to go to police. Call me back ASAP.'

Five seconds after I press send, Mum calls.

I'm calm when she picks me up from college. I waited in the car park. I went straight out to meet her, without trying to find Beth first or anything. Beth texts me. I don't reply. I don't want a circus; I just want my mum.

She's quiet as we drive. She's relieved with a slightly frantic edginess about her, as though I may change my mind at any moment.

I've walked past our local police station so many times in my life, but I have never been inside it.

We climb up steps to the glass front door which opens to what is a pretty standard reception area in an uncarpeted corridor. A couple of people sit grimly on plastic chairs in the waiting area. The police station is not like they are on TV. There's no shouting; there are no people being dragged off to cells.

There's a policeman at a reception desk that's closed off and raised, with a sliding window which he opens to speak to us. 'Can I help you?'

'Yes, please. My daughter would like to report a crime.'

The two people waiting are in earshot. Nothing comes out of my mouth. Mum looks at me.

I haven't thought this through. I wasn't expecting this. I wasn't expecting that I would have to actually spell out what happened, not in a public place like this. Could they not tell just by looking at me?

'Come on, Nina, it's OK. Tell him.'

I hear my voice, in an apologetic tone, utter: 'I've been attacked. Raped.'

'You've been raped?' he says, quietly.

'Yes,' I tell him.

Mum has her hand on my shoulder. She has read even more accounts of police indifference around rape than I have. She's ready to pounce.

'One moment, we'll get you somewhere more private, shall we?' He presses a buzzer and a colleague appears, a cheery looking older man, chubby with a moustache. They mutter for a moment and the older guy takes over at reception and we're taken to another room. It has a carpet, plastic flowers and a pretty print of a boating lake on the wall.

The policeman asks us to sit down and he takes my name and my address and the name and address of my 'alleged assailant'. I don't know Alex's surname or home address so I just tell him where Alex works.

'What happens now, Nina, is that we will contact Sapphire, our sexual assault unit, and they will send a SOIT officer. That's an officer specially trained in this field to take a statement from you. Now we can either do that today and you can wait until they are here, or if you prefer, you can go home and come back tomorrow when a SOIT officer will be here for you to give a statement.'

'We'll wait,' says Mum, then quickly remembers me. 'Is that OK, Nina? Just get it over with?'

I nod and me and Mum wait in the little room. We each grab a magazine from the rack. Neither of us read them. Her phone rings. It's Alan. Mum says, 'Hello, darling. Yes, we're here and waiting for a special officer who deals with this sort of thing to take a statement. No. No idea how long we'll be.'

I could be at the dentist. You'd never guess from their phone call what was actually going on.

Mum takes a gamble and runs out for sandwiches. She comes back with supplies from a posh sandwich chain.

We sit on the old blue sofa and munch them, drink our smoothies and share a chocolate brownie.

We wait there on the sofa.

'Funny places I've ended up hanging out with you in, Mum,' I say, trying to be chipper. 'Rehab, private police station rooms . . .'

'Yes,' Mum says with a grim smile and a squeeze of my hand. 'We should try a spa day soon for a change.'

Finally, the door opens and I meet Angela for the first time.

'Hi there, I'm Angela, I'm your SOIT officer. Have you been told what that is?'

We have, and Mum and me have also googled it on my phone. We nod.

'I'll be your first port of call. I will be there every step of the way of your complaint.' Angela is about forty, beautiful and black. Her voice, her manner, everything about her instantly makes me think I did the right thing coming today.

Angela has brought with her an Early Evidence Kit but it's pointless because it happened months ago.

'So it's too late to do anything about what happened?' Mum asks.

'No. It's not too late. Obviously it's too late for any DNA evidence, but we'll get a statement from you and go from there. There are rape convictions from historical cases often. Sometimes years back.'

I'm relieved, hearing this. This wasn't a rape down an alleyway half an hour ago. I'm not in shock. It's a relief the police are keen to get the ball rolling, taking me seriously.

A VRI – 'video recorded interview' – has been arranged.

'You sit with me and tell me exactly what happened in as much detail as you can. I will not interrupt you but when you are sure you are finished, I will go over what we need to get more detail.'

Angela is softly spoken and smiley but also quite businesslike. Now it's about facts; this is not about me crying on someone's shoulder. The police are not here to give me hugs; they want to know if the law has been broken, they want to know who, what, where, why. They don't want to know any other crap that's going on in my head. They don't want to know about Jamie or my dad or my drinking, unless it's relevant to their investigation. This is not therapy. This is not rummaging about in my feelings and dragging them out biting and hissing. This is hardcore.

There is a special room, a comfort suite, that smells of machine coffee. It has video cameras and microphones and I go in there with Angela and my mum. There is an Officer In the Case, a detective constable who sits somewhere outside, out of sight, but Angela explains that he can see and hear us.

I talk through all of what happened, from beginning to end, without Angela stopping me or interrupting, as promised. I tell her every little detail. I don't know if she needs to know I had borrowed Beth's dress, but I tell her anyway.

I tell her about the blow job, I tell her about the bouncer. I tell her about the alleyway, my blackout, the Muslim driver, my knickers in my hand, the puke on the garden wall. I tell her about Zoe and our party, I tell about the pictures on Facebook. I tell her about the film Zoe sent me of me being raped. That's what it was. It was a recording of me getting raped. I tell her I showed Jamie. I tell her I went to see Alex and I tell her that Alex gave me a lift and what he said. As I tell her all this, I do not cry. The atmosphere in the police station forces me to be businesslike. Black and white.

When I exhaust my memory, Angela asks me questions and I give even more detail. This takes ages. It's like when I colour something in felt-tip with Katie and no matter how careful we are, we still have to go back and fill in a few cracks. By the end, I'm exhausted. My phone is taken from me and admitted as the first piece of evidence.

So it's all out and in the hands of the law who I'm now forced to trust with handling the most terrible thing that has ever happened to me.

The next step is to 'seek authority to search his home'. He committed a crime that night, and now the police have got a section 8 warrant to look for more evidence of that crime.

All this is happening fast and it seems mad that I waited this long to tell. I was keeping his crime a secret for him.

Endless worries sweep into my head.

'Mum, what if they say, "Why did you get into his car, even though you say he raped you?"'

'You're not the one being investigated,' Mum says. 'Remember that.'

These are the things that I have learned:

1. *You can't put rape 'down to experience'.*
2. *You can pretend you weren't raped to everyone but yourself.*
3. *You don't need to be shaking and crying with your clothes torn for the police to take you seriously.*
4. *You can talk about having spunk in your hair in front of your mum without actually dying.*

Angela comes over the following morning, first thing.

'An initial investigation has unearthed that two complaints of a similar nature have been made against him by two separate young women. The cases were NFA, that's No Further Action, but the finding is significant.'

'Well, you can arrest him now, can't you? If he has history with this sort of thing . . .' Mum blurts out as she makes Angela an obligatory cup of tea.

'I'm afraid because they were NFA, and he wasn't convicted of a crime, we can't use it at this stage to add weight to our case.'

'Why were they No Further Action?' I want to know. 'Did they bottle it?'

'It could be that they chose not to pursue, or it's likely that they weren't able to find enough evidence to have a strong chance of conviction and the women felt it was best for them to leave it.' Angela accepts a mug of tea from my mum with a smile. 'What we can do is approach them, the women, let them know there has been another complaint, and they may feel able to give statements again so it helps your case.'

Mum, again, wades in. 'But they have to! If they know someone has been attacked, surely you can *make* them step up?'

'Mum!' She has no idea. 'You can't just grab them and force them to go through all that.'

'Indeed,' says Angela. 'We have to make sure their best interests are taken into consideration.'

'And the best interests of my daughter?' Mum is the most aggressive I've ever seen her, which is ever so mildly aggressive and still polite, but even so, it's excruciating.

'We have to make sure they're not too vulnerable. The best we can do is tell them what is going on and give them time to decide if they're able to open that door again. At best, they can be Bad Character witnesses.'

I think about these two other girls all day, thinking what it must be like to know what someone did to you and not see them punished. To know that the person who hurt them is walking around, going out boozing, to clubs and never giving them a second thought. In the mornings, when I sit and meditate before I start my day, I send these two girls my love and strength. It does *me* good; I have no idea if it does anything for them.

Angela gets in touch every time there's a new development. Although we try to get on with everything 'as normal', mine, Mum and Alan's lives have become a true crime series. It's on all of our minds. Although Beth can dip in and out, she chooses not to, so she too is a character in our cop show.

They have spoken to Hassan, the taxi driver, who confirmed I was falling about all over the place with my knickers in my hand and passed out in his cab.

The club didn't have any CCTV footage of that night but the police have spoken to the horrible security man who threw me out.

Alex had told him he was my boyfriend and that he would look after me.

The security guard wouldn't have thought twice about it. Why would anyone doubt posh, sincere Alex?

'On his phone were other recordings of that night,' Angela tells me. 'Both men are laughing and discussing how drunk you are. Alex is seen and heard on camera saying, "She's passed out! Wake up, love! You're about to have the fuck of your life."'

Angela delivers this news in her calm, kind voice. My stomach lurches, sickened. Mum's face crumples as she tries not to cry. Alan goes into the kitchen to attempt the world record for Longest Time Making Tea.

Jamie has been Skyping; Jamie is a 'significant witness' because he's the first person I told and showed the video to. I bet he's told Marcia. I bet she was all concerned and understanding and putting her hand to her mouth and saying, 'Oh my God! Poor girl!'

The police talk to Zoe too. Zoe is not well, Angela says. Zoe is suffering depression. Zoe has said that she was devastated when she found out I'd 'slept with Alex that night'. Slept with? She says 'slept with' when it was outdoors? When I was raped? We did not sleep.

I am so angry with her and rage at Beth. 'How could she still be trying to pretend he did nothing wrong? She's seen the pictures? She *knows* me? Why would I lie?'

Beth shakes her head. Zoe still talks to her but is guarded because she knows how close me and Beth are.

'Nina, she's not well, I mean really. When she talks about him, she sounds deranged. Everything is staring her in the face but she doesn't want to see it.'

Angela calls again. 'He's been arrested and charged with rape and sexual assault.'

'Right,' I say.

'Thank, God!' Mum says when I tell her.

So it's official. My experience has been validated by the law.

Alex is denying the charge. Denying everything. This apparently is going to make things a lot harder for me and I panic.

'His dad is rich: he's going to have an amazing, expensive lawyer!'

Alan gives my shoulder a little squeeze and says, 'So will you, Nina. I will make sure of that. Would anyone like some more tea?'

CHAPTER TWENTY-ONE

Jamie coming back to London is not entirely a surprise, not like last time. He's still messaging me a lot, asking me how I am.

He just turns up at our door. Mum hugs him, tells him it's lovely to see him. He's home for the rest of his gap year, without Marcia.

'She's staying to finish her studies out there. She wants to put our travelling plans on hold,' he tells me.

He asks me if I'm seeing anyone. A pocket of excitement I hadn't remembered I have stirs for a moment when I think of Robbie. 'No,' I tell him.

Julie and I have talked about me not needing to know the ins and outs of Jamie's life, no matter how much I'm dying to know. We have also talked about protecting myself, not allowing him to know everything that's going on with me, every thought I have.

Despite being initially pleased to see him, Mum is worried about Jamie being back and the effect it might have on me. 'Remember, what you need is a *friend* right now, Nina.'

I'm know I'm not totally over Jamie. I can't just slip into a friendship with him. He comes to the house a lot. He's got himself involved in all of this. He's quite chuffed at being a witness.

'You're a damsel in distress,' Beth says. 'You know how boys love a damsel in distress.'

'Yeah, but I'm not. I *was* when he left me. I was a damsel in shitloads of distress then, but I don't need him to be all protective of me *now*.'

I don't want him back. I don't have that desolate, desperate ache to be with him. My world sank to the bottom of the sea when he left me. But I've surfaced again. I'm afloat and he can think again if he thinks he's rescuing me.

'But you've already rescued yourself, haven't you, Nina?' Julie says in our weekly phone call.

Yep. Cringy, I admit, but true.

There is hope and excitement scattered around my life again. The Jamie-shaped hole is blurring, and soon will blend completely into all the other colours and shapes of my world. It's not The Great Sadness anymore.

I talk a lot to Julie about what's 'normal' and what is not. You don't know what 'normal' is when one of your parents is a drunk. You think everyone's family is like yours. The chaos, the unpredictable tempers, the high highs and the low lows. Screaming and shouting one minute, hugging and kissing the next. You don't know which way is up. You're told you are loved, but then you're screamed at, and told they wished you'd never been born. So if your parent is a drunk, it's normal for someone who loves you to make you feel hated.

If you're lucky, if you get the right help and support, later on, when you're grown, you work out that being treated like shit and called names is not love. It's a sickness that your parent had. 'Love' doesn't make you feel insecure and expendable.

He's out on bail, Alex. So is Spencer Turnbull, his mate. Turnbull has been charged with rape on 'Joint Enterprise', which means he encouraged and facilitated a rape but didn't actually take part. We are going to court and because they are both denying everything, it will be a fight.

'Of course they're out on bail, the filthy fucking posh-boy toe rags!' I have come to Belle and Trish's for supper; they too have walk-on roles in our ongoing police drama. They now know everything. I needed to get away from Mum who, since the arrest, has focused on trying to 'keep calm and carry on!'

'She must be going through hell, your mum. You're her baby. But she's one of those "brush problems under the carpet" types, eh? Doesn't matter what the crisis is, your head could fall off and your absolute main priority is to pretend everything is normal. There is no shame in crying your fucking heart out where people can see.'

When I get home, Jamie is in the kitchen with a cup of tea, talking to Mum. Irritation prickles me.

'You given him a key, Mum?' I try to sound jokey.

His face turns to me all concerned. 'Your mum has been keeping me in the loop.'

'Oh.'

Jamie wants to be kept 'in the loop'. Why has he popped round without telling me, without asking, and made himself at home with Mum as though nothing has happened?

'Have you been here long?' I ask him.

'A while. Got here just in time to read Katie a story and tuck her in. She's grown so much! I've really missed her.'

Mum 'leaves us to it' with a concerned look and Jamie makes more tea and says he needs to talk.

'Nina, it's been mad since I left. I've been on this, like, intense whirlwind and I come back now and see how much I left behind, how much I missed it.'

He reaches across the kitchen table and holds my hand. 'On New Year's Eve, before that awful message, what we shared, it was pretty cool.'

A few months ago, I was aching to be here like this with Jamie. But now, I feel cold towards him.

I'm quiet. My silence forces Jamie to continue. 'I went back to Hong Kong and Marcia was like, "Is everything OK?" and I said "yeah". But now, I'm not sure if it is. With her and me, I mean.'

Oh God. I still say nothing so he asks, 'Are you OK?'

'Yes, I'm OK, but this is . . . I don't know what this is.'

'I'm trying to say I know I hurt you, I'm sorry I hurt you.'

He didn't write, he didn't return my calls, he didn't respond to my long, pleading emails, begging him to talk to me, help me make sense of it. He flew away on that plane and everything we planned flew out of his mind. Then there was Marcia, long legs and 'intellectual equal' Marcia who represented excitement and opportunities that I did not.

He keeps talking and it's as if all that pain is parading in front of me again doing the can-can.

'I hurt you and I'm so sorry, you were my best friend and I fucked it up. I wanted to have an adventure, see what else was out there. That's the awful truth.'

'Yup,' I say. 'Yes, Jamie, that's pretty awful. But, you know, it is what it is. I'm OK. You're OK.'

'I feel so bad.'

'That isn't my problem, Jamie. I don't need to deal with your "I feel bad".'

'Fine. Fine. I know.' Jamie lets go of my hand, surprised by my coolness. I'm not being horrible, I'm not angry. I don't think this is what he expected.

'OK, Nina, look, I just want you to know I'm here for you, OK?'

He hugs me. A big bear hug. One of the hugs which for ages I longed to bury myself in again. But I am slightly stiff and I only offer a polite hand on his arm in reciprocation.

When the hug is over, finally, Jamie goes to leave and I say, 'Jamie, can you drop me a text next time? Before you come round?'

He raises his eyebrows and goes.

It's in the paper, about Alex and Spencer. I never read the *Ealing Post*, but Alan does. As I eat my Coco Pops one morning he solemnly puts the paper on the table in front of me, and says, 'I think you'd better know about this.'

'Oh my God!' My name's not there, of course, but 'local student' is and both of their names. It will still be obvious to a lot of people that this case is about me.

'Oh my God!' I say again.

'Now don't fret,' Alan says. 'It'll be tomorrow's chip paper.'

'Alan, it'll be online for ever.'

No wonder so many women don't report this stuff. Hard enough to get the words out of your mouth to tell your family, the police, without becoming 'news' for everyone to gawp over while they're having their breakfast.

Alex's picture is in the paper. He looks like a nice, good-looking, middle-class guy, out, having fun, laughing. You wouldn't guess what he'd been charged with.

I get messages on my Twitter and Facebook calling me a whore: 'lying fucking slag, ruining two innocent lives'. There's enough hate for me to make a pact with Julie to stay off social media completely for now.

'People are mental,' Beth says. 'They've got no clue and, by the way, you are so brave going back to college with all this crap going on.'

I'd been anxious about seeing Zoe, but she's no longer here.

Zoe's mum and dad took her out of college.

'She's really ill.' Beth's been to visit.

'What do you mean?'

'Skinny.'

'She's always been skinny.'

'No, but I mean so skinny it makes your eyes water. She doesn't eat. At all. Proper anorexic.'

'Oh my God.'

'I don't think she's seeing Alex anymore.'

Zoe's mum and dad have taken her to specialists and counselling.

She was almost as unlucky as me, meeting him that night.

'Men like Alex prey on vulnerable women; they have a sixth sense for them,' Mum says.

Robbie, since our date and the reappearance of Jamie on the scene, has kept a friendly distance from me.

He's seen the report on Alex's arrest in the paper. It doesn't take a genius to work out I'm connected to it and gossip at college is in overdrive. Lots of people have seen it. Everyone has seen it, actually. Isabelle and all the other teachers have been told exactly what has happened, at my request, but I have anonymity in law so the papers can't say the victim is me.

Robbie catches up with me as I walk to the bus stop one afternoon.

'Would I be being nosy or would I be being a friend if I asked about all of this?'

I have been thinking a lot about Robbie.

'Do you want to go for a walk with me?' I ask.

'I do, Nina. I definitely want to go for a walk with you.'

We get takeaway tea from the cafe. He pays for the teas. It's a little thing, I know, but I notice stuff like that. We pass a couple from college snogging on a bench and smile 'hellos' and it's an awkward 'that could have been us' moment. We walk quite a long way away from them before we sit down at our own, non-snogging bench.

When you are going to tell someone who cares about you that you have been raped, you have to be careful, you have to look after them. I've had time to adjust, but to Robbie it's going to be a shock, even though he probably suspects.

I don't know how to tell him but I want to tell him because I want him to know me, I want him to be more than just my friend. I'm sure about this. He's looking at me all cute and expectant.

He holds my hand. 'You don't have to tell me if you don't want to,' he says, and I think he means it but what happened isn't going to go away. If he's going to be in my life like a boyfriend – a tingle goes up my spine as I think this – then he needs to know what he's getting into. I can't go through a court case and deal with all of this without telling him. It would be like trying to hide a giraffe under a tea towel.

'I got drunk,' I begin and want to kick myself because I'm already taking the blame. I start again. 'I was drunk and I was raped and now the guy who did it and his mate who filmed it have been caught and charged.' That's what I say.

I tell him everything about that night. I tell him that the Facebook picture was not the whole story and I tell him about the other videos that the police found.

He tries not to cry, which is touching, but a bit awkward. I feel bad for telling him.

'I'm sorry,' I say and he blinks harder, his lashes wet.

He takes my hand and kisses it. 'I'm so sorry, Nina.'

I laugh. 'Why are *you* sorry?'

'I'm sorry because I absolutely adore you and I have never met anyone as beautiful or as brave.'

He doesn't know whether to hug me or not. So I hug him. We hold each other close and kiss until it starts to get dark. For once I do not worry about the future, about the court case I'm facing. Or whether a relationship with Robbie can last the distance between Bristol and Warwick University. It's enough to feel normal. Kissing a boy I really like on a bench in the park.

CHAPTER TWENTY-TWO

The call from Jerry, from rehab, comes out of the blue. He asks if I'm OK. I tell him I am and he asks if there's anyone with me. I tell him my friend Beth and her boyfriend Steve are with me. Robbie is with us too but I don't call him 'my boyfriend' yet so I don't mention him.

It's Max's birthday and the four of us are making him dinner. Well, Beth and Robbie are making him a special dinner. Me and Steve are arguing about DH Lawrence and whether or not he was a misogynist. Steve thinks he was. I tell him he's been hanging around with Beth too long. Beth throws a piece of cucumber at me.

'I have some bad news, I'm afraid,' Jerry tells me. 'It's Isla. She's had a terrible accident. I'm really sorry to tell you she's dead.'

'Dead' doesn't feel like the right word when he says it. All I hear when he says it is its strangeness, like he's said the wrong word.

A celebrity can be dead, your dad can be dead if he's been dead since you were nine, but someone you have drunk with and had sex with, and who was very much alive the last time you saw them, can't be dead.

I've not spoken to Isla for at least three months. I've been comfortably forgetting about her. Guiltlessly ignoring her texts and calls. Julie said that was OK. Julie said if Isla was contacting me when she was drunk, then it was OK to ignore her. And she *was* drunk. Every time.

She was deep in relapse, Jerry tells me. She had exhausted favours from family members and friends who could no longer cope with her drinking and puking in their homes.

'No one is to blame,' Jerry reassures me. 'The only thing you can do sometimes with an addict who refuses recovery is not to let them take you down with them.'

As Jerry talks, I think about Dad. I wonder if there was *any* way he could've been helped. Is it right to accept you cannot help someone? Should he have been forced into rehab? *Can* you force someone into rehab? Should Mum have chucked him out and changed the locks? I used to dread Dad coming home. You didn't know until you heard his footsteps whether he was going to be nice or whether he was going to smash something and scream at you. If I had been older, could I have fought my way to that part of Dad that wasn't a drunk and bring it out, love it out of him?

Isla, Jerry continues, was thrown out of her hostel. They don't like drunks to get drunk in homeless hostels. She was in Vauxhall, under the bridge. People saw her walking on the wall by the river, drinking from a bottle. A bloke talked to her, apparently, before she fell. What did he say? I wonder. What can you say? 'Excuse me, you're pissed and staggering precariously on a wall by the river. You might wanna come down, get a coffee and go back to rehab.'

He probably just said, 'You OK, love?' and she would have been too trashed to even acknowledge him and he would have walked off.

I wished it was a couple who had seen her and talked to her. I wished a fairly new couple who each wanted to impress the other with their compassion had seen her. They would have spent time getting her away from the wall, asking her if they could call someone, but no one did that. She fell into the river and drowned. She didn't jump, I was assured by Jerry. She had texted her brother and her ex-girlfriend Claire obsessively that night and none of the messages were remotely suicidal. She wanted to make plans for the following week. She was being a pest but apparently the family didn't think it was suicide. Wasn't it? What is doing the thing that wrecks your life, over and over again, if it's not a slow suicide?

She hadn't put stones in her pocket or left a tear-stained note, but Isla, in that moment, could take or leave her life.

Max drives me and Robbie back to my house and I tell Mum what's happened.

When I ask if Robbie can stay the night, Mum says, 'I suppose under the circumstances, that's OK.'

Later it's Robbie who comes with me to Isla's funeral, though he never met her. The sadness of the day brings everything back – about my dad and how close I came to following in his footsteps. But I survive and I do it all sober.

And life skips on. I study and I go out with Robbie; I play with my little sister and make up stories for her; I see my friends and Julie; and I go to my meetings. Then, in the midst of this New Normal, we get a date for the trial. It's two months away. Right before my A levels.

'This will be a tough journey,' Mum tells me.

Alan writes me a card and leaves it on my rucksack.

'It is impossible for me to express how proud I am of you. You are a credit to your mother, and a source of inspiration to Katie. Alan.'

We never mention the note, of course, but I put it in my box of memories under my bed alongside the photos of my dad and Katie's first drawings.

Angela comes to see us one Monday evening.

Two huge things have happened.

Zoe has gone to the police. She has shown them the email I sent her and she has handed in her phone with texts from Alex, ordering her not to speak to me, calling me terrible names and saying he would leave her if she ever came near me.

And there was also this text exchange:

'I just can't get the image of you shagging my mate out of my head.'

His reply was: *'She was snoring. It was like fucking a dying pig. It was shit sex with a passed out dirty whore. Forget it babe. Put it out of your mind. What does that slag matter?'*

Mum holds my hand. 'He's scum, Nina, absolute scum. The court will see that. Won't they?' She looks at Angela for reassurance.

The words *'It was like fucking a dying pig'* ring in my ears. A pig. He was talking about *me*. What did I do to make him hate me like that?

'Are you OK, Nina?' Angela asks.

I snap back into the room and nod.

'These are painful things to hear, I know. But they will help your case.'

Angela has other 'good' news. One of the two women who had previously made a complaint against Alex has come forward. She's given a statement, the police are looking into her case again and so strengthening mine. She was fighting him – that beautiful, brave woman, whoever she was, was fighting her corner again. We will show Alex that we are not pigs.

Miraculously, astoundingly, Alex has changed his plea.

Even his top-of-the-range barrister, who costs his parents an absolute fortune, isn't able to make a 'not guilty' seem realistic. Alex can't hide. Alex is done.

Alan gives the air a little punch when he hears the news then quickly lowers his hand and smoothes down the front of his cardie.

I go upstairs to my room and I stay there for a long time. There will not be a massive trial. I lie on my bed; the bed I have wept on, puked on, fretted and worried endlessly on, now feels like a magic carpet. I didn't know there could be a state different from that awful, knotted anxiety I have been wrapped in.

I lie there until it gets dark and there is a tiny tap on my door. Katie has come. Katie has not always been sure lately if she's allowed to disturb me but there is nothing in the world

I want more in that moment than for my little sister to come into my room.

'Am I allowed in?'

'Yeah, baby, of course.'

She jumps on the bed and clambers under the covers with me, hugging me tight.

'Mummy said you're sad again.'

'I was sad, but I'm mostly not sad now.'

'Will you get sad again?'

'Yes, one day. Dunno when. I'm happy now though.'

Katie nods wisely. She's thinking.

'Can we get some M&M's tomorrow?'

'We sure can, Katie.'

We snuggle up, me and my baby sister, and she says, 'Nina, will you tell me a story? And no cheating. It can't be one you've read before . . . it has to be one you're making up now.'

I lift myself up on my elbow to look at her. 'Can it be a true story?'

She nods.

I sink back down, thinking that one day, when she's older, I will tell my beautiful baby sister the truth about all that has happened to me over the past year, but for now she gets the bedtime story every child deserves, full of wonder and magic.

'Well, in that case,' I whisper, 'I'll tell you the story of the time I tamed a dragon.'

ACKNOWLEDGEMENTS

My thanks, first and foremost, to Cass and Vivie, who allow me to share their house and their toys. You endlessly entertain me with your exquisite humour. You frequently floor me with your wisdom. My two little heroes, thank you for hanging out with me. Neither of you are permitted to read this book until you are fifty-three years old.

Huge thanks to Gillian Green for her guidance, smarts and enthusiasm and to everyone at Ebury, who have been, once again, delightful to be published by.

Thank you to Damon Petitt at Off The Kerb for general brilliance and kind understanding when I turn up in the wrong cities et cetera.

Thanks to my dearest pal Penny, for letting me creep into her house while she was at work to write at her desk, even though she was herself in the middle of hard-core studying.

Thanks to Chloe Bayram for more than twenty years of astounding friendship and for always dancing with me.

Thanks to Hali and Mags for being the best neighbours a first-time author can have. I would love you both even if I couldn't peer into your houses.

Thanks to Laura Sadler, the most exquisite cook on the Isle of Wight and the warmest host, for listening to my ideas very early on.

Thanks to Mike Gunn, Nicky Arrowsmith, Jim and Georgia Tuckey for very helpful chats and to Elliot Steel and Tom Lucy for telling me: 'No, lady, teenagers don't say that no more.'

As ever, my love and thanks to Hadi Khorsandi, Fatemeh Khorsandi and Peyvand Khorsandi for inspiring me and for looking after the children while I wrote this.

Andy, to whom this book is dedicated: thank you for everything you did to help me, for caring so much about it and for sharing with me top class chatter and incredible music as I wrote this.

And finally, to all the people I have got drunk with, from the perfect strangers to the dearest friends – and of course, the comics, all those comics – those delirious nights: my love and thanks for your wonderful, terrible, heart-breaking and heart-warming company.